THE SAMOSA REBELLION

Shanthi Sekaran

THE SAMOSA REBELLION

KT KATHERINE TEGEN BOOKS
An Imprint of HarperCollins Publishers

Katherine Tegen Books is an imprint of HarperCollins Publishers.
The Samosa Rebellion
Text copyright © 2021 by Shanthi Sekaran
Interior art copyright © 2021 by Shehzil Malik
All rights reserved. Printed in the United States of America.

ISBN 978-0-06-305153-9

Typography by Laura Mock
21 22 23 24 25 PC/LSCH 10 9 8 7 6 5 4 3 2 1

First Edition

For my parents,
whose hearts have traveled oceans

MARIPOSA

Chapter 1

When I woke up this morning and looked out my window, the first thing I saw was a minuscule airplane, way up in the clouds. I wondered what it would feel like to soar that high, to slice through the sky like an eagle. Like a butterfly. Where would I go if I could spread my wings, hop on an air current, and cross a whole country? A whole ocean?

It's Sunday afternoon now, and I'm standing in the international arrivals terminal of the Mariposa airport. Dad's on one side of me, Amma's on the other. It's Paati we're waiting for—my grandmother, Amma's mom. She lives in India. Except now, I guess she lives with us.

The whole world is here. That's what it feels like. People swarm around the terminal, frowning up at computer screens. From a bright hallway, passengers stream out, their carts piled high with suitcases. They've all arrived from other countries. They look a little dazed, like they just woke up. Some find their families right away and rush over to them.

Some burst into laughter. One bursts into tears.

Amma holds my hand in both of hers, rubbing it like a good luck charm, her eyes glued to the hallway. She chews at her cheek, the way she does when she's nervous. She made me wear my kurta, which is basically just a long shirt with a little round collar. We bought it on our last trip to India and now it's too small and the sleeves dig into my armpits. Dad's wearing a suit and tie and he's sweating. It isn't even hot. We stand straight and still and we wait. We wait and wait and wait.

I try to remember what Paati was like. It's been three years since I last saw her. I remember her house with its wide veranda. I remember her wild white hair, her voice like a crow's, the way she'd grab my arm and hold tight to it whenever we walked down the road together.

We haven't been back to India since then. The shop keeps my parents so busy I hardly see them on weekdays. I think that's why Paati's coming—to keep an eye on me when my parents can't.

Amma shrieks. She drops my hand and points to the bright hallway.

"She's here," Dad says. "Your paati's here." He pulls at his collar and clears his throat.

I see nothing but a mountain of luggage, six feet high, rolling toward us. And then a hand shoots up and waves. The luggage stops. From behind it steps an old lady: blue sari, gigantic glasses, hair like a circus. Paati.

"Go." Amma pushes me forward. "Go help her."

When I get to Paati, we're the same height. She grabs my arm. "Who is this?" she asks. "This strange man?" She peers into my face and slaps me lightly on the cheek. "Hmph. Take these suitcases." Then she walks past me with a little jink in her step, off-kilter and uneven, like her legs are in an argument.

I watch her walk to Amma. Amma crouches down to touch Paati's feet, which is what people in India do to show respect. Paati catches her by the shoulders and pulls her back up, cups Amma's face in her hands, and for half a second Amma looks like a little girl. Then Paati pulls her into a hug. When they pull away from each other, Amma's face is flushed and wet, but she's smiling. Dad steps forward and bends down to touch Paati's feet. Paati lets him. I wonder if I should have touched her feet, too. We don't do that sort of thing in Mariposa.

On the car ride home, Paati falls asleep, her mouth hanging wide open, a jagged tooth poking out from under her lip. Her cheeks hang loose around her mouth, like samosa dough before it gets rolled out. Her eyelids are two lines lost in a sea of wrinkles. What would it be like, I wonder, to fly across the world to a new life?

Finally, we turn onto Mingus Avenue, my street. It runs right through the middle of Oceanview, which sits plunk in the middle of Pacific City, which is the biggest city—really the only city—in the country of Mariposa. Paati stirs. Her eyes open, and she looks at me, astonished, like she forgot she'd gotten on a plane and traveled across the world. I wave at her. The corner of her mouth curls into a half smile.

In Oceanview, every house is two stories tall and made of brick. Each one's crammed right up against the next, and the streets are so narrow that people string laundry lines from house to house. Our clothes hang over the street like parade flags. Drive down Mingus Avenue and you might see my dad's underwear flapping in the wind.

Paati stares past me, out the window, at the old brick buildings, the one crooked stop sign, the storefronts with awnings and painted windows. I wonder what she finds so interesting. A couple of men in hard hats—I've never seen them before—stand with clipboards, surveying the street. Aside from them, it's the same old Mingus Avenue.

Paati, though, she sees it all with new eyes, like a little kid. And like a little kid, she twists this way and that, try-ing to get a better look. "Butterflies!" she gasps. From the rear window trails a welcome parade of orange butterflies. This is Paati's world now, whether she wants it or not. This is Mariposa. I wonder what she thinks of it. I wonder what happens next.

Chapter 2

Snap.

No.

Snap. Snap.

Uh-uh.

SNAP.

"Quit it!" I swat at the air and miss. I crack one eye open, and there she is, the old owl, her gigantic glasses level with my face, her black eyes magnified behind them: Paati. Again, she snaps her fingers in my ear.

"Wakey wakey, Lazybones! Rise and shine, my boy!"

I groan and dig my face into my pillow. It's 5:45 a.m. I know this without looking. I know the sun outside my window will be as sleepy as I am, the sky barely light, the sorriest excuse for morning, and Paati's favorite time of day.

Want a one-word description of what it's like to share a bedroom with your grandmother? Weird. Superweird. Weirdest.

Now, just like every morning, she spreads two yoga mats on the floor between our beds. I sit up, rub the sleep from my eyes. "I thought old people were supposed to be tired."

"Giddy-up, Sleepy-chops," she says, patting the mat next to hers. "Time is passing." Time would pass much better if I could close my eyes and go back to sleep. But I tried that yesterday, and she splashed water on my face. So I roll off my mattress and land on the floor. I lie still, eyes closed, until she says, "Muki, begin, please. Warrior pose."

"Corpse pose," I answer. My favorite. She gets up, goes to the bathroom, and I hear the tap running. She comes back ready to throw water on me, but now I'm up, eyes open, legs lunging, arms shooting straight from my shoulders, solid as a warrior.

As the morning meanders through my bones, Paati calls out the poses and springs right into them. Her usual wobble is gone, her limbs speedy and precise. "Boat pose! Child's pose! Cobra pose!" I follow clumsily. "Straight legs, somberi! Are you a cobra or a kitty cat?" *Somberi* means "lazy," and I'd be offended if it wasn't such a fun word to say.

I have to admit, when my parents told me that Paati was coming to stay with us, to *live* with us, my first thought was *no*. No, no, no, no, no, no, no. And have I changed my mind since then? No.

Finally, she pats the mat next to hers. "Bridge pose," she says. Bridge pose. A week ago, when Paati first got here, bridge pose was impossible. Now I lie on my back and plant my palms above my head. With one light push, I thrust my tummy to the ceiling and my body rises into an arch, like an old-fashioned railway bridge. When I first tried it, I could barely get my butt off the floor. Little by little, though, I've worked my way higher. Every day, I get a little stronger. I'm kind of proud of myself, actually. Don't tell Paati that.

Today, my bridge rises tall and strong over a roaring river. I can almost hear it: the watery gurgle, the wheezing wind. Behind me, a mountain. Above me, the sky. I solidify. I become the bridge. I am so focused, so completely *the bridge*, that I don't notice Paati creep up.

"Ha *ha!*" She jabs me in the ribs and tickles me and I crash to the ground.

"Paati!" I holler. I grab at her legs but she leaps away.

"I got you good, somberi!" She pulls me to my feet, cackling, and wraps her arms around my shoulders. "And now you're awake," she laughs, giving me a squeeze.

Suddenly, she goes silent. Her arms turn rigid.

"What's wrong?"

She just stares out the window. At the end of her gaze I find something I've never seen before: it's small and black, with wings that flutter so fast I almost can't see them. It isn't a hummingbird, though. It isn't alive. Between its wings, it doesn't have a head or body, but what looks like— is it?—a camera lens. Next to the lens shines a steady red light. The winged camera hovers for a second, then drops and dodges, zigs and zags. Its lens spins one way, then the

7

other, like it's trying to focus.

"What *is* it?" I ask.

"I don't know," Paati whispers. She lifts a hand, touches the windowpane.

"It sees us. It's looking at me."

Paati yanks open the window. "Shoo! Po-dah!" she hisses. She leans out and smacks at the flying camera, which zips out of reach, its red light flashing. "Leave us alone!" The camera hovers for a second longer, then buzzes off into the brightening sky. We watch it shrink away.

"What was that?"

She puts a hand on my shoulder. "Nothing to worry about," she says, her fingers trembling. "Nothing at all."

"Dragonflies!" Dad's in the kitchen, yelling over the growl of the blender. "You saw one!" He's trying to act casual, I can tell. A mound of gluey-looking chutney leaps and falls in the blender's glass jar. He turns it off, then opens it and pokes a spoon in. "They're very high-tech, no? Where was it, this Dragonfly?"

"Outside my window. What did it want?"

"Oh, who knows," Dad says. "Probably just to see your shining face."

Paati gazes out the kitchen window, strangely quiet. I walk over and stand next to her. Even with Dad acting like it's nothing, we know we saw *something*.

Finally, the sun rises and the morning cracks open

like an egg, spilling yellow light all over Mingus Avenue. Down on the sidewalk, I spot Amma. She drags open the shop's metal grating, unlocks its glass door, and stands there examining her storefront. Even from up here, I can see how tall she is, how her braid falls like a fat black snake down her back. I'm not sure how someone as little and wonky as Paati could have made someone like Amma—perfectly correct in every way, as strong and straight as a high-rise building.

Paati cranks the window open, and a clutch of butterflies lands on the sill. "Good morning, my beauties," she sings. Since she arrived, the butterflies have been flocking to our window every morning, perching on the clothesline, an excited dozen of them, sometimes more—more than ever before. Today brings us orange-and-black monarchs. They greet us with a quick dance of their wings.

Paati's been here a week, but it seems like she's always been here. She kind of just plopped into this life, like Oceanview's always been home. And Oceanview just opened up and pulled her in, like she wasn't different at all, like her bright saris and pom-pom of frizzy hair were the most ordinary things in the world. Now, as far as I can tell, she's staying forever.

"About Paati," I begin, watching Dad pour a slow river of coconut chutney from the blender to a bowl. "Can't I just call her Grandma?" Paati's not the best name, to be honest. It's Tamil for *grandmother*, but we all know what it sounds like.

"You will call her Paati and only Paati," Dad says. "We didn't bring you to this country to forget where you came from."

"You didn't bring me to this country at all. I was born here."

"You're right." He throws some mustard seeds into hissing oil. "If you'd been born in India, you wouldn't act so fresh." The mustard seeds pop and hop in their pan. Dad sifts them out and tips them into the chutney.

Paati walks back to the stove. "Time to eat, Muki," she says. "You'll be late." She opens a steamer full of idlis. With a butter knife, she carves one out and hands me the steaming dumpling. It's shaped like a flying saucer and fits precisely into the curve of my palm. It's almost too hot to hold. She takes another one out, pinches off a piece, and dips it in the chutney. Before I can stop her, she pops the idli into my mouth and pats me on the cheek. I don't mind. Food tastes better when it comes from her.

Chapter 3

"Mingus Mouse!" Fabi. She calls up from the sidewalk, dressed in a scratchy blue school sweater and a gold tie, identical to mine. When we walk to the subway station Fabi stays, as usual, a step and a half ahead of me. "How come you didn't come to breakfast?" she asks. "We had plantains."

Fabi Calderón is my best friend. Before Paati arrived, I'd spend mornings in the Calderón kitchen while Mr. Calderón read horoscopes from the newspaper. I'd chew on sweet, crispy plantains and hear what was in store for Gemini.

"I couldn't come over," I say. "I wanted to, but my paati—" I catch myself.

"Your what?"

"My grandmother."

"Your potty?"

"Forget it, Fabi." With Paati here, I'm supposed to be home for breakfast. Now, suddenly, my parents are talking about *family time*, about *learning respect* and *getting to know*.

It's a one-hour subway ride from Oceanview to our school, the Marble Hill Preparatory Academy. They give scholarships to kids like me, kids from Oceanview and Wormwood and neighborhoods that aren't packed with money. Most of my friends go to the regular school in Oceanview, but when I got the Marble Hill scholarship, my parents were so proud that there was no way I could *not* go. I'm just glad to have Fabi with me.

On the train, she grips the subway pole and swings from side to side. "Did you see it this morning?"

"The Dragonfly?"

"It buzzed right up to our window. Flip almost fell out trying to catch it." Flip is Fabi's little brother. He's nine and chubby and smart and has spent his entire life following us around.

"What do you think they're for, the Dragonflies?" I ask.

"Newspaper says security. They're like little flying policemen."

"They just fly around and spy on us?"

Until this morning, I'd only heard about the Dragonflies. They first started showing up after a soccer game that went bad. Really bad. Stuff was broken and vandalized all over town. Our shop window was smashed. A few days later, we heard about the Dragonflies, a way for the government to watch over the city, to be everywhere and nowhere, all at once.

We arrive at Marble Hill Station. "My life's pretty boring," Fabi says, exiting the train. She has to shout over the noise of the station. "I don't know who'd want to watch me."

Maybe it's the Dragonfly, maybe it's Paati moving in, or maybe it's just being twelve, but I can't shake the feeling that a big change crouches just around the corner, waiting to pounce. Something—*something*—is on its way.

At the school entrance, a long line of cars waits to drop kids off. Students flow through the massive front doors. Some kids can say that their parents went here. Their grandparents, too. Some kids don't even have to think about fitting in. But if you're a kid from Oceanview, you've got three ways to survive this school. First: Be funny. If you make people laugh, you're pretty much welcome anywhere. Being funny comes with risks, though. If you decide to try it, you really have to nail it. Like I said: risks. The second way: Be good at sports. I like soccer. I like it enough to be sort of good at it, but sort of doesn't cut it, not at Marble Hill Prep. The third way: Blend in. Press mute. Disappear. I walked onto MHP's campus the first day of school, saw the kids around me with their leather backpacks, listened to the way they talked to teachers, the way they talked to each other, and I knew I'd never be like them. So I went with option three. Like a leaf-tailed gecko, I blended into the wood-paneled walls. I speak when I'm spoken to. I eat lunch with Fabi and whoever else she brings along. I'm nice to people. People are nice to me. If I stopped going to school one day, I'm sure no one but Fabi would notice.

When the clock flashes 9:04, we stand for the pledge of allegiance. *My heart lives in Mariposa. . . .* We've been reciting this pledge every day since we were five, but I stopped hearing the words to it a long time ago.

Later in the afternoon, in civics class, Miss Pistachio hands out assignment sheets for our Spring Project. I've been dreading this project all year. We heard about it from last year's sixth graders, who heard about it from the sixth graders before them. *Pistachio will destroy you*, they told us. *Civics One will take over your life.*

At the top of the page, the topic: *MY COUNTRY IS.*

"My country is what?" blurts Box Tuttle, the biggest, freckliest kid in our class.

"That's for you to decide, Boxwood," she answers. She stands at the board, her pale cheeks flushed pink, her red-framed spectacles perched on the tip of her nose. "What is this country? What is Mariposa to you?" Box just blinks at her and sticks his pencil between his teeth.

"You'll be working in pairs," she says, and goes on to describe the rest of the project. Great, I think. Pairing up means I'll be working with Raju. Teachers always pair me with Raju. We're both Indian, so they assume we're friends.

"The project will take four weeks to complete. You can cover any subject you want—government, the arts, history,

14

even science. But your study must *commit to a lens.*" She says that a lot: *commit to a lens.* I'm not totally sure what it means. I think it has to do with how you see the world, but not through your eyes. More through your brain, and maybe your heart.

"I'll call out the research teams now," she continues, "but *please*, let's maintain order until the entire list is read out." She moves quickly through the names. Fabi gets paired with the class president. Raju's paired with Box Tuttle. They high-five. I'm relieved.

I'm so busy being relieved that I don't hear Miss Pistachio call my name. But I do see that every boy in the class has whipped around to look at me. And every girl has whipped around to look at Tinley Schaedler. Miss Pistachio keeps calling out names, but no one's listening. I pick up my pencil, stare down at my desk, and draw spirals across my notebook until everyone's turned back around again.

Could this be right? Have I just been paired with Tinley Schaedler?

Maybe you don't understand who Tinley Schaedler is. I'm not sure if *I* understand who Tinley Schaedler is. Tinley Schaedler is one of those girls everyone refers to by their first and last names. She's never just Tinley. Tinley Schaedler strides down the halls of MHP like a queen, her friends trailing behind like court attendants. I don't know all their names. I just call them the Tinleys. They wear matching hairstyles every day, Tinley Schaedler and her

Tinleys. Today, they all wear ponytails.

Tinley Schaedler is one of those girls everyone knows something about. She's only a sixth grader, like me, but even the seventh and eighth graders turn to watch her when she passes. Even the teachers trade little jewels of gossip about her. We whisper and we watch; all of us at Marble Hill building our collective encyclopedia of knowledge.

Tinley Schaedler, in the front corner of the classroom, cranes her neck to look over at me, like maybe she forgot who I am. She smiles and gives me a wave. I don't know what to do.

Chapter 4

When school lets out, Fabi and I run for the subway. We switch trains twice between Marble Hill and Oceanview. The whole trip takes about an hour. The train starts out nearly empty and every stop feeds in its own kind of passenger: a few office people in suits, followed by factory workers who fill the car with talk and laughter. The closer we get to Oceanview, the slower the train seems to move. I'm sweaty and thirsty when I bang through the door to the shop.

"Eeeeeasy," Buff mutters. He stoops low, stacking candy bars by the register.

"Are you allowed to do that?" I ask. Amma never lets Buff restock the candy bars, not since the day he ate five of them.

Buff ignores me now and carries on. He's got a new haircut, spiky on top and shaved around the edges, with a lightning bolt carved into the side of his too-long head. It's not a good look for him. Behind the counter, the television is on, and so is our president, Birch Bamberger. Everyone calls him Bambi. He has white hair trimmed close to his scalp, a tidy white beard, and a big doofy smile that makes you want to smile, too.

Bambi stands behind a podium. Cameras flash. He's wearing a blue suit today, and pinned to his chest is a golden butterfly. Two women stand at the checkout counter, gazing up at the screen. One of them puts a hand to her heart and sighs. "Have you ever . . . ," she says, and I don't really know what she means, but I can see how she feels, her eyes wide, standing with her hand on her heart like that, like she's saying the morning pledge.

Buff sits glued to the screen. People go on and on about how charismatic the president is. Just a regular, good guy. "Do you think I'm charismatic?" I ask Buff.

He turns to me, his eyes glazed over. "Do I think you're what?" He frowns. "You feeling all right, buddy?"

I wonder sometimes if I'll grow into more than I am— someone smart, brave, powerful, someone who could charm anyone into anything. I suspect I won't. I suspect that what I've got is what I've got. Buff's eyes are back on the television. The camera pans to the audience, where people hold up signs: *Mariposa for Mariposans. Butterflies In, Moths Out.* They have a hardness in their faces that takes me back to the night of the soccer fight, back to those angry, shouting mouths.

"Buff?"

"Mucus."

"Why are they talking about moths and butterflies?"

Buff's green eyes rest on me for a few seconds. "I guess it's about who's always lived here, and who hasn't," he answers. "Like, this is Mariposa, right? Butterflies are *from* here, right? And moths aren't. But they compete for the same . . . nectar."

"Bambi's not talking about insects, though, is he?"

He looks down at the counter. "No."

"He's talking about people," I say. "Who are from here. And not from here."

Buff nods. He waits for the two women to leave, then turns to me. "Look, Muki. Your parents probably won't tell you this. But I respect you, you know?" He sits down on his swivel stool. "So the moths and the butterflies, right? A Butterfly is a Mariposan. Someone whose grandparents lived in Mariposa."

"But my grandmother lived in India, and I'm still Mariposan."

He raises a finger. "That's where you're wrong. I mean, that's how it used to be, right? Born in Mariposa, you were Mariposan. But now, you only belong to this country— you're only a Butterfly—if both your grandparents are from here. Like mine are. Otherwise, you're a Moth."

"So I'm a Moth?"

"'Fraid so." He swivels from side to side. "Nothing wrong with being a Moth, though."

"But what does it mean? What's going to happen?"

"To you?" He stops swiveling. "I guess we don't know that yet. This is sort of the first time they're doing any of this."

"And nectar? That's money, right?"

"Well, nectar is opportunity, I guess. With the Moths taking all the jobs, the space, the money, there's not much left anymore for Butterflies."

Mariposa's a small country, but it has a lot of money. It has lots of jobs, so people come here from other parts of the world. There's this thing called the Mariposa touch. It's like the Midas touch. Success just sort of . . . happens here. But what Buff's saying doesn't make any sense. My parents and I, Flip and Fabi, all our neighbors in Oceanview—we don't take up much space. For sure we don't take up much money. And jobs? My parents own the shop. They're the ones giving Buff a job.

Before I can say any of this, the shop door opens and I hear Paati's familiar shuffle, the tinkle of her gold bangles. I turn around and there she is, wrapped in a shawl. "Buff." She nods.

"My lady," he answers, and sweeps his arm grandly toward the back of the store. "Your throne awaits." At the head of aisle two sits a folding chair. Paati's taken to sitting there, for hours on end, half foreman, half security guard, half mascot. That's three halves.

She settles into her chair and nods up at the television.

"What is this Bum-burger saying now?"

Buff smirks.

Moths and butterflies. I have no reason to believe a guy with a lightning bolt shaved into his head.

Suddenly, my stomach takes over. I forget about Buff and Bum-burger and Butterflies. I'm hungry. I get a monster sort of hunger sometimes. Upstairs, in the kitchen, Dad's making samosas. He and Amma sell them in the shop. Every morning, they put a sandwich board on the sidewalk: *Hot chai and samosas!*

"Hello, Thumbi," Dad says, standing at the stove. Thumbi means little brother. There's no big brother in our family. Just me. "How was your day?"

"Hungry."

He raises an eyebrow. I go to the fridge and pull out the peanut butter.

He's just rolled a gigantic sheet of dough onto the counter. Right now, it looks a little like our island. The four corners bulge out like butterfly wings. Dad pulls a knife from the butcher block, runs its blade along each side of the butterfly, and cuts away the bulges to leave a clean, wide rectangle. Then he sweeps the blade across the dough, down the dough, until he has a sheet of perfect squares. He's light and fast with the knife and doesn't even stop to measure. He knows, almost without looking, how to cut away the mess, how to make the thing clean and straight and perfect.

21

"Do you ever get tired of making samosas?" I ask.

"What do you mean, Thumbi," he says absently, like he's hardly listening, as he mashes a wooden spoon into a big pot.

"I mean, you used to be a scientist, right?"

Dad was a chemistry student in India when he met my mom. He got a master's degree, married Amma, and moved across the ocean for a job in Mariposa. "Why aren't you a scientist anymore? How come all you do is run a shop?"

He puts the wooden spoon down and looks at me. "I don't really look at it that way, Thumbi."

"What way?"

"As *all I do*. Your amma and I have our own business. It's a lot of work. It takes all my brainpower sometimes. Sometimes it's a lot harder than my job in the laboratory."

He pronounces it *la-BO-ra-tory*.

"But why did you leave the—the LA-boratory? Did they fire you?"

"No," he says. "I quit."

"Why? Did Amma make you?"

He doesn't answer. Instead, he pulls the lid from a large pot on the stove. Blossoms of steam float to the ceiling. I can smell the potatoes and peas, all mashed together, seasoned and ready to plop into the center of each samosa. "Well, Muki," he says at last. "I suppose it's because I could only rise so far there. With my degree, with my background . . ." He shakes his head, like he's trying not to think of something.

"Maybe you wanted to do your own thing," I offer.

He looks up.

"Maybe you didn't want other people telling you what to do all the time. Maybe you wanted to be in charge. Right?"

He smiles. "Come here."

He hands me a spoon. "You do the masala," he says softly. "One spoonful for each square." We work side by side in silence, plopping yellow potato masala onto squares of dough. When that's done, he takes a dropper, releases one drop of water on each side of each square, and smears the water along every edge. He leaves a few at the end for me to try. Finally, quicker than I've seen him do anything, he bundles each square into a tidy pyramid, fat and full and ready to fry.

"You see," he says as the oil on the stove starts to smoke. "I use chemistry every day. This oil. This heat. These samosas. Just a series of Maillard reactions. Cooking is chemistry."

He picks up a pyramid of dough. "My control group." He drops it in the frying pan. The oil gets giddy, fizzes and pops, and the samosa, within seconds, turns golden.

Amma and Dad work hard at everything—the samosas, the shop, keeping their customers happy. I asked them once if the Mariposan touch would make us rich. *Ha!* Amma scoffed. *Getting up every day at dawn, working until midnight. Every single day. That's your Mariposan touch, Muki.*

I reach for a samosa now, and Dad doesn't stop me.

"So these won't make us rich," I say.

He raises an eyebrow.

"So why do we make them?"

"Interesting question," he says, but doesn't answer right away. "I think we do it because people want samosas. Simple. And because it's something from our old life that we can bring to this new life. It makes us a part of this place."

I blow on the samosa. When I bite off the tip of the pyramid, steam pops from the flaky crust, just like I knew it would. It burns my lips a little, but I can't wait. The first bite is always the best.

Chapter 5

Saturday morning. Paati wakes me up for yoga and we end
with breathing exercises. We sit with legs crossed, pinching
one nostril closed and inhaling with the other, then closing that one and exhaling with the first. Today, when she
closes her eyes, I stop doing what I'm supposed to do and
just watch her. I wonder why she's come all this way, to our
poky little home, why she left behind everything she knew.
Paati breathes rhythmically, counts twelve breaths, touching her thumb to each joint on each finger, the Indian way
of counting. She opens one eye. "Somberi . . . ," she mutters.

Later, from the kitchen, I hear the tinkle of her prayer
bell. She spends a few minutes every morning praying to her
collection of framed pictures: Lakshmi sitting on a giant
lotus, Vishnu reclining on a six-headed python, Ganesha
with his elephant head and jolly belly.

Outside my bedroom window, a breeze rustles the
clothesline, hung today with a green sari, a red sari, and

Dad's blue shirt, whose sleeves wave around like they're trying to make a point.

Butterflies have settled between the hanging clothes. Slowly, their wings open and close, open and close. At the other end of the clothesline, Fabi's window opens and she leans out, her hair blowing loose around her shoulders.

"Rapunzel, Rapunzel."

"Shut up," she says. "Soccer?"

"Sure."

Flip pops into the window. "How did *you* get paired with Tinley Schaedler?" he asks. He leans so far out I worry he'll fall.

"How do you know who Tinley Schaedler is? You're not even at our school!"

"*Everyone* knows who Tinley Schaedler is. She's famous."

"What are you talking about?"

A few minutes later, Fabi, Flip, and I pump our bikes up Oceanview Hill. I duck as a Dragonfly whizzes low, red lights flashing, just inches from my forehead. I count five Dragonflies on Mingus Avenue today—a lot more than usual.

"It's no big deal. We're just doing this dumb project together."

"You know it's a big deal," Fabi says. "You *know* it."

"Tinley Schaedler," Flip pants, "has her own car and driver. She can go wherever she wants, whenever she feels like it. Also, her dad's on TV all the time. If you ever watch

Bambi? Look behind him. You'll see Tinley Schaedler's dad."

I've never paid attention to the people standing behind the president.

"And her dad? He has a glass eye. And he's a ruthless interrogator. He's made the world's most notorious spies cry like babies. You think he really has a glass eye?"

Fabi sails up Oceanview Hill on her rusty red bike. Flip's legs pump hard at the pedals, and I hang back to ride with him. When we get to the soccer field, Fabi's already dribbling her ball along the perimeter.

The Marble Hill and Quimby Corner teams are wrapping up their practices. Oceanview used to have a team, too. Not anymore. After the big fight at the soccer stadium, pro soccer was canceled, and so was kids' soccer. Only Marble Hill and Quimby Corner were allowed to continue. Now they only play each other every weekend. As for the Oceanview kids, we just play when we can, where we can.

As we watch the teams pack up, Flip pulls out the red ball he's had for as long as I've known him. It's never not in his pocket. He bounces it hard against the ground and watches it arc high in the sky. Bounces and watches, bounces and watches.

Raju walks by. "Hey, Mucus."

"Hey, Cookie."

Raju turns and swipes my ball from my feet, then boots it as hard as he can. It sails over the field and vanishes into a creek bed. I hate when he does stuff like that. Chasing after the ball, I spot Box Tuttle running to catch up with him. They're both wearing green team jerseys, numbers twenty-one and twenty-two. Over by the bleachers, Box's mom waits with her lipstick smile, her big wave, car keys dangling from her fingers.

We make our goals from jackets and hats, whatever dented juice boxes happen to lie along the sidelines. Soon, other Oceanview kids will trail in. If we're lucky we'll have ten or more, enough for two teams, and we'll play until dark, until the air snaps cold and the dinner smells warn us it's time to get home.

By the time we finish, the sun has dropped below the horizon, but it's still light out. We bike up Oceanview Hill. Behind me, I hear a buzzing. "Dragonfly!" I shout. We pick up speed, hurtling down the road that will take us home. Mingus Avenue draws closer, but when we get to it, Fabi wobbles on her bike, and turns left instead of right. The Dragonfly buzzes away and out of sight.

"Where you going?" Flip yells.

"I see something!" she yells back, heading toward the East Hills. We pump harder to catch up with her.

Fabi's right. Something's happening. A line of trucks has pulled up along a wide expanse of land. This used to be a bare, rocky lot with a thick fringe of poisonous oleander bushes growing around the edges. Now the bushes are gone, replaced by a high fence. It's covered in razor wire, curls of it that climb from ground to sky, metal spikes ready to rip into whatever flesh it finds. Beyond the razor wire sit three fat black tents. Farther down, a cinder-block building rises row by row from the ground. A cement mixer churns out heavy fumes. Fabi finds an opening in the fence and squeezes through it.

"Fabi!" Flip calls. But she's already zoomed ahead. Flip and I squeeze our bikes through and follow. A few construction workers stand at one end of the lot, but they haven't noticed us. Flip and I catch up to Fabi, who's speeding past the tents like she's trying to catch something.

The air in this place is dusty and dry. It's like we're in a different town, a different planet, even. A hot wind whips the tents, rippling the black cloth and spraying dust into my eyes and throat. I stop to cough. I spit on the ground and the taste of cement spreads across my tongue. Fabi keeps speeding ahead.

She screeches to a stop in front of the cinder-block building. She's looking at a low billboard when Flip and I catch up with her. There's so much we don't understand about this place, about these tents, about all of this, but then I see something I do recognize. On the billboard is a picture of a moth. It's painted gray against a black background, its wings turned down, its head bulbous and eyeless. I know what a moth means. Outsiders. Next to the moth is a list of letters. GBR, PHI, ARG, BRZ, GRN. At the very bottom of the sign, painted in small, neat capital letters: *PACIFIC CITY DETENTION AND REMOVALS.*

"What do you think it means?" Fabi asks.

"I think we'd better go," Flip says. "I don't think we're supposed to see this."

"I know what the moth means," I say. They turn to me. "The moth is us. It's our parents."

"What are you talking about?" Fabi asks.

"We're Moths. People who are new to Mariposa."

"I'm not new to Mariposa. I was born here."

"You're new enough," I say. "And I am, too. Our parents aren't from here. Right? Neither are our grandparents. So we're the Moths. But Mariposans—they're the Butterflies. They belong here. This country is theirs."

Matching frowns flash across their faces. "But I'm *from* Mariposa," Fabi says, her voice so quiet it's almost a whisper. "I'm a Butterfly."

Flip studies the sign, then turns to me. I'm suddenly the one who knows things. "What'll they do to us? Is this bad?"

The thing is, when no one tells you anything, there's no way to know when things are super bad, and when they're pretty much okay. So sometimes, everything seems bad. What we see here, today, seems bad for sure.

"HEY!" A voice from the other side of the lot. "GET OUTTA HERE!" A man in a hard hat barrels toward us. He's picked something up—a sledgehammer? An ax? He's running so fast his hat flies off his head. We hop on our bikes and race toward the man, because it's our only way out. Back in his direction, back through the gap in the fence. I can see the gleam of his bald head, the red rings around his eyes. He bares his teeth and clenches his fists. I can hear every huff of breath. He's about to nab us when Fabi reaches the gap in the fence. With a sharp turn, she's through. Flip follows. I slip through the fence, but my sweatshirt catches. My bike crashes to the ground and I crash down on top of it. A spike from the razor wire drags along my hand.

"Fabi!" The man's just a few inches away. I scramble to my feet and jump on. He grabs for me, but I bolt away. He slams to a halt. I speed off. "You don't belong here!" he roars.

My heart thumps in my ears, even when the man has faded, even when I find Flip and Fabi waiting for me. We bike slower now. No one's coming after us. Ahead, the road stretches empty and calm. I don't look back at the fence, at the tents, at whatever that place was, but I can feel it looming behind me, taking up space and air. I can feel a ripple in the atmosphere, and I can hear the man's voice: *You don't belong here.*

The last threads of twilight finally snap, and the sky turns black. We're not close to home. I imagine Amma standing at the window, seething. I imagine Dad, his hands on his hips, his brow furrowed, picking up a flashlight to come look for me.

We bike down the flats to Mingus Avenue but even this

flat road tires me out, like I have cinder blocks strapped to my calves. I'm not used to knowing things. I never knew knowledge could be so heavy.

Later, I lie in bed, staring through the dark at my soccer posters, and listen to Paati snore. Sometimes, when the snoring gets really loud, I ball up a sock and throw it at her. I aim for her belly, not her head, so she won't wake up. Usually, the gentle thump of the sock stops her snoring. Amma would be furious if she knew I did that.

I think about the letters I saw today. GBR, PHI, BRZ. There's something familiar about them, and I can *almost* see what they stand for. When I close my eyes, the letters swim behind them. As I start to drift off, the door opens. Amma comes in, sits on my bed, and picks up my bandaged hand. "Better?" she asks.

"Yes." No one was mad when I got home. I told Amma I'd cut my hand on some thorny bushes by the soccer field. She seemed to accept this.

Now she starts to smooth my hair down and I start to fall asleep. But then, in my mind, a question sits up and blinks awake. The question stands and starts pacing my brain. It knocks on my eyes until I open them. It tickles my lips until I move them. "Amma?" My mouth is so sleepy I can hardly form the word.

"Yes, Muki?"

"Am I a Moth?"

Her hand stops. "What did you say?"

"Am I a Moth or a Butterfly?"

"It's late, Muki. Go to sleep."

But the question isn't going to let me sleep. "Tell me. I'm a Moth, right?"

"You were born here, Muki. You are Mariposan."

"But we're Moths. Like, with the new names they're using? We're Moths?"

She sighs and says nothing, and I think she's probably not going to answer until she says, "Yes, Muki. By that naming system, we would be Moths. You and me and Daddy and Paati."

"But Buff's a Butterfly."

She sighs again. "Yes. Buff, of all people, is a Butterfly." We're quiet for a minute. Thinking about this, I guess.

"Amma?"

"Yes?"

"What's going to happen?"

"Well." She goes quiet. For a long time. I can hear her trying to decide whether to tell me the truth. "Well. They're thinking, Muki, of sending the Moths away."

"Sending them away? Where?"

"Back to the countries they came from. Or back to the countries their relatives came from, a long time ago."

"But that's not fair."

"Of course it isn't."

"But they told us we belonged here. They told us we

were Mariposan, and now—"

"Muki, don't get upset."

"*Amma.* They can't just send us away like that! That's not going to happen!"

"Shhh. You'll wake your paati."

I look over at Paati, a rumbling hill of sheets. "What will they do with Paati?"

Amma doesn't answer. She starts stroking my head again. "Time to sleep," she mutters.

"Amma?"

"Yes?"

"We saw something today. Me and Flip and Fabi."

"What did you see?" Her fingers on my scalp nearly put me back to sleep.

"We saw these . . . tents. Behind a razor wire fence." Her hand stops again. "And a sign with a moth on it. And letters. But I didn't understand them."

Her fingers lift away. "What were the letters?"

"I remember a few, I think. GBR? GRN?"

Her voice winds up tight now. "Muki? Are you telling the truth?"

I nod.

She goes to my desk and gets my notebook and a pencil. Then she sits down next to me and switches on the lamp. "Can you draw what you saw?"

And so I do. I piece it together very carefully in my memory, then draw it out for her. The moth on the left—I draw this well. I pencil in the letters on the right. I hand the notebook back to her. "My god," she whispers. She says it again. "My god."

"What is it? What does GBR mean?"

Her forehead falls into her hands. "I can't believe they're doing this," she says. "They're actually doing this."

My heart starts to thump. "Doing what?"

"Muki, this is a very important discovery. I'm proud of you."

"But what did I discover?"

She takes my chin in her hand. "Never go back there again. Do you hear me? Never!"

Her voice is shrill, but her eyes are bright with love. I know I've done something good, whatever it is.

"You have to tell me."

"I will tell you, Muki. I will tell you everything soon. I just have to think about what this is. But you—you've done good work. No more thinking for you. Okay? Just sleep."

"Okay. Will you pet my head again?" I can tell she wants to jump up and bust out the door and go tell Dad what I found, but she doesn't. She sits and strokes my head until I'm calm again. Paati's snores grow loud enough to fill the room.

"Does she always snore like that?" Amma asks.

"Pretty much."

"And you can sleep with this noise?"

"I have my ways."

Her lips twitch at the corners. "You have your ways."

I take the sock off my left foot, ball it up, and toss it at Paati. It thumps off her belly and she stops snoring. Amma puts a hand on mine. "Well," she says, "that seemed to work."

Chapter 6

What's your anti-power? An anti-power is a good quality that can sometimes be bad for you. Amma's anti-power is honesty. Dad's is kindness. Paati's is bossiness. Authoritativeness, Dad calls it. Really, it's bossiness. My anti-power? It's shape-shifting. It's the power to blend in, to get along with everyone. Flexibility, I guess you'd call it. A go-with-the-flow attitude. Sometimes, though, that go-with-the-flow attitude? It lands me in certain situations.

Imagine, for example: Tinley Schaedler lying on her back on my bedroom floor, her socked feet up against the wall, her fingers braiding the teeny-weeniest braid into her flame-colored hair. And imagine this: Muki Krishnan, sitting petrified on the chair by his desk, watching Tinley Schaedler braid the teeny-weeniest braid into her flame-colored hair. Now stop imagining. Because that's what's really happening.

Tinley Schaedler arrived this morning in a car with

gullwing doors. Gullwing doors are those doors that hinge at the top and open *up* instead of *out*. I've seen lots of gullwings at the school drop-off circle, but you don't see cars like that in Oceanview. When the gullwings opened on Mingus Avenue, they nearly knocked into the buildings on either side of the street. Flip and Mrs. Calderón leaned out of their window to watch. Buff came out of the store. Mrs. Demba and two customers ran out of Dembubbles to watch the doors rise and rise and Tinley Schaedler step lightly from the car. A man got out of the driver's seat. He wore a suit, and judging from the color of his skin, I don't think he was Tinley's dad.

When Tinley walked up to the shop, it seemed like all of Mingus Avenue had come out to watch her. I watched from my window. She didn't seem to notice any of the attention, but she did seem a little confused. First, she stood outside the shop. She looked up and down the street. I don't think she understood that our apartment was above the shop. I think she was expecting a house like hers. She said something to Buff, who stood gawking on the sidewalk, and he walked her to our stairway door. That's when our buzzer buzzed.

And now Tinley Schaedler has made herself at home on my wooden floor. I'm grateful, for the first time, that Amma made me clean my room before Paati arrived. I'm starting to see that people clean their floors for a reason, the reason being that Tinley Schaedler could show up at your house any minute of any day and want to lie down on them.

She gazes at my World Cup poster, the one with little pictures of all the national teams. "So your parents have the bodega downstairs," she says, trying to piece together the facts of my life. "But you guys *live* up *here*. So you get to live right upstairs from where your parents work?"

"Yeah. I guess so."

"Where are they now?"

"I don't know, actually. My mom wasn't in the shop. My dad's out, too. But usually they're around." Paati's home. I can hear her clanking in the kitchen.

"You are so lucky." Her eyes cross a little when she peers at her braid. "I only see my dad at night. He's always gone in the mornings."

"What about your mom?"

"I don't have a mom," she says quietly.

"Oh."

"She got sick. When I was five. She died."

"Oh." I don't know what to say.

We sit silently and all I can hear is the rush of blood to my face. The house has gone quiet, too. If I wasn't so brown, I'd be bright red. This wasn't in the Tinley Schaedler encyclopedia. I don't know anyone whose mother has died and I wish I knew how to say something good. But when I look down at Tinley, she doesn't seem sad or uneasy. Maybe she doesn't need me to say anything.

And then a sound rises from the other end of the house.

It starts quietly and gets louder. A tinkling bell. Paati's puja bell.

I panic. "SO HOW DO YOU LIKE SCHOOL?" I bellow. Maybe Tinley won't notice.

Her eyes get wide. "What's that?"

"WHAT'S WHAT?"

"What's that sound?"

"I DON'T HEAR ANYTHING."

"It's a bell ringing!" The bell is getting closer. The bell is coming down the hallway.

"Oh. It's nothing. It's just a fire alarm."

Tinley scrambles to her feet. "There's a fire?"

That's when Paati opens the bedroom door. She stands there, bell in one hand, a small brass pot in the other, a banana tucked into her elbow. She looks right at Tinley. Tinley looks right back at her. Paati walks up to her, places the brass bowl in Tinley's right hand, opens its lid, pokes her finger in, and presses the finger to Tinley's forehead. A smear of red powder is left behind, crimson against Tinley's pale skin.

Paati just touched Tinley Schaedler. Just walked right up and smeared kumkuma on Tinley Schaedler's forehead. Does she have any idea what she just did? Tinley's eyes are so wide I'm worried her eyeballs will fall out. But she doesn't look mad. Or scared. Just confused. Paati turns to me, dips her finger in the pot, and swipes my forehead. A crumb of red powder drops onto my nose. Then she pulls the banana from her elbow, hands it to Tinley, pats her on the cheek, and steps out of the room.

Tinley turns to me, holding the banana.

"I don't—I can't—" That's all I can say.

"That's prasadam," I finally manage, pointing to the banana.

She examines it. "No. It's a banana."

"Prasadam is what you get after you do puja. After you pray. It's like . . . a blessing."

"It's like a blessed banana?"

"Yeah. Exactly."

"And I get to eat it?"

"Yes."

"And I get blessed when I eat it?"

"Right."

She looks at the banana with a new sort of respect, then opens it and takes a bite. I'm not about to tell her that she's supposed to share it with me. I don't even get a chance to worry about what to do or say or think, because from my window, I hear Fabi. "Mingus Mouse!"

Tinley follows me to the window.

Fabi's about to say something, but when she sees Tinley Schaedler, her jaw drops open.

"Hey," I call.

Fabi stares back, pulls a strand of hair into her mouth, and then she's gone. Tinley and I are left staring at her empty window.

"Was that Fabi Calderón?"

"Yup."

"She lives right there?"

"Yup."

"Huh . . . and is this where you hang your laundry?"

"Yup. Well. My parents do. I'm not that good at it. When I try it, people end up with underwear on their cars." Tinley laughs, and that feels good.

The line hangs with a rainbow of Paati's saris. Amma's started wearing Indian clothes, too. Shortly after Paati arrived, Amma pulled from her closet a big box that smelled like mothballs, and soon, orange and yellow and red saris replaced her drab old pants and shirts. The house is brighter now. The street is brighter, too.

Just then, as if they've heard the news about Tinley Schaedler, the butterflies descend. They land on the laundry line, a row of orange monarchs.

"Oh wow," Tinley says. "They're amazing!"

So far, Tinley's encountered a blessed banana, Fabi Calderón, and a flutter of butterflies. She leans out the window, looking up and down the street, searching, I guess, for more wonders of Mingus Avenue.

Finally, she turns back to my room and sits down. "It must be fun having Fabi right there," she says.

"Yeah. It is." I'm more relaxed now. "She has a little brother. They're pretty much my best friends."

"I thought Raju was your best friend."

"Why would you think that?"

She tilts her head to think for a second. "I don't know. I just assumed."

"It's because we're both Indian. That's why. You shouldn't assume things about people."

She opens her mouth to say something, but stops. She stares at the wall, and I hear, suddenly, the echo of my own voice, how angry it is. I don't mean to sound angry.

"I mean . . ." I'm searching for something, anything, to say. "People think we're best friends because we're both Indian, but we're not. Our parents are but we are definitely *not*."

She looks at me and nods. "Yeah. He hangs out with Box Tuttle mostly, right?"

"Yeah."

"Who's kind of a jerk, honestly."

"Yeah." Pause. Long pause. "Sorry. If I sounded mad."

She shakes her head. "So what about this project?"

The project. I'd almost forgotten. "I guess we need a topic."

"Yes! A topic would be good."

We stare blankly at each other.

"My country is," I say.

"My country is," she repeats, stretching out the last word, waiting for an idea to hop onto the end of it.

"How about Mariposan history?"

"Like all of Mariposan history?"

"Yeah."

She scrunches up her nose. "I think that's too much for one project. How about tourism?"

"Sports? Swimming pools?"

"Ice cream? An entire project on Mariposan ice cream!"

"Let's make a swimming pool full of ice cream in the shape of Mariposa!"

As I lose myself in thoughts of ice cream swimming pools, something happens that's never happened before. A monarch butterfly flies in through my open window and lands on the corner of my desk.

Tinley gasps. I don't dare move. I've been looking at butterflies my entire life, but I've never seen one this close up.

"Is it a girl or a boy?" Tinley whispers.

For the first time, I'm seeing how velvety butterflies are. This one, boy or girl, has gold wings that seem to be lit from the inside. Drawn across its wings are the thinnest black lines, branching off thicker ones, like a map of rivers and streams. The edges of its wings are black with white spots. Little hairs shoot off its belly. Two black antennae and a long dark proboscis droop down from its head. "I can see its eyes," I whisper. "They're looking right at me."

"Muki," Tinley whispers. "I have an idea."

I can't pull my eyes from the butterfly's. I can almost hear it breathing.

"Butterflies," she says. "*Mariposa* means 'butterfly.' Butterflies come from Mariposa. Let's do our project on butterflies."

I look at Tinley. She's right. There's no other reason for this butterfly to land in my room, to sit here looking at me. He's a messenger.

"Okay," I say. "Let's do a project on butterflies."

It's well past lunch when Tinley Schaedler picks up her phone and tells it to "Call George." Seconds later, the blue gullwing car pulls up.

"He's been waiting for you all this time?"

She shrugs. "I guess." She still has a patch of red kum-kuma on her forehead. She checks it in the mirror, perfects the circle with her pinkie, and puts her coat on.

We walk out to the kitchen and find Amma, Dad, and Paati sitting at the table. Amma smiles warmly. "You must be Muki's school friend. How is the project coming, Muki?"

Tinley extends a hand, the way an adult would. "Hi, I'm Tinley Schaedler," she says, giving Amma's hand a hearty shake. "It's lovely to meet you."

Amma's face darkens. The smile vanishes. She pulls her hand from Tinley's like she's touched a hot stove. Tinley drops her own hand, surprised.

"Muki." Amma turns to me. "Please go get ready for dinner."

I look at Dad, who's watching Amma. Why isn't he saying anything? What's wrong with my parents? Dad clears his throat and heads to the fridge. Only Paati gets up, takes Tinley by the hand, and leads her to the door.

Tinley Schaedler stands at our door, and I've never seen her look like this—unsure, off balance. "Okay," she says. "So, um, I'll see you at school?"

I'm just as lost. "Yeah."

"Okay, then." She gives me a small wave and musters a smaller smile, then makes her way, slowly, down the dark stairs.

When I turn around, Amma's face is all daggers. I've never seen her this angry. Behind the anger, just faintly, flows a river of fear. "Never," she begins, "never, never, *never* bring that girl to this house again. Do you understand me, Muki?"

"But why?"

She takes a sharp breath in and lets it out slowly. She's trying to stay calm. "This has gone too, too far." Tears spring to her eyes. "You must be very careful, Muki. Very, very careful. That's all I can tell you."

"Mom, she's not my girlfriend. We're just working on this project."

Her eyes pop wide. "You will work on the project at school. Never here! I will not have her here."

I turn to Dad, who is concentrating very hard on whatever's on the stove. He won't even look at me. That's how scared he is of my mom. I turn to her and match her glare with mine. A second later, I'm on the stairs, out on the street, running. No sign of Tinley Schaedler. I hear footsteps behind me. "Muki!" It's Amma. I'm not stopping.

I barrel down the sidewalk, the pavement sending shock waves up my shins as I run, and the pain feels good.

When I slow down to catch my breath, I hear footsteps again. I swing around to find Amma running clumsily in her house slippers, her hair falling out of its long braid. She stops, out of breath. "You have to listen," she says between gasps. "You have to listen to us, Muki."

"I don't have to do anything I don't want to do," I say.

"This time, for your own safety, you do."

"What do you mean?"

"Tinley Schaedler," Amma says, "has a very dangerous father."

"I know that. Our whole school knows that."

She shakes her head. "You don't know. He's dangerous to us. To *us*."

"What do you mean?"

"The Butterflies and Moths—the camp you went to. The sign with the numbers. General Dogwood Schaedler is in charge of that, Muki. He will take us away as soon as—"

"What? He's really taking us away?" Panic, like a spinning top, starts to whirl and tremble inside me. "What do you mean? What's he going to do?"

Amma puts a hand up. "No one's taking us away yet," she says, straightening up, breathing normally now. "Okay? We'll be fine. We just don't know where things are going. We have to be very careful—"

"The general's dangerous, but that doesn't mean Tinley

is. She's just a kid. What's she ever done to you?"

"But we don't know yet. What to think of anything. We don't know—"

Amma's just telling me the truth, like she always does, and usually the truth makes me feel better. But now it doesn't. Now the truth has many voices, and I don't know which to believe.

"We will be fine, Muki."

"You tell me we'll be fine, and then you tell me people are dangerous. How can Tinley be dangerous if I'm going to be fine? How can both those things be true?"

"I told you—" She takes my hand and I try to run, but her grip is solid.

"Why can't I just do a stupid school project, Mom? Why can't I just have someone over without you being weird? Why can't things be *normal*?"

I hear the buzz of Dragonflies behind us. When I turn around, there's one, two, three of them. Three Dragonflies, their cameras trained on me, their red lights blinking. This isn't security. I feel like this street, Mingus Avenue, isn't mine anymore. Oceanview isn't mine. Pacific City isn't mine. Mariposa isn't mine. It belongs to them now: to Bamberger, to the Butterflies, to the Dragonflies, and to everyone who somehow decided that I don't belong. I don't feel better for knowing the truth. I feel furious.

The Dragonflies buzz louder than ever, and one swoops close enough to graze my head. I've had enough. I yank my hand from Amma's and pull off my shoe. I throw it at the Dragonfly. It hits. The Dragonfly dips, falters, bleeps, and buzzes, its red light flashing.

"Muki!" Amma hisses. She grabs me by the shoulders.

I jerk away from her. "I hate you!" A sob rises in my throat and I turn to run, one shoe off, all the way back home.

Chapter 7

I burst through the kitchen door, still full of fight. I want Dad to be mad at me, because I want to be mad at him. I want to be mad at everyone, but when I stomp inside, the kitchen's empty. But a moment later, I hear a shuffling sound. There he is, my dad, on his knees, rummaging deep in a kitchen cupboard, muttering and growling to himself. "Dad!" It feels good to be angry. But I have nothing to say, so this comes out: "What's for dinner?" Those are not fighting words. He untangles himself from the cupboard, stands up, looks at me with a face as blank as a dead computer, and I know I shouldn't have asked.

"Where is your other shoe? And where's your mother? She ran after you, no? Even after you spoke so rudely?"

I have no answer, just a long, snotty sniffle. Dad leans back into the cupboard, pulls out a package of cookies, and whacks them on the counter. "Dinner." He doesn't get mad that often. He never yells. The cookies mean that he can't deal with me right now. Still, they're cookies. I grab them and run to my room.

Lying on my bed, I slide a whole cookie into my mouth. I *never* get cookies like these—not even for dessert, and definitely not for dinner. Mom says they're packed with preservatives. The sweet biscuit breaks against my cheek, the chocolate crumbling into the cream. I almost forget to be mad. I think about going to Fabi's. What if I moved in with Fabi and Flip? The Calderóns, they're always happy to see me. They never get mad at me. They wouldn't have embarrassed me in front of Tinley Schaedler.

Paati comes in. She lowers herself onto my mattress, creaking and grunting and calling out the name of every Hindu god. When she's settled, she heaves a big sigh. "This isn't an easy time, Muki. Especially for you."

I stare at the ceiling. I can't be mad at Paati. "Why does she have to be like that?"

"Your amma cares about you, more than anything."

"So? What's the point if she doesn't understand me? She doesn't even *try* to understand me. Nothing I think matters."

"Maybe that's true. She's stubborn like a water buffalo."

We're quiet for a while.

"This Tinley, she's a school friend, no?"

I shrug.

"But not a good friend. A new friend. A girl everybody wants to be friends with."

"How do you know?"

"I'm smarter than I look." She grins and pokes me in the ribs. "Let's go find your shoe."

I sit up, and that's when I see it. On my old World Cup poster: the letters from the sign at the Moth camp! GBR, with a little British flag next to it. BRZ, with the Brazilian flag. ARG, with the Argentinian flag. Those letters at the Moth camp stood for countries. I knew I knew them! I look up at Paati, who holds her hand out to me, waiting.

Paati clutches my hand as we walk down Mingus Avenue. With her limp, she spends as much time moving sideways as forward. I'm too busy thinking of those country names to care. Will they be dividing Moths up by the country they came from? Will they be sending us away?

"I see it!" Paati cries. My blue lump of a shoe sits halfway up the street. I try to untangle my fingers from hers, but she's a lot stronger than she looks. We end up running, slowly and awkwardly, together.

As I tie up my laces, Paati gazes around her. "Muki, what do you know about this Demba?"

"Mrs. Demba? She owns the laundromat. Dembubbles."

She clicks her tongue, as if I've said something ridiculous.

"Why do you want to know?"

"Take me to her."

We walk a few doors down to the brightly lit laundromat. The sign in the window, the one that reads *Demba's*

Dembubbles, has started to chip and fade, and through the letters I see Mrs. Demba herself, sitting on a folding chair and reading a magazine. When she sees me, she lowers her spectacles and gasps. "Well, well, look who found his way back!" She springs up and pulls me into a ferocious hug. "Where have you been, Mr. So-and-So!"

"At school, like always," I say, but my mouth is squished into her shoulder, so it comes out more like *A shool, luk awuzh*. The giant tumble dryer's on, the one with the round window. When I was a kid, I'd stand and watch it, hypnotized.

That's when Mrs. Demba spots Paati. She stiffens, looks her up and down. Paati gives Mrs. Demba the once-over, too. The two ladies find each other acceptable, I guess, because Mrs. Demba reaches out a hand and takes Paati's. It's not really a handshake, just a holding of hands. She disappears into the back and comes out with two cans of orange soda. She spanks the side of the vending machine and down falls a bag of potato chips. When I try to refuse, like I've been taught to do, she tuts at me and shoves the chips into my hands. "Go ahead, my prince." She turns to Paati. "You have a good boy here, my friend."

"I know," Paati says curtly. She settles into a folding chair and pops open her soda. "That's why I came to Mariposa. I came for Muki."

This surprises me, but it doesn't surprise Mrs. Demba. She nods, eyes half-closed, like she knows exactly what Paati means. "I'm glad to meet you," Mrs. Demba says. "It's good to have another old goose around, you know."

Paati lets out a laugh. "Old goose, indeed," she says. I eat my potato chips and drink my orange soda, and Paati, Mrs. Demba, and I watch the big dryer, where a stranger's clothes jump and tumble.

When we get up to leave, Mrs. Demba turns to Paati. "Anything else?"

Paati gives her a look heavy with meaning. "Eyes open," she says.

Mrs. Demba's smile falls. She nods. "Eyes open."

Out on the sidewalk: "What's *eyes open*?"

Paati releases an orange soda burp.

"Paati! Come on. What does it mean?"

"What does what mean?"

"Eyes open! You said it to Mrs. Demba!"

"Po-dah," Paati says, squinting up at butterflies on the clothesline. She says that a lot, *po-dah*. It's basically Tamil for *Get outta town*.

"Paati, come on. Be serious."

She glances down at me. "Those sugary drinks make you difficult."

Clearly, I'll have to figure this one out on my own.

When we get back to the house, I cross the street to Fabi's. "Mingus Mouse!" I call. On the clothesline, the butterflies startle. A few leap off the line and hover midair. Fabi comes down.

"What's going on?" I ask her.

She shrugs. "Why were you walking with your grandma?"

"I don't know."

"Why were you holding her hand?"

"I don't *know*." I wish she hadn't seen that.

She grins. Flip comes out. "Yo."

"Have you noticed your parents acting weird?"

"They're always weird," Fabi says.

"It's just that—I don't know. I was just with my grandma, right? And we go to Dembubbles, and Mrs. Demba's there, and everything seems normal, but then they say this thing to each other."

"What thing?"

"Eyes open."

"Huh?"

"Eyes open."

"Eyes open? That's it?"

"And they both knew what it meant. That's what it seemed like. Like it's a code. Or a password. Or a secret message."

"Eyes open," Fabi says. She looks up and down the street, then leans her face close to mine and whispers. "I think you need a hobby."

Flip stops bouncing his ball. "I believe you, Muki."

"Thanks."

"No problem."

"Your parents are acting normal, though? Nothing weird?"

He shrugs. "Parents are weird, man."

Fabi turns on her heel and goes inside. Flip follows. Maybe she's right. I need a hobby.

Chapter 8

My door opens. Amma walks in and leans against the wall. She looks—I'm sure I see it—the tiniest bit sorry. I expect her to come over and give me a hug, but all she does is toss a white shirt at me. "Get dressed, please. We're going to Raju's for dinner." And she's gone again. I flop back down. All I wanted was for her to sit down with me. I put the shirt on, though. We do this every few Sundays, and it's never what I want to do.

All four of us pile into our car and we're off. Dad curses and honks for twenty minutes, until we pull up to the gates of Raju's neighborhood, a pristine pocket of Marble Hill, just a few minutes from school. The guard at the gate gives our car a suspicious once-over every time we pull up, like he's never seen a Honda before. Then he hands us a guest pass and waves us through.

Marble Hill isn't like Oceanview. First of all, there are no Dragonflies in Marble Hill, no one watching. Also, in

Oceanview, almost everyone is from someplace else. We all have different skin colors, all different shades of brown. But it's not like I go around thinking about being Indian, any more than Fabi thinks about being Salvadoran, any more than a monarch thinks about being from the family Nymphalidae. We just fly around and do what we do.

But now, suddenly, we've had a big fat label stuck on us. We're Moths. And the funny thing is, when one group is labeled, other groups get labeled, too. I've started to notice things I'd never seen before. Like how Butterflies seem to all be white, and Moths every other color. How Butterflies are either very rich or very poor, but Moths sit right in the middle. Moth families are like my family. They work. They have enough, and not much more.

I wonder what it's like for Raju, a Moth surrounded by Butterflies. It probably doesn't bother him. It wouldn't have bothered me, either, to be honest, if Bamberger hadn't started sticking us with labels.

When we roll up to the house, Raju's shooting baskets above his garage with Box Tuttle.

"Hey, Mucus," Box calls.

"Hey . . . Box." I keep reminding myself to come up with a good insult for Box Tuttle. Either way, his name is Box. That seems bad enough.

I've known Raju all my life. Pictures exist of us as babies, side by side in our car seats, two scowling brown lumps with black hair and cheeks like samosa dough. Raju's full name is Raju Rajarajan, which, roughly translated, means *King, King of Kings*. Dad calls him Posh Spice.

The front door swings open and there stands Raj Uncle. Raja Rajarajan, father of Raju Rajarajan. I couldn't make this stuff up. Raj Uncle hugs my dad around the shoulders. Then he clasps his hands together and gives a little bow to my mom and Paati, and says, "Please, please." He leads us into the house.

The Rajarajans' front entrance is covered in mirrors, so the house looks three times bigger than it is, and it's huge to begin with. We take off our shoes and I work my toes into the soft plush of their white rug. I love how it feels between my toes, against the balls of my feet. It's like stepping on kittens.

"Is that my Muki?" Sonal Aunty's squeaky, shrieky voice travels from farther inside the house. "Is that my Cookie-boo-boo?"

Sonal Aunty is the human equivalent of a jelly dough-nut. She's round and soft, filled with sweetness and coated in powder. She emerges with her arms outstretched, like she hasn't seen me in a year. She hugs me to her and pulls freely at my cheeks. "Look at you!" she snarls. "Just look at you!" She squeezes my face like she's trying to juice me.

Finally, mercifully, she notices Paati and lets go of me. In one swift swoop, she falls at Paati's feet. Paati, a little startled, pats Sonal Aunty on the back and coaxes her gently back to standing.

Having performed her welcome ritual, our hostess invites us in, just like Raj Uncle, saying, "Please," smiling modestly, and motioning to the living room.

"Muki," she says to me, "help me bring the chaat."

In her kitchen, which, for the record, is bigger than our whole apartment, she arranges a selection of crackers and cheeses and cookies on a three-tiered tray. She puts every cracker, every square of cheese—everything she possibly can—into miniature muffin wrappers. And while she's at it, she turns everything she can into muffins. She's made omelet muffins before. She's made pinto bean muffins before. Today, she places a collection of small brown muffins on the tray.

"Are those chocolate?" I ask.

"Chicken curry," she answers. I gag.

Between the kitchen and living room hangs a curtain of glass beads. They tinkle and clack as I walk through them. First, I take the tray to Amma. "Try the chocolate muffins, Mom. They're really good."

Amma picks one up and takes a bite. She blinks rapidly, holds her napkin to her mouth, and manages to swallow. I grin at her. She is not amused.

That's when Raju comes in, sweaty, holding a basketball, Tuttle-free. "Chicken curry muffins!" he shouts. He bounds over and takes three.

Upstairs, Raju has his own bedroom and bathroom and a playroom just for his toys, a game console, and a sixty-inch television *just* for his game console. Normally, after eating, our parents gather in the living room for tea and Raju and I go up to his room to play video games. But today, Raj Uncle stops us. "Boys," he says. "We'd like you, please, to join us in the living room."

I glance at Raju, who gapes back at me. He doesn't know what's happening, either. Sonal Aunty brings out a plate of sugar cookies, each in a little muffin wrapper. Amma clears her throat and begins. "As you know, we've been living in Mariposa for a long time now. Longer than you've been alive." She glances at Sonal Aunty, who nods. I've never seen her this serious. "We've always loved this island. It felt, very quickly, like our home, and we've been happy here."

Raju turns to his parents, powdered sugar smeared across his cheek. "Are they moving?"

"Nobody's moving," Amma says. "But the country, in a way, is moving." She looks suddenly sad. "It's not the place we came to fifteen years ago."

Raj Uncle clears his throat. "Maybe you've heard of this . . . this business with the Butterfly and Moth?"

I nod. Raju looks clueless.

"Well. Raju. It seems we are the Moths. We only arrived here fourteen years ago, you see."

"I don't get it."

Raj Uncle explains.

"So what does that mean?"

"Well, the plan—the president's plan, that is, is to send

the"—Raj Uncle clears his throat again—"is to send the Moths to other countries."

"Like back to India," I say.

"Well, this is the thing, Muki," Dad chimes in. "Remember those letters you found?"

The answer clicks together. "Those are the countries they're sending us to."

The adults all turn to me, staring.

"I saw those letters at the camp, and then on my soccer poster," I explain. "I thought maybe those were countries people were from. But no. Those are the countries they might send us to, aren't they?

"That's what we think," Dad says. "Great Britain. Brazil. Greenland. Argentina."

GRN. Greenland. Of course. "Why those countries?"

"Those are countries this country has been giving money to."

"So they're paying Bamberger back now," Amma says. "They're doing him a favor. By taking us in. By accepting the *Moths*." Her lip curls with disgust.

"Wait," I say. "So they might send us to Greenland. Not even to India." Not that India is any more my home than Greenland is. I try to picture that country on a map. Mariposa's in the Pacific Ocean. The closest continent is South America. To get to Greenland, we'd have to travel way up and to the right. Farther up and farther right than I've been in my whole life.

"That's what we think, Cookie," Sonal Aunty says. "We think that it's easier for them just to send us to these countries they choose, rather than send each of us back to the country we came from. To figure all that out. So much work. . . ." She trails off.

"But that won't happen to us, right?" Raju's paying attention now. "I mean—we'll be okay. Right?"

"Of course we'll be okay, Cookie," Sonal Aunty says.

Amma and Dad exchange a look. "I think we should be honest, Sonu," Amma says. "There's a chance—"

"We don't want to worry you, my cookies," Sonal Aunty cuts in, "but we want you to know this. We're going to need your help. You will have to be big boys for us, okay?" Raju and I glance at each other. He looks worried.

"Okay," I say.

"Raju?"

"Okay."

Amma sighs. "It's going to be a busy time. Muki, we'll be delivering samosas from the shop. Lots of deliveries, for the summer season. That's why Paati came to join us—to help take care of you. You know how busy it usually gets. But if things get too—busy"—her voice breaks a little—"if we get very busy, Muki, and we can't come home one day, I don't want you to panic. Okay? I want you to get on the subway to Marble Hill, and I want you to come to Raju's house. You'll stay here with them."

"Okay," I say again. I try to read the feeling in the room,

but I can't. I try to figure out if I should be afraid, but I can't. I know what Amma's saying, though. "This isn't really about you getting too busy, is it? They might take you away. They might put you in that camp we saw." And now I know: this is definitely fear I'm feeling. It churns in my belly.

The adults gaze at each other for a long time. For a little too long, like they've forgotten Raju and I are even there. "And what about me?" Raju pipes up. "If they take you away, Mama, will I go to Muki's house?"

"Yes, yes, Cookie-boo-boo," Sonal Aunty coos. She squeezes closer to Raju and covers his head with kisses. "You will go to Muki's house, and you will be fine. We will all be fine. Okay? I promise." Sonal Aunty and her powdered-sugar promises. I know they'll melt to nothing if Bamberger takes my parents away.

Raju slumps back against the sofa. "Can't I just go to Box's house? Muki doesn't have a game console."

"What about Paati?" I ask. "Will they take her away?"

"No one's being taken away yet, Muki." Dad takes my hand in his. "I'm sure everything will be fine. We just want you to be prepared, that's all."

I look at Paati, who's happily munching on a chicken curry muffin. A hundred little specks of light bounce off her glasses, thrown down from the chandelier above. I imagine her in one of those black tents, alone and surrounded by strangers, missing us. I imagine a day when Dad doesn't come home. I look up at the chandelier, and it sends knives into my eyes. My head throbs. I look at Sonal Aunty, who smiles sweetly at me. Too sweetly. There's a big hole inside me and it's filling quickly with fear. Fear tastes like a stale chicken curry muffin. It shoots from my stomach to my mouth and before I can stop myself, I bend over and throw up. All over Sonal Aunty's nice white rug.

That night, Paati sits on her bed, dragging a brush through her white mop of hair. It rises from her head like fizz, wiry and wavy, until she pulls it back into a bun. It's dark in my room, but the full moon hangs right in the frame of my window. I have a thousand questions. As if she senses them, Paati asks her own question, in a calm and quiet voice. "How did we get here, Muki? Do you know?"

It started with the soccer fight, I tell her. I break it down for Paati in three steps. First, the game: East City versus West City. Second, the fight: Fistfights in the stadium. The crowd sort of folding into itself, bodies twisting, arms flailing, until the fight spilled onto the field, then into the streets. Smashed windows. Ruined storefronts. In Marble Hill, a statue of Mariposa's founder, Elmwood Rumrunner, ended up with a jar of grape jelly on his head, purple goo glopping down his face. I thought that part was funny. The president did not. And that's when the third step started: the crackdown. Pro soccer ended. Youth soccer ended. The Dragonflies. Moths and Butterflies. And now the camps. What's next?

After a pause, Paati sighs. "Well, I suppose the details are correct. However."

"However what?"

"This Moth-and-Butterfly business? That started brewing in Bum-burger's bean brain long before the soccer game."

"It did?"

"Oh yes. That president does not give one flying falooda about smashed windows, my boy. Or that statue of Emily Rumbottom."

"Elmwood Rumrunner." Paati's right. There's one thing I've never talked to anyone about. It's something I've hardly wanted to think about. East City was down a few goals, and the game was moving along like any game. But about halfway through the second half, something changed. I saw it in the East City stands. Their fans, dressed all in red, started a chant. Its words were hard to pick out at first, but then I understood: They were yelling at West City's center forward. They were yelling about his skin color. They were telling him to get out of their country. The way they moved had changed, too. They started pumping their arms up and down in exact syncopation. Their faces were dead serious. Their voices became one voice, their faces one single angry white face. They moved like a robot army and sent chills down my legs. This wasn't a soccer game anymore. Not to them.

I never thought soccer fans cared about skin color or

what country a player was from. I never thought soccer had anything to do with Moths or Butterflies. It was just a game. It was the world's game. It was the best game. But I watched it happen, real-time, on TV. Sometimes, when I close my eyes at night, those faces, those arms, come charging back at me.

I speak carefully, since I've never said these words aloud. "There are people in Mariposa who hate people like us. Who want us to go away."

"Yes, in a way," Paati answers. "But it's not all people in Mariposa. There are many good people in this country. And really, the problem is, some people's lives are not very good, Muki. They have trouble finding their futures; everything seems impossible when they don't have the money or the good luck they need. They're unhappy with the state of their lives, and so they look for someone to blame."

"And Bamberger's right there, telling them where to point a finger."

"Correct. He used that terrible night as an excuse to do what he wants to us. He used it to make people afraid of us. And when people are afraid, Muki, they'll close their eyes and let the president do what he wants. As long as he makes them feel safer."

"So the fight wasn't the real problem. It was just an excuse to start talking about Moths and Butterflies. To send Dragonflies into the city."

"Bum-burger was just waiting for that fight. He saw his

chance to take control and make this country into something different."

I study Paati through the dark. She looks very serious. Then she snaps her fingers.

"But don't look so worried, my boy. Everything will work out in the end."

I wish I could believe her.

A minute later, she's snoring. Through the window, I see butterflies on the clothesline again, more tonight than I've ever seen before. My head gets heavy. This mattress is lumpy and thin, and Paati's snores are loud, but this day was too big and my mind is too full. As Dad says, my suspension needs to settle. I close my eyes.

I open them. I can't sleep. One hour passes, then two. My mind sprouts its own pair of wings and flies out the window, over the ocean, all the way to India, where I can see Paati's house so clearly it's almost like I'm there. I see the floor tiles, beige and speckled with black and gray. In the living room: her ceiling fan, its blades spinning slowly, barely bothering the air, clicking with every turn. I spent long, boring days in Paati's big, quiet house, watching that ceiling fan go round and round.

From outside, I hear a clang and—*whoosh*—I'm back in my room. I sit up. The clock reads 3:10 a.m. That was the clang of our front door closing. I'd know that sound anywhere—awake, asleep, with or without wings. I listen closer and hear the low rumble of an engine. A car on

Mingus Avenue at this time of night?

Slipping out of bed, careful not to bump Paati, I go to the window. A little past our shop sits a silver pickup truck. There's a woman standing on the sidewalk, leaning into the truck's open window. I can barely make her out, but there's something familiar about her—her hand on her hip, her chin jutting just the way—just the way— "Amma!" I gasp. Paati stirs, snuffles, turns over.

I'm about to rap on the window and call to her, but I stop myself. I want to see what she does. And so I watch, silently, as she steps away from the car window, tucks something into the sleeve of her sweater, and swings back around to the house. She lets herself in the front door, and a few seconds later I hear her bedroom door close.

I turn to Paati. She's awake now, sitting up and blinking at me, confused. "Paati, it's Amma," I whisper. "She was down on the street, talking to a car!"

She slumps back down. "Po-dah," she mutters, and falls back asleep, snoring.

Chapter 9

I don't sleep at all. Not a wink. Not a blink. At 5:45, Paati gets up, raises her hand to snap her fingers, but sees that I'm already awake. "Not bad," she crows, and spreads the yoga mats.

After yoga, as Paati bangs around the kitchen, I stay in corpse pose, just staring at the ceiling. That's when Amma sticks her head in the room. "Fabi's sick today," she says. "You can take the subway on your own." She pauses, looks at me lying on my back. "Well?" Her eyebrows jump up her forehead. "Any plans today? Breakfast, maybe? School, perhaps? What do you think, sahib?"

"Amma?"

"What?"

"Nothing."

When I roll to my feet, the questions get up with me. The questions follow me into the shower. They sit with me at breakfast and walk with me to the station. They stand next to me in the subway car, filling my head, pushing against my ears, pulling my eyelids closed.

Somehow, I fall asleep. Can you believe that? I fall asleep on the subway train and almost miss my stop. The funny thing is, I fall asleep standing up, holding on to a pole, and when I wake up, there's a man holding me up by the elbow, like it's no big deal, like kids fall asleep standing up all the time. I blink awake, yank my arm from him, still confused. He looks down, winks, and moves down the car to find a seat. He opens a book and doesn't give me another look. I'm one stop away from Marble Hill Prep. I spend the rest of the ride staring at the man, feeling like I've seen him before. He's white, with blond hair pulled back into a ponytail. His eyes are a strange blue. He wears red pants. I've never seen anyone in red pants.

At school, I do everything I can to avoid Tinley Schaedler. I can't believe it was only yesterday that she was lying on my bedroom floor. I don't look over at her side of the classroom at all, and I mean *at all*. I have a headache by the end of the day.

When I get home, I'm ready to put my head under a pillow and go to sleep, but Fabi calls to me from her window, and suddenly soccer and sunshine sound exactly right.

"I thought you were sick," I say.

"I'm okay now. Tummy bug."

I tell her about last night, how I barfed on Sonal Aunty's sofa, onto their magical white carpet, how Sonal Aunty threw her hands up and shrieked, and all at once the grown-ups were dashing around, grabbing napkins, sopping up my mess. But I don't tell her about the conversation with my parents and Raju's. I don't tell her *why* I threw up.

"Maybe you had the same bug," she says.

"Maybe."

When Flip, Fabi, and I get to the field, the Marble Hill and Quimby teams are packing up and heading out. They practice on our field, because theirs was destroyed in the riots. Theirs is just a mud pit now, so they moved to ours. Must be nice to be on a real team that plays real games, with a real coach and uniforms.

As Raju and Box walk past us, I see this: bright yellow butterfly decals on the chests of their green jerseys. When Raju sees me staring at the butterfly, he covers it with his hand. Then he leans in and says something to Box and they both laugh. Suddenly, all I can think about are the tents at the camp, my parents' worried faces, the East City fans, their faces oozing hate. *You're no butterfly*, I want to tell Raju. Normally, I'd just think it and let him pass. But today, something boils up inside me, like hot milk in a saucepan. Before I can stop myself, I yell, "You're no Butterfly!" Raju stops walking. He gathers the fabric of his jersey in his fist and stares back at me. Then he walks over to where I'm standing, Box stalking behind.

Raju stands just inches away from me now. "What did you call me?"

"I didn't call you anything. I said you're not a Butterfly. You're a Moth like me."

He leans in so close his hot breath sails up my nostrils. "I can be what I want to be."

"Hate to break it to you."

That's when Fabi steps in. "Cut it out, Muki." She pulls me away from Raju. "Let's play." Raju stares at me, walking backward. I stare back at him until he turns around.

"Forget about him," Fabi says. And for a while, I do. The pound in my knees when I run feels good. The thwack of the ball as it flies off my foot feels good. I want to keep running. I want to use up all the energy I have, to run and kick and shout until I'm so wrung out I can't think. By the time we ride home, my head's a lot clearer. But the mixed-up feelings—they're not all gone. They stick to me like burnt milk to a pan.

Chapter 10

Tuesday afternoon, as I settle into my desk for civics, Tinley Schaedler walks up to me. "We need to work on our project," she says. Her words are crisp. All business.

"Okay. Um, today?"

"After school. I'll meet you at your locker." She turns and walks away. And then she's back. "I have no idea where your locker is. Just come to mine." And she's gone again.

Everyone knows where Tinley Schaedler's locker is. As we walk down the hallway, I try not to notice people watching us. We're like Moses parting the Red Sea, if the Red Sea were a sea of sweaty, staring middle school kids. Outside, at the school pickup zone, we wind through SUVs of every shape and color until we reach hers—royal blue with gullwing doors. Her driver hops out and opens the car door for us.

"Hi, George," she says.

"Tinley kid," he answers.

"This is Muki."

George gives me a nod.

As soon as she's buckled in, Tinley grabs a phone from the back-seat pocket and plips away on it. She doesn't say a word to me. It's like I'm no more a person than the leather backpack beside her.

Butterflies. I think about the butterfly that flew through my window. I think about how excited Tinley was to see it. I felt, that day, like I was showing her something new, with the butterfly, my window onto the street, even Paati's banana. I felt like maybe she was interested in my world.

We come to the familiar gates of Raju's neighborhood. Other cars pull into other garages, and I see kids I recognize from school. Soon enough, we pull into the mouth of the Schaedlers' long and winding driveway. It's lined with trees that filter the sun, spilling freckles of light along the ground. We pass over a little bridge, and when I press my nose against the window, I glimpse a creek trickling past. In the distance are tennis courts and a swimming pool, and past those, a small house with a yellow door, really no bigger than the shop. I'm surprised. I'd expected a mansion.

"Is that your house?" I ask.

She glances up. "That's George's."

We carry on, past another house like George's, and another. We pass a second swimming pool. "You have two swimming pools?"

"Three. There's an indoor one, too." The trees close in,

and soon the sunlight's blocked out completely. When I look up through the window, there's just a canopy of green. At last, we push through a final thick tunnel of trees and emerge in a clearing. Here, the sun rains down on an enormous house. *House* really isn't the word for it. It's bigger than any house I've ever seen. It's more of a castle, made of the same yellow sandstone as our school, with a turret at the corner. I expect to see a knight perched there, on the lookout for invaders. No knights, but a guard dressed all in black stands at the front door.

At the side of the house sits a low black panther of a car. "Whoa," I say. "That's a Bugatti."

Tinley snaps to attention. "Papa's home?" She drops the phone and cranes her neck to see. "George! Papa's home!"

"Sure is."

The car has barely stopped when she presses a button on her door, ducks under it as it opens, and rolls out onto the driveway. She scrambles to her feet and runs to the front of the castle. I watch her heave open the front door and slip inside. George glances back at me. "Better get inside, kid."

I slip through the heavy front door just as it closes.

Inside, the house is dark. Tinley is nowhere. The first thing I notice is the smell—like old damp stone, but not in a bad way. There's something earthy and watery and fresh about this smell. I take a deep sniff, let it fill my nose and chest. A staircase winds up and out of sight. On the wall at the foot of the stairs hangs a large photograph of a woman holding a little girl. The woman throws her head back in an openmouthed laugh. The little girl does the same. I know, right away, that this is Tinley's mother, and in her arms is Tinley. Tinley got her orange hair from her mom. I wonder what it's like to see this picture every day.

A hunger cramp reminds me that I have no idea where to go next. I open room after empty room and find Tinley, at last, in a vast, red-carpeted parlor. She stares at her phone, earbuds in, her feet up on a sofa.

"Hey," I say.

She ignores me. My stomach growls more insistently. I think of samosas. A samosa on a plate with a cold glass of milk. I try to act calm, but the hunger rises like a dragon woken from its nap. "Hey," I try again. "Could I get something to eat?"

"Ask the kitchen staff," she mutters, and flaps her hand toward a far door.

I find no trace of a kitchen, just more cold and cavernous rooms. The cold seeps right into my stomach, right into my bones. The hunger hurts now. The dragon is awake. The dragon is *hungry*.

I stomp back into the parlor to find Tinley. "Hey!" I say louder now. I walk right up to her, and I can't believe I'm doing this, but I pull her earbud out of her ear. She wrenches herself up, stares at me. A flash of fear, then fury, passes over her eyes. I step back, drop the earbud.

"Sorry," I say. I'm out of breath. I can't believe what I've done. "I'm sorry. I'm just hungry. Like really hungry. Could you show me where the kitchen is?"

She stands and gives me an icy, endless glare, and leads me through the first door, then through a swinging door, one I didn't see before, into a humongous kitchen.

"Lee's out," she says quietly.

"Who's Lee?"

She doesn't answer, just leads me to a colossal fridge and yanks it open. She pulls out a packaged sandwich for herself and hands one to me. Then she fills two glasses from an *automatic chocolate milk dispenser* and I think I might faint.

At the big round kitchen table, we eat our sandwiches and don't say a thing. I take my last sip of frothy, cold chocolate. "So, should we start?"

She shrugs, pulls a lock of hair over her shoulder, examines the bristly end of it.

I decide to just ask. "Did I do something wrong?" She looks up at me. "Are you mad at me?"

"I don't know," she says.

But I know. Of course I know. "Was it my mom?"

She shrugs, then nods.

"My mom wasn't nice."

She nods more vigorously, and I think I see tears spring to her eyes.

"Yeah. I don't know what was wrong with her. She's usually really nice to my friends. Like, nicer than she is to me."

"It's happened before," Tinley says. "My dad says it's because of him. People are angry at him, but they take it out on me."

"Why're people angry at him?"

"Oh please, I don't know," she sighs. "Whatever the president's doing. I don't pay attention to that stuff."

"Oh."

"I like meeting people's moms, though. They're usually nice to me."

"I think my mom's upset about the Butterflies."

"Our project?" She stares openly, like she has no clue what I'm talking about.

"You don't know about Butterflies? And Moths?" I search her face. I'm pretty sure she isn't joking. She just doesn't know. "So, when you wanted to do a project on butterflies, you really just wanted to talk about butterflies?"

She rolls her eyes. "That seems obvious. What else would I be talking about?"

I hesitate. I almost don't tell her. "So. There's this other thing happening." And I tell her everything I know. Her eyes get wider and wider as I walk her through the news.

"So you might have to leave?" she asks.

"That's what people are saying. My dad says maybe it won't go that far." This doesn't make either of us feel better. We sit quietly for a minute. The thing I like about Tinley is that she can be quiet. She doesn't talk unless she has something real to say.

Finally, she does speak. "That doesn't seem right," she says.

"Hey," I say, pulling out my butterfly book. "Should we get something done for this project? In case I stay in the country long enough to get a grade?"

She smiles. "I'll show you what I found in the reading room."

The reading room, as big as the school library, sits in dreamy gloom. By the bookcase, Tinley turns on a big lamp. Now I can see its ceiling, which soars to a high, painted dome.

"Look at this," Tinley says. From a low shelf, she pulls a large black box. When she opens it, a cloud of dust billows out. I sort of expect a fairy to zing out, with a twinkling wand and hummingbird wings. No fairies, though—just a moth we've surprised. It flutters from the box and up to the ceiling, its wings sprinkling more dust. From the top of the box, Tinley pries a cardboard layer, revealing a white platform stuck with pins. Held beneath each pin, a butterfly: dead, velvety, and incredibly still.

"Are they real?"

"Yes."

"And dead?"

"Obviously."

I touch one, gently, sure it will crumble, but it doesn't. It's so soft I can hardly feel it. I recognize the orange monarch. The yellow swallowtail. The purple hairstreak.

A voice booms through the shadows. "Where's my girl?" Tinley jumps up and peers at the door. Then she yelps, runs across the room, and leaps into the arms of a mountainous man. The general.

"Papa, come meet Muki." She pulls him into the lamplight.

"Muki," the general says, his voice a crisp baritone. He has close-cut dark hair and eyes as big and round and brown as Tinley's—real eyes, not glass. He's wearing a green uniform, and on his chest is a gold butterfly, just like the president's.

I swallow hard. "I'm here to work on a project with Tinley."

He charges at me with his hand out. My first impulse is to run. But then I realize he just wants to shake my hand. A buried memory claws its way up: Dad teaching me how to shake hands. *Firm grip, head up, look him in the eye.* The general's grip is crushing but I manage not to cry out.

I stand there looking at everything but him, massaging my right hand with my left. "Of course," he says. "Muki." He doesn't smile. His back is so straight I think it might bend back the other way. "General Dogwood Schaedler. You can call me General Schaedler."

"Hi."

"Welcome," he says dryly.

His eyes land on the box of butterflies. "You found them, I see." Tinley pulls him over. "These are native Mariposan, all these butterflies. My grandmother collected them." He crouches down, places a finger on one of the labels, handwritten in spidery cursive.

He looks up at me. "Are you good at school, Muki?"

"I have a good vocabulary." I wonder if this is the right answer.

"You know how I like to test a person's intelligence?"

"How?"

"We play a game."

"A game?"

"Blackjack." A cool smile slips across his face. "You ever play blackjack?"

"My dad taught me. But it's not like—"

"Join me at the table," the general says, and turns on his heel.

"Papa?" Tinley looks up from the butterfly box. She watches her father, nervously, as he pulls a chair out from a table and sits in it.

"Come with me, Muki." It's an order, not a request. I obey. The general won't stop looking at me.

"Comfortable?"

"Yes." No. My mouth has gone dry. I look to Tinley but she's absorbed in the butterfly box. The general pulls a deck of cards from his pocket and starts to shuffle them, then stops and presses a button on the side of the table. "Lee. Tea, please," he says.

"You a tea drinker?" he asks.

"No," I answer, just as serious, "but my dad makes it every day."

The general goes quiet. His gaze sharpens. I feel like he sees all the way through me, to every dumb idea that's ever swum through the petri dish of my mind. All I can do is sit there and squirm, like a bug on a pin.

Footsteps at the door, a throat clearing. "Thank you, Lee," the general says.

I've never seen a butler before, but I'm pretty sure this is one. He doesn't wear a tuxedo with long tails, the way they do in books. This one wears a blue-and-white-checked shirt and an apron around his waist. He carries a tray to our table and puts down a pot of tea and a cup.

It's hard to make anything out in this low light, but when I look up, I know I've seen him before. The blond hair, tied back, the nose that looks like it's been broken maybe twice, reset long and crooked. I almost gasp out loud. It's the man from the subway, the one who held me up when I fell asleep standing. I look past his apron to his pants, and sure enough, they're red.

When he sees me, he stops short, but only for a second. For a microsecond. He stares at me but speaks to the general. "Would your guest like some juice, sir?"

"Muki?"

My throat is coated with sand. "No, thanks."

Lee peers at me now, like he's trying very hard to figure something out. The general snaps his fingers for his attention. "That will be all."

The butler moves silently out the door, but he throws me one last glance before he exits.

The general deals the cards. Two for me, two for him. "Blackjack," he mutters, "is a deceptively simple game. It can tell me a lot about a person."

I think about the rumors. Is this how he used to interrogate people? Did he make cold-blooded spies cry with games of blackjack?

"So you go to Marble Hill. You started just this year?"

"Yeah, this is my first year." I don't tell him about the scholarship.

"Going all right?"

"I'm good at fitting in."

"Are you, now?"

"It's my anti-power."

"And an anti-power is?"

"A good thing about you that can make things hard, sometimes."

"Interesting." He doesn't ask how fitting in works against me. Instead, he pours himself a cup of tea.

I look down at my cards again. Ten and two—twelve. Not exactly a winning number, but not small enough to ask for another card without worrying.

"I'd like another card," I say.

"You tap the table, Muki."

"What?"

"When you want another card, you don't say *I'd like another card*. You tap the table and the dealer gives you one."

"Oh."

"And when you don't want any more cards, you say *I stay*."

"Okay."

He sighs. I tap the table.

"So your dad plays blackjack and makes tea. Where's he from?" he asks.

I think about not answering. This is General Schaedler asking, after all. I'm not sure what my answer will mean. I turn my card over and it's a three. That gives me fifteen. I decide to just say it: "India." The general deals himself another card. "But if you asked him, he'd probably say he's Mariposan."

His eyes snap up to meet mine. "Would he, now? And how long has he been here?" He keeps his eye on me as he reaches for another card and looks at it, stone-faced.

"Fifteen years."

He cocks an eyebrow. "Fifteen years must seem like a very long time to you."

"Not really. But long enough."

"Long enough for what?"

"Long enough to call Mariposa home." My heart has climbed into my throat and sits there, holding its breath.

"The Schaedlers have been here a long time, Muki. A long time." He stares at his cards.

I tap the table. My heart climbs back into its little cage. I'm calm now. Strangely calm. "How long have the Schaedlers been here?" I ask.

"Hundreds of years. I can trace my ancestors back to the very first settlers."

"That must feel great." I pick up my card. It's a two. I have seventeen now. It's a high number—close to twenty-one but not a sure winner. I'm not sure what to do.

The general picks up a card, glances at it, and lowers his gaze to my hand.

"What are you going to do, Muki?"

I look him right in the eye. Head up, firm grip. "I'm going to stay."

"Papa!" Tinley's growl makes us both jump. "Papa, we have a project to do. Muki, I am not going to do this project all by myself while you and my dad . . . play cards!"

The general's face softens. The lines around his eyes crinkle as he turns to his daughter. "Sorry, Blossom," he says. "It's not often I get to meet your friends." He holds his hand out, and she leaps up to take it. "I'll let you get back to work now."

When the general turns back to me, his smile drops, but his eyes still sparkle. He picks up my cards and his, and without turning them over, he shuffles them into the pack. He sticks the deck in his jacket pocket, stands up, and walks out the reading room door, leaving his teacup and an empty chair.

I remember something then. "Tinley, can I use your phone?"

Tinley points to a phone on a far desk. I pick it up and dial home. I tell Amma a bald-faced lie while Tinley Schaedler watches and listens. *Just staying after school to work on the project. We're at school, Mom. I'll be back before dark.*

I sit back down.

"You just totally lied to your mom," she says. A slow, sly smile spreads across her face. "That was cool."

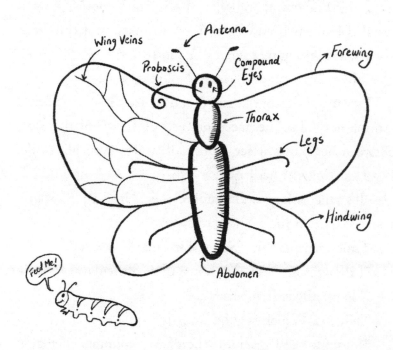

A couple of hours later, I'm back in the gullwing car, George driving, Tinley in the back with me, phoneless. On this ride, the silence is comfortable, so comfortable that I think of something to say: "I like that picture near your front door. Of you and your mom."

"Oh. Yes. People say I look like her. I have her hair and my dad's eyes."

"Do you remember her?"

She thinks about this before answering. "I remember she laughed a lot. I remember she had this crazy laugh. Papa says it was like a goose honking."

I think about that house, its infinite rooms, how it smelled like earth and time. I try to imagine a tiny little Tinley, a laughing mother, a sick mother.

"How does your mom laugh?" Tinley asks.

I try to answer, but I can't. I'm not sure when I last heard Amma laugh. I see her face, the vertical worry line that runs between her brows. I see her small smirk, even her smile. But I can't muster her laugh.

"It's kind of high and strange," I lie. "It's like the sound you make when you're about to sneeze."

Tinley accepts this. "Sorry if my dad was weird."

"I thought he was never home during the day."

"He usually isn't," she says.

"Mine is. Which is good, mostly."

"I used to see Papa a lot when I was younger." She goes quiet again, and I wonder if she's thinking of her mom now. "He used to take me to the beach. Almost every afternoon."

"Really? In Pacific City? I didn't know we had one."

She tilts her head at me. "Come on. You know we have a beach."

I shrug.

"I mean, we're an island. We have beaches."

I'm getting uncomfortable. She's peering at me like I'm an alien specimen. "Well, I've never been to one. Okay?" We sit in silence for another few blocks. "What's it like?" I finally ask.

"It's fun. It's kind of cold. I mean, the water's really cold. You just have to get used to that part. And around sunset, the air gets cold, but when it's sunny, P.C. Beach is the best place in the world."

"What do you—do there? Like, make sandcastles?"

"Sure. And go in the water. Play in the waves. Papa used to surf. He used to come out of the ocean and shake himself dry, all over us, like a dog." She laughs at the memory. "My mom would surf sometimes, too. She was good at digging holes."

"I can't imagine your dad surfing."

"He did," she says. "We just go to the beach club now. We don't go in the water. No one plays in the sand. People just drink and talk and drink and talk, like they could do anywhere. It doesn't even matter that they're at the beach. No one even eats. They just have shrimps in a glass with tomato juice. Which is gross. And that's about it."

I definitely have questions about the shrimps in a glass, but just then George pulls off the highway at the exit marked

Oceanview. "Almost home," I say.

"Should we work at your house next time?"

"Probably not."

"Okay," she says quietly, fiddling with her lock of hair. "If it's okay for you to come over to my house, that's fine with me."

"It's not exactly okay," I say. She heard me lie to my mom, after all. "But I like it at your house."

"Well, I like it at your house."

Now she's the one lying. I'm sure of it. "You like my house?"

"Sure. It's warm inside. And it's right above a shop. And there are butterflies outside your window. And I like your grandma. And I think it's nice you all live together. I sort of wish I had a house like that."

"I don't believe you. You get to live in a castle."

She shrugs. "It's more of a castillo."

"That's just Spanish for *castle*."

"There's a difference. Believe me."

George drops me off at the edge of Oceanview, five minutes from home. I don't want the spectacle of an arrival on Mingus Avenue, and I definitely don't want Amma to see me get out of the gullwing car. I run down my road just as dusk turns to dark. I'm back in the kitchen just as the idlis come out of the steamer, and I'm seated at the table, hands washed, just as Amma sets down a bowl of coconut chutney.

« »

90

After dinner, Dad sends me down to collect the chai dispenser. We clean it every night, fill it every morning.

"Mukaroni and Cheese," Buff calls from the storage room.

"I'm here to get the chai thing," I answer.

"Knock yourself out." The dispenser is empty. We don't worry about Buff drinking the chai. *Can't stand the stuff,* he said once. *Can't stand the smell.* Only Buff could hate the smell of chai. But as Dad pointed out, Buff's favorite food is a french fry sandwich, so maybe it's not that surprising.

When I reach behind the counter to unplug the dispenser, a long, thick roll of paper falls out. The paper itself is thin and yellowing, like an old treasure map. *What if it is a treasure map?* the voice in my head says. I peek into the storage room, where Buff is deep into a magazine. Then I unroll the paper and spread it on the counter. Wide purple lines cut across the paper—a street labeled *Mingus Ave.* This is no treasure map. This is Oceanview.

The next page leaps into color, with computer-generated drawings of wide, clean sidewalks. Three computer-generated ladies walk down the sidewalk in hats, holding shopping bags. They're not smiling. They don't seem to be having a very good computer-generated day.

I stare at the drawings. They say *Mingus Ave.,* but where are the brick buildings? Gone. The laundry lines: gone. The sweet, cluttered street I've known my whole life: gone.

"Hey!" Buff stomps in. "Put that down!" But it's too late. I've seen everything. He grabs the drawings from me and rolls them up.

I back away from the counter. My feet want to run upstairs, away from Buff and that roll of paper. But I have to ask: "It says Mingus Avenue there, but what is it? It doesn't look anything like—"

"We're tearing it all down," he says.

"Tearing it all down? Why?"

He stares hard at the floor. The lightning bolt on his head jumps a little each time he clenches and unclenches his jaw. "We're starting over, Muki. We have great plans for a new Oceanview, new shops, new houses, new everything." Who's *we*, I wonder.

"What's wrong with our old shops?"

He leans in, lowers his voice. "No more bodegas. No more laundromats. Just high-end clothing stores. A luxury car dealership. Fancy restaurants. Oceanview's finally getting classy." A slow smile spreads across his face.

"I don't think my parents would want to run a clothes store."

Buff doesn't say anything, just clears his throat and taps the roll against the counter. And that's when I realize: Amma and Dad won't run anything on the new Mingus Avenue. They won't be here, in the new Oceanview. And neither will I.

Buff walks to the window and looks out at the street.

"These dingy old buildings. These laundry lines. These sad little businesses. Dembubbles . . ." He shakes his head. "Who even uses laundromats anymore?"

"Probably lots of people," I say. "People love Mrs. Demba. And lots of people love the Wongs' place. And lots of people love this shop."

"Lots of freeloading Moths like this shop," Buff sneers.

I feel like Buff's just punched me. I wait for him to snap out of this. I wait for this to turn into a joke, but he just gazes coolly back at me.

"You think we're freeloaders? My mom and dad gave you a job."

He shrugs this off. "Look, you guys are all right. All right? It's the rest of 'em."

"The rest of who?"

He looks up at the ceiling, out the window. He won't look me in the eye. "People hear about the Mariposa touch, they come here to our rich little island and they use it and abuse it. They suck out the nectar and leave us dried up. Empty."

I look around at my parents' tidy shop. "Do you really think that?"

For a second, he looks ashamed, but he puffs his chest back up again. "You wouldn't understand."

"I mean, yeah, sometimes my mom's kinda mean to you, and Mrs. Wong's always double-parking and blocking up the street, and half the time Mrs. Demba's vending machine doesn't work. But do you really think we're—bloodsuckers?"

"Freeloaders."

"Well, do you?"

He finally looks me in the eye. "Like I said, it's complicated." He snatches up the plans and rolls them up. "You weren't supposed to see this anyway."

I pick up the tea dispenser. "Well, I just did. So."

"Don't tell anyone!"

"I make no promises." I walk out.

I don't tell anyone, but not because Buff doesn't want me to. I'm just trying to figure out who to tell and how. Amma and Dad? I find them in the kitchen, still sitting around the dinner table. I have to tell them. They have to know.

But the moment I decide to tell them, Paati starts talking about my grandfather, Tha-tha. I didn't know Tha-tha all that well. He died last year. He liked to read. When we visited Chennai, he'd sometimes call me out to the front veranda of his house. He'd put his book down and take my hand in his, and we'd sit there without talking, and watch the people and rickshaws and bicycles pass by.

Now the three of them sit quietly, staring down at the table. Finally, Dad perks up. "Did I ever tell you, Muki, about the first time I met your amma?" I sink into my chair and pull my sweater up over my nose.

Amma perks up, too. "Yes, yes. You should have seen it! Your father walked up to me," she says, "and asked me to go to the coffee stall with him." She makes a face. "I said no. Who was this fellow? Boldly asking to have coffee? I had never seen him before. I didn't know his family. So."

"So I told your amma to go see a movie with her friends. And *I* would go to the same movie at the same time with *my* friends. This was our love life, Muki." I pull my sweater all the way over my eyes. The thought of my parents dating makes me want to disappear. Through the weave of my sweater, I see Dad smile warmly at Amma, and Amma smile back at him.

I won't tell them now. Not now.

Chapter 11

For the rest of the week, I watch Amma and Dad for signs of worry. I stay hush on the Mingus Avenue news. I'm just a kid, I tell myself. Let the grown-ups worry. They're the ones who made the trouble in the first place. And just like that, the worries lift and drift away, like steam from a subway vent. Life returns to normal. A new kind of normal.

Every morning, as I leave for the subway, Buff enters the shop. He holds himself straighter, a smug little smile stamped on his face. I suspect the smugness lasts until Amma comes down and starts telling him what to do. That much hasn't changed.

Around the city, orange-and-black Butterfly flags spring up outside buildings and houses. One morning, I see a Butterfly flag flying from the flagpole at school. That same afternoon, I walk past Miss Pistachio in the hall, arguing about something with Mr. Pinto, the principal. The next morning, the flag is gone.

Soon, something new starts to brew in Pacific City. It starts, for me, on a Monday afternoon in civics, the last class of the day, when kids start watching the clock, waiting and wishing for the end. Miss P. stands at the front of the room. She smooths down the front of her green dress and waits for the bubble of conversation to quiet. "Butterfly Day," she says quietly.

She looks around the classroom and doesn't say a word, just turns to the board and writes *May 5*. Two weeks from now. Then, crossing her arms over her chest, she begins. "Butterfly Day is a day to celebrate Mariposa and Mariposan identity." Something about her voice sounds robotic, like she's memorized these lines. "Butterfly citizens will be invited to participate in a parade through downtown, which will begin at three o'clock. Colorful dress is encouraged. Applications for parade floats may be submitted at City Hall." She sends out a tight smile. "Okay?"

Fabi raises her hand. "What if you're not a Butterfly?"

Miss P. blinks very fast. "Non-Butterfly residents may watch the parade, but not participate. There will be a special spectator section for those residents."

I raise my hand. The entire class turns to me. "Will there be a Moth parade, too?"

Again, the tight smile. "I don't think so, Mukesh."

Fabi raises her hand. "Could we start one, if we wanted?"

"That's something to discuss with your families," Miss

P. says. Then her smile softens and widens. "It's a lovely idea, Fabiana."

Fabi turns to look at me. We both get it. We're invited, but we're not invited. I look over at Raju, whose cheeks have gone pink. He doesn't look at me or Fabi. He keeps his eyes on his notebook.

Box Tuttle raises his hand. "When are they making the Moths leave?" The room heats up. In my chest, a rubber band stretches tighter and tighter.

"Shut it, Box," Fabi growls.

"I'm just asking, Fabi. When are you leaving?"

"Boxwood Tuttle! That's enough!" Miss P. hisses.

"Yeah, Box," a voice says. I realize, too late, that it's mine. "Don't talk about what you don't know about."

That's when Raju turns to me. "There's no point denying it, Muki." His eyes burrow into mine. "All of Oceanview's heading to Greenland soon. Better pack a coat!" A smattering of giggles, a smirk from Raju, and the rubber band, stretched to its tightest point, snaps.

I spring from my chair and pull Raju to the floor. The classroom erupts like a mess of seagulls, kids all over us, yelling and cawing. I have Raju around the neck. Miss P. is shouting in my ear, and I'm pulled off him. I'm on my knees, panting. Miss P. holds one of my arms, Fabi the other. Raju stares at me, shocked. He touches a hand to his neck, streaked with a long red scratch.

« »

School is over. The classroom is empty. Raju and I sit at our desks. Fabi's here, too. She isn't in trouble, but she decides to wait with me. Miss P.'s gone to get Mr. Pinto. I imagine news of the fight getting back to Amma and Dad, back to Paati. I can see the shame on their faces, the confusion. *This isn't at all like him*, they'd say. And they'd be right. This isn't like me. I don't know who I am right now, but I'm sure not me.

"Muki," Fabi says quietly. She eyes the window for signs of Miss P. "You can't do stuff like this. You can't, either, Raju."

"But Box Tuttle—"

"Forget Box Tuttle. His dad just bought the school a new pool. Box Tuttle can do what he wants. But you? Me? Kids from Oceanview? One slip and we lose our scholarships. We're back at Oceanview Middle."

"I know," I say. "But maybe we're gone anyway. Maybe they really are sending us away."

Fabi shakes her head. "Until they do, I'm here. I'm not getting expelled."

It hadn't occurred to me that I could get expelled. If that happens . . . I imagine telling my parents. I go hot and cold and want to cry. Maybe if I do cry—

Miss P. walks in. No sign of the principal.

"Where's Mr. Pinto?" Raju asks.

"I decided not to involve him," Miss P. says. "I just needed a minute to calm down."

"We're not in trouble?" Raju asks.

"Oh, you're in trouble," she says. "With me."

Raju sits back, lets out a whoosh of air.

"Well, you don't need to look so relieved," she says. Her face hardens into an iceberg. I've never seen Miss P. like this, craggy and cold and angry.

"What's going to happen to us?" I ask. She turns to me. A second later—I don't know how I do this—but a second later, the iceberg starts to melt. She softens, looks down at her hands, at the bare, pale fingers. Then she rummages in the pocket of her green dress and pulls out a cell phone. "Who here has a phone?" she asks.

"I do," Fabi says.

"Take down my number, Fabiana."

"Why?"

Miss P. looks from me to Fabi to Raju. "Just in case. You never know." She jots something down, and Fabi blips it into her phone.

"Can we go now?" Raju asks.

"Not yet." She clears her throat. "I haven't really planned what I wanted to say," she begins. "I can only imagine, though, that this might be a hard time for you." Raju's face goes pink again. "I'd like all three of you to be part of this parade. You are as much a part of our school as anyone."

"So we can be in the parade?" Fabi asks.

Miss. P. looks down, scrunches and stretches her fingers. "No. I'm sorry. You can help make the float, of course.

And you'll be able to watch from the Moth section."

Fabi stands up, looks Miss P. right in the eye. "That's not good enough for me." She picks up her backpack and runs out the door, past the frosted-glass window, her footsteps echoing down the hall.

Miss P. turns to the window, her cheeks drooping. Then she sighs and sits down at the desk next to mine. She leans over, looks at me, at Raju. "Never again, you two," she says. "Do you hear me?"

We nod.

To my surprise, her eyes fill with tears. One leaps off her lid and streams down her cheek. "Okay, then. You're free to go."

And that, I guess, is our after-school punishment. Raju scrams down the hall and bangs through the school's front door. I look around for Fabi, hoping she waited for me. She didn't. At the steps to the subway, I'm so lost in my head that I don't hear anyone behind me, until, "Hey! Wait up!"

I turn. It's Fabi. She stomps past me down the steps, staring straight ahead.

I wait till we're on the subway platform. "What's wrong?" I ask.

"Can you believe her?"

"What—the parade thing?"

"So messed up." She shakes her head.

"I think she felt bad," I say. "I think she was trying to say sorry—"

"She can keep her sorry," Fabi snaps. "If she can't change anything, I don't want to hear it."

On the train, we share a pole. A sheen of sweat coats Fabi's face and beads above her lip. We're both quiet for a while. As we leave Quimby Corner Station and move into Moth neighborhoods, the people on the train get browner, the talk around us a little louder. She stares hard at an ad for a plastic surgeon, and I try to think of something funny to say about it, but then a single tear drops from her eye. She blinks quickly, swipes at her face with the back of her hand. I freeze. I know how to do jokes. I don't know what to do when girls cry.

One teardrop, then two. They drop off Fabi's eyelashes like rain from an awning.

I search my memory for what Dad might do, what he's done in the past when Amma's been upset. I can see Amma angry, annoyed, but never crying. I'm about to tell Fabi to stop crying. I'm about to tell her not to worry, not to be upset, but then, out of nowhere, Dad's voice: *Never tell a woman how she should feel.*

"How do you feel?" I ask.

"Mad. I'm mad. Who are they? Are they better than me?" She looks me in the face, like she's really asking me. "Are they?"

"No, Fabi. Those Butterflies aren't better than you."

People around us look up from their phones. I can feel them listening, but I don't care.

"They're no better than any of us. If anyone's better than anyone, it's you." I'm not lying when I say this. I'm not even exaggerating. I don't know anyone who comes close to Fabi—she's smart and great at soccer and funny, and she doesn't care what the world thinks. And she's good to her brother, and real with pretty much everyone, no matter who they are. That's the thing with Fabi—she knows she's a hundred percent, so she doesn't pretend to be what she's not.

She sniffs, wipes her nose on her sweater, looks at the stain on her sleeve. She makes a face. I smile. She cracks a smile, too. I want to tell her that things are going to get better. But I don't know that for sure, and Fabi, she'd see right through that line. So, for the rest of the ride home, we're quiet.

Walking down Mingus Avenue, I remember there's more bad news. I almost forgot, after everything that happened at school. I don't want to tell her, but I need to tell someone.

"I found something yesterday." My heart starts to pinball around my chest. "They're going to bulldoze Mingus Avenue. Like, get rid of all of it. And change its name."

"What do you mean?" She stares me down, hard and serious, in that Fabi way.

I tell her.

"No. Come on. No one's coming to Oceanview to stay in a hotel."

"I found the plans. They were all drawn up, like on

computers. It even showed these ladies with shopping bags."
This is the crowning detail, for some reason, in my mind—
the shoppers who look like they were imported from Marble
Hill, who walk down Mingus Avenue like it's theirs, only
theirs, and always has been.

"So they're getting rid of all this? The houses? My
house?" She looks up at the brick buildings, the laundry
lines.

"Yeah. I don't know when. But, yeah."

"Shut up," Fabi says. "That's the dumbest thing I've ever
heard."

"Dumb but true."

She looks me over, still deciding whether to believe me,
I guess. We get to the shop. "You want to come over?" I ask.

"No, that's okay. I think Flip's home alone. Soccer later?"

"Sure."

She doesn't move, though, just stares at the ground looking so sad I wish I could hug her. I *could* hug her. I just . . .
can't. I pat her on the shoulder. "See you later."

"Okay," she says. We're about to part ways when I hear
a commotion in the shop. Through the window, there are
about twenty people gathered around the counter, looking
up at the television.

Fabi's parents are there—both of them. Flip, too. Mrs.
Wong and Andrew from down the street. Mrs. Demba,
looking worried, pokes her fingers into the tight gray bun at
the top of her head. Buff's at the front of the shop, his arms

crossed, chomping on gum, his eyes bugging out of his head. He's the only one smiling. On-screen, Bamberger stands at a podium. He's in the PCFC soccer stadium, the same stadium where the big fight broke out. The camera zooms out to the stands rammed with people. They're perfectly quiet. Peppering the crowd are orange-and-black flags. I spot a sign that says *Nectar Now.*

When the camera zooms back in on Bambi, I search for Tinley's dad. And sure enough, I spot him standing behind the president. He's out of focus, but I can make out his square head, his dark hair. Inside, a little leap of excitement. I *know* him.

But then I listen to what the president's saying. It's funny how you can like a person, or think you like them, and then realize that they probably wouldn't like you. The words coming from Bambi's mouth are nothing new. He talks about a New Mariposa, a Mariposa that will be wealthy and beautiful, a Mariposa for Mariposans.

I look around at all the familiar faces. Tonight, they're heavy with worry. I have known these faces all my life. Mrs. Demba moved here from Senegal. Her kids are way older than me, but they still used to play with me, even when I was an annoying little kid. Mrs. Wong once gave us a whole crate of paper cups for chai when we ran out one busy Sunday. Mr. and Mrs. Calderón give me Christmas presents every year. They make sure to invite me over for rosca cake on Three Kings' Day. These aren't the people who should leave Mariposa. These people *are* Mariposa. They're my Mariposa, anyway.

"We'll begin here," Bambi goes on, "in Pacific City, our capital, this great metropolis, this exemplar, this oceanic jewel." He lets his words settle over the crowd. "You will hear more in the coming weeks about our camps. You will begin to see population enforcement officers on the streets. They'll be hard to miss. All in black. Great new uniforms, with black helmets. I call them my Crickets." An appreciative murmur sweeps through the stadium. "They will answer to my best generals." Behind him, General Schaedler stares straight ahead. "The Bambergers came over with Captain Elmwood Rumrunner, many generations ago. We have always fought to defend this country, and I aim to do the same."

He looks down at his feet, taps the podium, as if he's thinking deeply about something. The crowd waits. "I'll tell you something about moths—real moths, the insects," he says thoughtfully. "They're a predatory species. And when they attack their prey, they attack them in the eyes. They suck their blood through their eyes." He lets that sink in for a second. "We have been blinded long enough, my fellow Mariposans." He spreads his arms. "My Butterflies." His arms drop to his sides. "We have welcomed the Moths of the world to our prosperous island, and what do we see now? Poverty. Misery. We see good Mariposans—people whose ancestors sailed the very first ships to this island—living in the poorest neighborhoods. We see their children going to the worst schools. We see them without jobs. Butterflies, this is your land. I'm here to give it back to you." The crowd in the stadium erupts. In the shop, one man, a customer I don't recognize, claps high in the air.

The speech ends soon after that, and the crowd in the store disperses. Only our friends stay behind. Buff gets back to work, smiling to himself and whistling. I wish I had something mean and smart to say to him, but I don't.

Dad turns to the Calderóns, the Wongs, and Mrs. Demba. "Tea?"

Chapter 12

When we file out of the shop, no one looks at Buff or says a word to him. All nine of us tromp up the stairs to the apartment.

"Fresh, hot samosas, coming up!" Dad calls cheerfully. The next thing I know, we've all squeezed into the kitchen. Amma busies herself with the tea, pulling every mug we own from the cupboard. Paati sits back and closes her eyes. "That Bum-burger," she mutters. "He's a bum-faced buffoon. A bean-brained baboon. A blown-up balloon."

Flip starts bouncing his ball against the ceiling. When he fails to catch it, it ricochets madly from floor to wall, bouncing under chairs, getting lost again and again. From the fridge, Dad pulls a big bowl of potato filling. "That's what you put in samosas, isn't it?" Flip asks, eyeing the potato mixture.

"That's right. Samosa masala," Dad says.

"Sa-mo-sa. Ma-sa-la," Mr. Calderón says. "That feels good to say."

"But what *is* it?" Flip asks.

"A masala is just a mix, Flip. In this case, it's potatoes and onions and peas and spices. But masala can be anything, anything that mixes well together."

"Like peanut butter and jelly."

"I suppose."

"And all of us on Mingus Ave., right? We mix well together." Flip bounces the ball against the wall and gets a good rhythm going.

Dad drops three samosas in hot oil. "You're a smart boy, Flip. You might be a poet."

Mingus Avenue masala. My eyes meet Fabi's. She's thinking the same thing, I can tell. We have to tell them, but I can't bring myself—

"They're destroying Mingus Avenue!" Fabi shouts.

The adults stop talking and stare at her. "What did you say, Fabi?" her mother asks.

But Fabi just sits there, her lips squeezed shut, like she's afraid of what else might fly out if she opens them.

"That's not funny, Fabiana," Mr. Calderón says. "There's no need to be so dramatic." The adults gaze at her for a moment longer, then return to the business of eating and talking, more quietly now.

I think about letting Fabi's declaration fade back into the walls of this kitchen until it stops being true. I wish it would, but truth always beats wishing.

"Fabi's right," I announce.

Again, the grown-ups go silent. Forks freeze midair. Everything in the kitchen is still. I stand up and say it again. "Fabi's right. It's true. She's just telling you what I told her."

"What's true, Muki?" Dad folds a samosa without looking at it. He drops it in the hot oil.

"What's happening, kids?" Mrs. Calderón asks.

"I found out about the plans. I know they're going to take our shop away from us and tear it down and tear down our house and demolish all of Mingus Avenue and they're probably going to change the street name—"

"Muki, slow down," Amma says.

"—because Buff says they will, and they're going to put a hotel here and fancy stores for ladies with shopping bags and parking meters—"

"Muki!"

I stop.

"Slowly. Explain."

I look from Amma to Paati to Dad, from the Wongs to the Calderóns to Mrs. Demba, each face curled into a question. I explain.

Amma blinks at me, her mouth half-open, like she doesn't know who I am. I turn to Dad. I've never seen him like this, his chest heaving up and down. He turns to the table. "Has anyone heard about this?"

No one has.

"Buff had these printouts?" Mr. Wong asks. "The shop boy?"

I nod.

Mr. Wong says to Mrs. Wong, "Why would they give Buff the plans?"

The adults look at each other for a long, quiet moment.

"One more thing," Mrs. Calderón says, shaking her head. "You think you know what you're dealing with, and then they add one more thing to the pile."

"Who's *they*?" Fabi asks. Her mom gazes at her, but she doesn't answer.

Amma clears her throat so loudly I jump. "Never mind who *they* are or what *they* are doing. I think we know what this means." She stands up straighter, hands on hips. "It's time to get down to business. It's time to really begin."

Mr. Calderón's eyebrows jump. "You mean—"

"Yes. Precisely. Vikky?"

Dad fishes three samosas out of the oil and drops them on a paper towel. "I think you're right. I think it's time to start."

"Hold it!" Flip says. He begins to pull frantically at his pockets. "My ball! Where's my ball? My little red ball?"

Fabi groans. "Oh, come on, Flip."

"Fabi, what did you do with it?"

"Nothing! Why would I want that ball? I hope you lost it forever."

"Don't say that, Fabi! Mama! Where's my ball?" Tears rain down his cheeks.

What follows is a good amount of sighing, some

screeching of chairs, and a general squabbling ruckus as all of us start looking for Flip's ball. It's nowhere. Our kitchen isn't big. There are no hidden corners, nothing for a ball to hide behind. Somehow, it's vanished.

"I'm sorry, Flip," Amma says. I can tell she's fed up— with Bamberger and Buff, with Flip's ball and the dips and downs of the evening.

"Don't worry, mi amor," Mrs. Calderón says. She pulls Flip to her lap and wraps her pillowy arms around him. "We'll get you a new one."

Flip digs his face into his mother's shoulder. "It'll never be the same," he says. "I've never lost that ball."

"Please," Fabi says. "You lose it constantly."

We sit around the table, the room quiet, except for Flip's snuffles. Even the oil in the frying pan stops popping. I'm sad for Flip. He never quite gets what he wants, but he's happy, most of the time, just to hang around with Fabi. *Flip's right*, I want to say. Things will never be the same.

Chapter 13

Mr. Wong's the first to get up. "We should go. I'm sorry about your ball, Flip. It must have been a very special—"

"Just one minute!" Mrs. Demba shouts. There's a sudden shuffle at the table as she pulls apart the golden crust of her samosa. "Look at this!" She raises her hand high in the air, Flip's little red ball clutched between her fingers, coated in potato.

Mrs. Demba puts a hand to her cheek and laughs. Tearfully, Flip takes his ball back and wipes it on his shirt. He kisses it and puts it in his pocket.

Everyone relaxes now that Flip has his ball, and the Wongs take their plates to the sink. They hug my parents and say goodbye.

"I'm off also," Mrs. Demba says. "Too much action for one night." She pats my cheek. "Don't worry about any of this, sweet prince. It will all come out in the wash. And I should know!" She laughs, does a twisty little dance at her own joke, and then she's gone, too.

Only the Calderóns are left. They turn to Amma. So does Dad. She's obviously in charge here, but in charge of what?

"So," Amma says. "What's next? What's first?" There's a seat for her, but she paces the kitchen, hands behind her back, like a general.

"We need to get word out," Dad says. "First, that the operation's beginning."

"Operation? What operation?" I ask.

"Yes," Mr. Calderón says. "That should happen tonight. Should I text everyone?"

"No," Amma says. "They're tracing our cell phones. I'm sure of it."

"You are?" Dad asks.

"If they aren't already, they will be soon. No cell phones."

I stand up. I need to know. "What's going on? What is this?"

The adults all turn to me. "We're trying to stop this from happening, Muki. We're trying to keep them from sending us away."

"But *how*?"

They stare at me blankly. Amma carries on. "Getting the word out. Emails?"

"No."

"Letters?"

"Too slow. And too visible."

"I think," Dad says, "we'll have to rely on word of mouth."

"Really?" Mrs. Calderón says. "That seems impossible."

"Wait!" I cry. "I have an idea!"

The table turns to me. "Flip's ball," I say. "Flip's ball hid in that samosa. Our messages could hide in samosas."

The room shatters with laughter.

"You're so creative, Muki," Mrs. Calderón says.

"Good one, Muki," Mr. Calderón adds. "Thanks for breaking the tension."

Even Amma slides over and gives me a little hug. I am one hundred and ten percent offended. It's clear they're not taking me seriously. And I'm *not* creative. I never have been. This is just a good idea. But the parents go back to messaging routes, contacts, information channels. They pull in close to each other and begin to speak quietly, making lists, nodding, rubbing at their eyes.

I look to Flip and Fabi. They've been staring at me, openmouthed, all this time. And I can see it in their eyes. They get my idea. They're ready to take me seriously.

When the Calderóns leave, I go to my room. Paati follows. She sits down on her bed, lets out a glorious belch, and lies down, gazing out the window.

"You people," she says. "Worrying about every little thing. I'm not worried."

"You should be."

"Po-dah. I have seen this all before."

"When?"

"Oh, you know when. The war."

"The war?"

"The Second World War," she says, like the Second World War was no big deal. "What happens one time will happen twenty times, Muki. That is the way of the world." With this, she takes off her glasses and puts them on her nightstand.

An hour later, I'm tucked in, lights out, when Amma enters the room. I pretend to sleep. She sits on my bed for a few minutes, then kisses my forehead and walks back out. When the door closes, I open my eyes. From across the room, Paati: "I knew it. You weren't sleeping."

"I thought *you* were sleeping."

"Just resting."

"How'd you know I wasn't sleeping?" I ask.

"Usually, you snore."

"I don't snore!"

"You snore like a Tata tractor, my dear."

"Paati?"

"What, Muki?"

"You snore like a broken bulldozer."

"Muki?"

"Yes?"

"You snore like an elephant with a cold."

"You snore like a motorboat with a microphone."

"You snore like a confused rooster."

"Paati? You snore like a chicken . . . who snores."

Paati giggles. "That one was no good."

"I know. I ran out of ideas. Paati?"

"Yes?"

"I'm not tired."

"I'm not tired, either."

We both lie very still. From the kitchen, I hear the rumble of a rolling pin, the clattering of pans. Samosas will be fresh and ready for the shop tomorrow. Between these brick walls, nothing's changed. That's what I think about as my head gets heavy and I drift off to sleep: Nothing has changed yet. I am home.

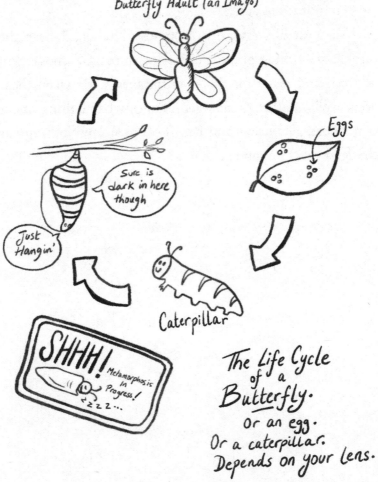

The Life Cycle
of a
Butterfly.
Or an egg.
Or a caterpillar.
Depends on your lens.

Chapter 14

The next day, I remember last minute that I'm going to Tinley's after school. I grab my sketchbook—really just a notebook, but I've been filling it with sketches of butterflies. I also grab two of last night's samosas from a big tray in the fridge. I know I'll be hungry when I get to Tinley's house, and I don't want to ask for food again, and it's basically been carved into my brain that I can't eat in front of someone without sharing. Hence the two samosas. But really, I could eat both on my own.

"I'm going to Tinley's," I tell Fabi after school. "Do not tell my mom. Please."

"*Tinley?* You call her *Tinley* now?"

"Come on."

"*Fine.*"

When we get to Tinley's, we head straight for the kitchen, and I remember my samosas. "I brought food," I say.

"Good. I don't think Cook's reloaded the fridge for the week."

"You call your cook *Cook*?"

"Yeah. Don't you?" She grins at me.

"I call my cook *Dad*."

"We call Cook *Cook* so we can tell her apart from Lee. I mean, you know, when we talk about them. Obviously we can tell them apart in person. We used to call George *Driver*. But then Dad got his own driver, so we started using their names."

"How humane of you. You could just use the cook's name, you know. That's how people tell each other apart normally."

"Well, sure. I guess."

I must be staring at Tinley or something because she turns to me and sighs. "What now?" she asks.

"I don't know. You live in a *castle*."

"A castillo." She opens the fridge.

"You call your cook *Cook*."

She stands in front of the open fridge and looks at me. "And?"

"And what?"

"What's your point?" Tinley pours us two glasses of chocolate milk.

"I guess I don't have one." I unwrap the samosas.

"What in the world!"

"Samosas."

"But what are they?"

"I don't know. Just try one."

She takes a samosa and holds it up to the light, like she'll be able to see through it. Then she takes the daintiest bite off the top corner and chews, carefully, with just her front teeth. She nods.

"It's good," she says. She takes a bigger bite. This time she gets a mouthful of the potato, and her eyes pop a little wider. "Did your dad make these?"

"Yeah."

"Lucky. I don't think my dad can even make toast."

"He does other things."

I'm lost in samosa happiness, trying to not eat so fast, gulping at my milk, when Tinley starts to make a weird gagging, hacking sound. She's bent over her plate now, spitting out clumps of potato. Reaching into her mouth, she pulls out a long, thin strip of paper.

"Whoa!" she gasps. "What is this?"

My heart starts pounding. This is not supposed to happen. This is not normal. She drops the strip of paper on the table, and it sits there, a little bent, shining with spit and chewed-up potato. It's not regular paper. It's covered in plastic, like some of the posters at school.

I reach out and pick up the white slip. I'm so freaked out that I'm not even grossed out. Tinley's coughing, breathing hard. "What is it?" she says. "Show me."

There's writing: *Oculi aperti*.

"What does that mean?" I ask.

"I don't know," she says. "Let's ask Lee."

"No! Wait." I have to think carefully. And quickly. Who put this here? Amma or Dad. Last night? Is this a message in a samosa? Of course it's a message in a samosa. That's exactly what it is. Then it dawns on me: This is it! This was my idea! A secret message. And the first person to see the secret message? Tinley Schaedler. Daughter of the general, Bamberger's right-hand man.

"Where's your dad? Is he here?"

"I don't know. I don't think so."

"Good."

"Why?"

"I can't say."

"Do you think it's code for something?" she asks. "Or another language? I learned French when I was little. This isn't French."

"It isn't Spanish."

"Oculi . . . that could be Latin. Remember we learned those phrases in civics once?"

"I don't remember this one."

"No. Same."

"What kinds of dictionaries do you have in that reading room?" I ask.

"Every kind." Her face lights up. "Every kind of dictionary."

We run for the reading room, leaving our samosas behind. "Wait!" I cry, just as we exit the kitchen. I head back to the table, back to my samosa. "I might have one, too." I dig in, rip apart its golden crust, and sure enough, I find the same message. *Oculi aperti.*

At the far end of the reading room, Tinley pulls a rolling ladder across a bookcase. She climbs up to the top of the ladder, reaches high, and yanks at a red book that's tightly wedged on the shelf. The book pulls free, and she almost falls but she catches herself and climbs down.

"First word," I say, "*oculi.*"

She skims the page with her finger. "Oculi . . . eyes. Eyes!"

Of course. "Eyes open!"

"What?"

"It's what Paati said to Mrs. Demba."

"What who said to who?"

"Aperti. Just look it up."

She sticks her tongue out a little as she riffles through the pages. "Aperto . . . aperti. Open! Eyes," she says. "Open." And her own eyes pop wide open. Tinley's whisper booms across the half-light: "Eyes open."

"Eyes open."

"What does it mean?" she asks.

"Just what it says. Eyes open. Look out. Be ready."

She lets out a small gasp. We stare at each other. The room goes silent. All I can hear is the tick, then the tock, of the clock on the wall.

The door clangs open and Tinley jumps.

"Hello, scholars." It's the general. I can't see him, but I know the voice, its rumble like distant thunder.

"Papa," Tinley whispers. She doesn't jump up to hug him this time. She watches him approach, grabs the samosa messages before he sees them.

The general walks halfway into the room, a mug in his hand. "How goes the butterfly research?"

"Fine," Tinley says, her voice chirpy, higher than usual.

He looks at the two of us, and I wonder what he sees. Amma can always tell when I've done something I wasn't supposed to. *Your lips close very tightly and your eyes grow very big*, she once told me. I relax my mouth. I squint my eyes.

"What are you two doing?"

"Just looking up some Latin. Butterfly names. Latin names for butterflies."

That was an excellent lie. Maybe she *won't* tell her dad.

He smiles, relaxes. "I'm home a little early, I know. Muki, Tinley doesn't see me very much during the day. It must be a little strange for her."

"Why're you home, Papa?" Tinley asks.

"It's still light out. The days are getting longer." Which doesn't answer the question. "I thought I'd show you something for your research. Have you seen the butterflies of Mariposa, Muki? The real ones?"

"Sure. They're in Oceanview all the time, right outside my window."

"Huh. I didn't know that about Oceanview."

"There are probably lots of things you don't know about Oceanview."

"Muki," Tinley warns.

The general stands up. "Come with me, Muki."

I don't move. Something tells me not to move.

He's buttoning up his jacket. Clearly, he expects me to follow. "Muki? Proceed. Tinley?"

Tinley stands and walks on uncertain feet. My heart beats faster.

"Where are we going?" I ask.

"Follow me."

Now I plant my feet and don't move. The general turns around to face me. His brows furrow, his mouth sets in a stern line. "I said, follow me."

"Muki," Tinley whispers. "It's fine. Just come." She takes my hand and pulls me forward.

The general leads us to the kitchen, where he opens the door to a large pantry.

"Papa, what are you doing?"

He doesn't answer, but reaches around a loaf of bread, jiggles something with his hand, and all at once, the wall of the pantry pulls open. "Wow!" Tinley jumps. "I've never seen that!" The opened wall reveals a new wall, and in that new wall is a door—shorter than most doors, and narrower. The general looks back at us and raises his eyebrows.

"It's a castle," he says. "What did you expect?"

I turn to Tinley. "So much for your castillo."

Hunching down, we squeeze through the door, through a maze of hallways, each narrower and darker than the last. The floor slopes downward, and that damp, muddy smell intensifies, like we're burrowing deep into the earth, closer and closer to its core. Finally, we get to an even smaller door. It comes up to my nose, and it seems to be stuck in its frame. Grunting and puffing, the general pushes his entire body against it. It opens.

When I step through the door, the world opens into a forest of towering trees, sunlight peeking through their blue-green leaves. We walk down a path bordered by high, wild bushes. In the distance, I spot the high clock tower of MHP's main building. We're not so far from school.

Branches spring into my face and puddles of muck suck at my soles. Finally, we get to a clearing, and we stop.

"Take a look around, Muki."

Next to me, Tinley beams. "Do you see them?" she asks. "They're everywhere!"

But when I look up, all I see are trees. They smell minty and so strong I'm getting dizzy. Strange flowers droop from their branches. But they're not flowers.

They're . . . butterflies.

Butterflies!

There must be a thousand of them here. They hang off the trees, so many clustered together that they seem to form a new kind of gold-and-black-and-spotted animal.

Others dance from branch to branch. One swoops down and brushes my cheek.

"Wow," I say. And I keep saying it. "Wow. Wow!"

"Hush. Listen."

We stand still. Wings rustle, like leaves in the wind, like a gentle rain. Here, in this grove, we could be anywhere. A different planet, even. A universe free of generals and Crickets and Dragonflies. If I could stay here forever, I would.

Tinley walks over and stands next to me, and I wonder if she understands, at least a little, what it's like to be me—a Moth standing in this grove of butterflies, in this forest, in my city, in Mariposa, my only home.

On the walk back to the castle, butterfly wings still rustle in my ear, like a song I can't unhear. Eyes open. For what? The general holds down the high grasses to let me pass through. "Muki, what can you tell me about butterflies?" His face is set and solemn.

"I could tell you a lot."

"Oh, could you, now?"

"Did you know monarchs taste bitter and disgusting to their predators because of all the milkweed they eat?"

"I did know that."

"Did you know butterflies can't fly if their body temperature goes below eighty-six degrees Fahrenheit?"

"Sounds reasonable."

"Did you know that a group of butterflies is called a kaleidoscope?"

"A kaleidoscope of butterflies."

"Yup. And did you know butterflies can taste with their feet?"

"I did not."

"Did you know butterflies eat poop and drink tears? And did you know butterflies are people's souls, according to the ancient Greeks? And that in the Middle Ages, when a woman wanted to have a baby, she'd eat a butterfly because people thought that would bring a new soul into the world? Also, some butterflies use ants as babysitters. And some butterflies come in colors the human eye can't even see. And some have fake heads. To confuse predators. And some smell bad. Also to keep away predators."

"What do they smell like?"

"I don't know. Probably poop."

"But poop might only smell bad to humans. It may not smell bad to a butterfly's predator."

"So maybe it smells like humans."

We arrive at the castle. Back through the narrow hallways—somehow they seem even smaller now. When I step out of the pantry, I halt. It's Lee, the butler, the man with the red pants. He's standing at the kitchen table, where Tinley and I have left our samosas. I spot him leaning over the samosas, prodding at one with a fork. When he sees us, he straightens. He clears his throat and starts to say something, but stops.

"Good day, Lee," says the general.

"Good day, General. Tinley." He leaves the samosas where they are and slips out of the kitchen. That's when the general turns to me.

"Muki."

"What?"

He picks up a corner of a samosa and nibbles at it, then looks down at me quizzically. "You seem to know a lot about butterflies. What can you tell me about moths?"

I pause. *Firm grip. Look him in the eye.* "Nothing," I say. "I don't know anything about moths."

On the car ride home, Tinley hands me the samosa messages. She slipped them into her sock when the general barged into the library. I stick them in my pocket now.

My plan is to march straight up to Amma and demand an explanation for the samosa messages. But when I walk into the shop, something feels different. It's hard to pin down, at first. The aisles look the same, the tower of toilet paper in the corner, the Fruit Snax display by the door. Amma's sticking orange discount stickers on the milk that's about to expire. It all seems normal, until it hits me: Amma's working the aisles, doing the jobs that Buff usually does. She's working quickly and angrily. Her face hangs with worry. Where's Buff? I turn to the checkout counter. And there he is, wearing a crisp white shirt and an orange necktie. I've

never seen Buff in a tie. I've never seen a smile like the one now smeared across his face.

"Good evening," he says. He crosses his arm and sniffs.

"Hey." Next to his tie is a name tag—not the sticker kind you get on the first day of school, but a gold badge, shaped like a butterfly and pinned to his shirt pocket. I move closer to read it. *Buffington Garbanzo III, Ambassador of Commerce.*

I start with the most obvious question. "Your name's Buffington?"

"It's a family name." He sniffs good and hard.

"What's a—what's an ambassador of commerce?"

His eyes sparkle, like he's been waiting all day to be asked. "It's a government appointment, Mucus, my man. The orders came down from President Bamberger himself, in fact."

The orders, I think. Like he's in the army.

"As a government-appointed ambassador of commerce, I'll oversee the shop's transition of ownership."

"What does that mean?"

He reads my face. Maybe he can see that I'm getting worried, because he mellows out a little. His shoulders sink the tiniest bit; his voice loses its irritating edge. "It means that eventually, Bodega Bodega will be owned by a Butterfly, right? Moths won't own any businesses soon."

"But why?"

"Well—"

"Buff!" Amma's voice quivers. She's standing behind me

131

now. Buff stops talking, opens his mouth, but says nothing. Amma jabs her roll of orange stickers at him. "I think that's enough, Buff. Don't you?"

"Yes, Mrs. Krishnan."

Amma turns to me. She doesn't look too happy to see me, either. I can almost smell the smoke trailing from her ears. She won't be answering any questions about samosas tonight, and I won't be asking them. My questions form a quiet line and file obediently out the door. And so do I.

Chapter 15

That night, I perch on the end of Paati's bed, gently, so I don't wake her. She snores like a predictable engine. Outside, our laundry hangs motionless. Across the way, Fabi's window is dark. I think of what I saw today: the butterflies hanging like honeycombs off the eucalyptus trees, the friendly music of all those wings, the weird magic of that hidden grove.

From nowhere, a butterfly swoops down and lands on the windowsill. It's bright green, except for two black spots. I look closer. This is no butterfly. Butterflies rest with their wings closed, and this guy sits on the windowsill with his wings flat and open. This is a moth. "Hello," I whisper. He has a furry little face and long green tails that dangle from the bottom of each wing. I feel a twinge of brotherhood with this moth. Misunderstood. Just trying to live his life. "You're not so bad." He looks right back at me. *Not so bad yourself,* he seems to say. He isn't fancy like a butterfly, but he's caught the moonlight and glows. He's beautiful in his own way. He flies off, and I get in bed.

A few hours later, something startles me awake. Footsteps. Were they real or in a dream? Sometimes I dream about doorbells and wake up convinced that someone's at the door. This time, though, the footsteps sound real. From outside, rising above Paati's snuffles and snores, I hear a car engine. And just now, I hear the groan of our one creaky floorboard. Those are real feet, not dream feet. My clock reads 2:43 a.m. I get up.

At the bottom of the stairs, the door stands open, just a crack. A cold wind whistles through, and I can hear the murmur of rainfall. No time for shoes or a jacket. I go out.

The cold shoves me awake. The ocean fog has rolled in, and I can hardly see past my own hand. Within seconds, I'm drenched. It's raining so hard it's raining *up*. No one's out here. No car. This is crazy, I tell myself. The wind blew the door open, that's all. But just as I step back inside, I hear the car again.

Here it is, creeping down Mingus Avenue. A silver pickup truck, here for Amma again. But where's Amma? I twist around, trying to push the mist from my face. I call her name. Rain pelts the ground like gravel. I can barely see or hear.

The next thing I know, I'm at the truck's door, banging on the rain-spattered window. The door opens.

And here she is. Amma steps out, leaving the car door

open, rain running down her face, her eyes wide with disbelief. "What are you *doing*? *Muki!*"

The disbelief starts to look more like anger. Yes, this is
definitely anger.

"Muki! You're dripping wet. What do you think you're
doing running around the street in the middle of the night,
and with no coat on?" She looks down and gasps. "No
shoes?" She whacks me on the arm. "Go. Inside! Now!"

But I don't go. I stand where I am. I cross my arms.
She's blocking the driver. "Who's in the car?" She turns to
look back at the truck, and that's when I see him: Lee.

From the driver's seat, Lee sees me, too. We stare at
each other, letting the night fog fill our mouths.

"Well, stop staring like two giraffes. Muki, go inside."

"What's he doing here?"

"Who?" Amma asks, as if it isn't obvious.

"Tinley Schaedler's butler."

She turns back around to Lee. He looks at me, looks at
her, and throws his hands up.

"Mom."

"What."

"*Mom.*"

"It's complicated, Muki."

"Let's go upstairs. All of us." I glare into the car. "Lee,
too." And like two kids in trouble, they grudgingly obey.
Lee turns off his engine and runs with us down the street,
back up the stairs, and into the house.

The lights are on now, and the house is warm. Dad's in the kitchen, sitting at the table, sipping a cup of tea. "Well, look who's here," he says. "Three drowned cats." Lee walks over to him and shakes his hand.

"Tea, Lee?"

"Sure."

While Dad fills the kettle, Amma pats herself dry with a dish towel, looking out the window, as if she's alone in the kitchen and lost in her thoughts, as if her son and husband and Tinley Schaedler's butler aren't sitting right behind her. I turn to Lee. "I know you."

"Yes, Muki, you sure do."

"You're the butler."

"We like to say *house manager* these days. But sure." He yawns, leans back, and stretches his legs wide. Nothing about him is very butler-like now.

"And I saw you on the subway that time. When I fell asleep standing."

"Yeah. I know. Strange to think that was you."

"You didn't know who I was? You just held up a random sleeping kid?"

"Well, yeah. I didn't know what else to do. I looked up, and there you were, about to topple over. . . ." He trails off, then looks hard at me, leans forward in his chair. His eyes are the exact blue of toilet bowl cleaner.

"How do you know my parents?" I ask.

"I've never seen anything like it, a kid just falling asleep on his feet like that."

"I've never seen anyone with red pants before."

"Technically, they're salmon."

"So how do you know my parents?"

"You've got good parents, kid." He speaks with a kind of drawl. "The first time I met them, your mom brought a cup of tea out to my truck. I mean, who does that?"

"My mom."

Dad brings Lee a cup of tea now.

"'Course, I took it home first to test it wasn't poisoned," Lee says.

"How'd you test that?"

"I fed a little to the general's cat."

"That's a terrible thing to do, Lee." Amma seems to have woken up to the room. She turns to him. "If I wanted to kill you, I have simpler methods than poisoned tea."

I study Lee. "For a butler, you're not very good at answering questions."

He takes a sip. "Okay. You want to know how I met your parents? Just by delivering messages to them. People doing what we do, we don't really *meet* each other. It's not like we have mixers."

"What do you mean?" I ask. "*People doing what we do. What are you doing?*"

Amma cuts in, "And why would I kill you, Lee? You're

the closest person we have to the center."

Lee looks worried, darts his eyes at me.

I turn to Amma. "He thinks I don't know anything." I turn back to Lee. "I know things."

"Muki's the one who told us about the Moth camp. Right, Muki? And then the plans for Mingus Avenue."

Lee nods at me, raises his cup high. That's when Paati wanders in, blinking into the bright light of the kitchen. Lee gazes back at her, then remembers his manners and hops out of his chair. "No, no," she says. "No ceremony for me. You sit." She sits down next to him.

Dad continues. "There are other places, it seems. Not just Mingus Avenue. Other old neighborhoods will be mowed down and rebuilt."

"Marble Hill?"

"No," Dad says. "Not Marble Hill. Neighborhoods more like this one." Moth neighborhoods.

Amma turns to Paati. "You should get back to sleep. Why are you awake?"

"I was hungry," Paati says.

Amma puts a hand to her stomach. "I'm hungry, too. Starving."

"Me too," Dad says. "Muki?" But he knows the answer. I'm always hungry.

"Let's eat," Amma says. "Let's really eat." From the fridge she pulls containers, sticks them in the microwave, and a few minutes later, we have a table full of food—chicken curry and purial and pachadi and crispy murukkus. She slices a cucumber and places a few pieces on each plate, with a squeeze of lemon. Paati drops a spoonful of mango pickle next to each mound of rice. For a good ten minutes, our only goal is to eat, to put food in our bodies. We all eat with our hands, even Lee. He eats like an amateur, though, getting rice between his fingers, spilling grains back onto the plate. No one shows him how to hold his food above his top knuckles, how to use his thumb to push it neatly into his mouth. But no one minds how Lee eats, because as long as we're eating, we don't have to worry about Butterflies or Bambis or Buffs.

I wait until the end of this midnight feast, for the pause that happens just before my parents get up to wash their eating hands, when their food has dried to a crust on their fingers and conversation has dried to a crust on their tongues.

"Hey!" I shout. The four of them jump in their seats. "Sorry. I didn't mean to shout."

Paati starts to get up. "Paati," I say, trying to sound authoritative, like Miss P. "I think you should be here for this." I look ceremoniously around the table. Then I take the two messages from my pocket, *Oculi aperti*, and place them on the table.

Lee stares at the messages. Amma stares at the messages. She blinks again and again, her lids moving faster and faster, fluttering like butterfly wings. "Muki?" she says at last, picking up a slip of paper.

"I took two samosas to school today, to Tin—to eat after school."

She nods. She looks at Dad, who drums his fingers on the table. Again, they flip their mental coins—heads: truth, tails: lie.

They speak at the same time.

Dad: "It's just a receipt." Amma: "You deserve to know."

They stare at each other. Amma wins. "Muki." She turns to me. "You deserve to know what's happening."

"You're using my idea. You're putting messages in the samosas," I say. "That's what's happening."

Dad gives Amma a warning look—the look he usually saves for me, but she bobs her head in agreement. "Mukesh. Yes, it's true. We used your samosa idea. It was a very good idea."

"Very good," Dad agrees.

"But that's as far as you can go. We're trying to stop what Bamberger has started. He's planning to send thousands of families away from this country. Families who have built their lives here."

"I know. So Lee was here tonight to pick up these secret messages." I turn to him. "Is that what you were doing?"

"Lee, don't answer," Amma says. "This isn't one of your adventure books, Muki. This is serious. And dangerous. Too dangerous for you. You can't do anything. You can't know anything." She leans in until her nose almost touches mine. "Is that clear?"

"No."

She sits back and heaves a great sigh. "Well, it's going to have to be clear."

"The samosas were my idea."

"I know."

"It's not fair. I'm not a baby."

"I know."

"So I can be part of it?"

"No. Absolutely not. You will have nothing to do with any of this revolution business."

"It's a *revolution*?"

"Ay-yoh," she moans, and grasps the sides of her head. "You will stay out of this. Okay? Do you promise?"

"Mom—"

"Muki."

"Amma. You have to let me know what's happening. Even if I don't get to do anything. It's safer for me to know." Brilliant. "That way I won't accidentally give anything away." I look at each person around the table. "Information is safety." Genius.

"The boy has a point, Sindu," Dad says.

"I agree," Paati says.

Amma looks at Lee, who puts his hands on his knees and shrugs.

"Fine," Amma sighs. "Fine! Lee? Go ahead. Tell him."

"Okay." Lee clears his throat and scratches his cheek, thinking. "Here's what we're trying to do. The Moth camp?

The place with the tents? That's basically HQ for Bamberger's whole operation. So what we're trying to do is infiltrate their HQ, get people on our side one by one, until we have enough."

"And then what?"

"And then, if it all works out, we gather our people and take over the camp. We arrest Bamberger. We replace him."

"Why can't you just build an army and invade?"

"Working from the inside's a lot more effective. You build alliances. You raise sympathy. We could try attacking from the outside, but if we don't have cooperation with the inside, we won't have much of a chance."

"What will they do? The allies on the inside?"

"That, I cannot tell you. Scratch that! I *can*. But I won't."

"Hold it," Amma says. "If we're going to tell him everything, we're going to tell him everything." She opens the brown bag she was handing to Lee and pulls out two foil-wrapped parcels. She unwraps the first.

"It's a bao!" I whisper. I recognize the plump, chewy dumpling from the Wongs' restaurant. With her hands, she parts the white dough, letting its shredded green filling fall out. She digs a finger deeper into one half and pulls out a slip of paper, coated in plastic, just like mine. She looks at it before handing it to me. There's a name on the slip, one I don't recognize. "Who is this?"

"That's someone at the Moth camp who's willing to

help us. See the little square next to the name? That means they're a safe contact."

She unwraps the next packet. This one's an empanada. "Is that from Flip and Fabi's house?"

She nods and pulls the empanada apart. This time, Dad reaches over and fishes out the message. It's a triangle, the number 27, and a flag. "See the triangle here? Government. And the number twenty-seven: that means we have twenty-seven recruits inside the government. Twenty-seven people willing to help."

"You mean sabotage something?"

"Maybe. If it comes to that. And we'll need the military, too. Or some big part of the military. Enough to give us a fighting chance."

"Like General Schaedler? Could we get General Schaedler on our side?"

"Probably not," Lee says. "Others. Maybe."

"What will people on the inside actually *do*, though?"

"For one thing, they'll help us gather the weapons we'll need."

"Whoa."

"Yeah. That's why your parents want you out of this." I try to imagine my parents with weapons, Amma manning a tank, Dad a cannon. I can't.

"We're building public sympathy for the resistance, too," Dad says.

"I can help with that! I'm good at resistance."

"I know."

I study Lee. He looks like your average Mariposan: he's white, he has these round eyes, a long nose. His wet hair falls in loose yellow ropes around his face. He's probably a Butterfly himself. "Why are you helping us?"

He thinks about this. "I don't have a great answer for that, buddy. I just don't like what's happening in Mariposa. I don't like that Bamberger's blaming people like your family for the country's problems. I'm trying not to let it happen."

"That's a good answer," I say.

"Yes," Amma adds. "I think that's a very good answer." She reaches out and takes my hand. "We're not sure what's going to happen, exactly, but we need allies where we can find them."

"It takes more than three people to overthrow a government, Muki," Dad says. "It takes a lot of people working together, planning, and deciding when and if we're going to turn the tables." He glances at Amma. "It's a complicated plan, and it could very well never happen."

"But it very well could," Amma says, a glint in her eye. "It will happen very, very slowly. And then very quickly. There will come a day when the resistance is big enough, strong enough. So strong that Bamberger will have no hope of a fight."

"But will he fight? Will there be war?"

"We don't know."

I look from Amma to Dad. I've never seen them look so serious. I've never seen their eyes so bright.

"Wait a minute." Something clicks into place. "You didn't bring Paati here to babysit me while you were at work. You brought her here because you're mixed up in all this. Because—because you don't know what might happen to you—"

"Muki, I don't want you to worry about all that," Amma says. "I'm in charge of these operations, you know. Which means that no one is getting *mixed up* in anything. As long as I'm running things, they'll run just fine. We'll take care of ourselves."

I want to believe Amma. She was smart enough, after all, to bring Paati here before Bamberger started with his Moths and Butterflies, before the camps were built. I want to know that we'll be okay.

Paati laughs softly. "It seems your parents are rebels, Muki. You never thought of it, did you?"

"No. I don't know." I never thought of my parents as anything but my parents. But now, *rebels*. They're part of a *rebellion*, like people in history books. Here's what I do know; the thought comes to me all at once. This rebellion isn't happening on a battlefield. There won't be cannons. This rebellion is happening at home, in the kitchens of Oceanview. Late at night, after bedtime. Early in the morning, before work and school. My parents, the Wongs and

Calderóns, other parents around the city. Butlers. They're saying *You will not do this to us. You will not pull this country apart.*

Without another word, Amma gets up and clears the mugs from the table. She starts washing the dishes, stacking them to dry.

A new question pops up. "Why Latin? Why not just say *Eyes open?*"

Amma thinks about this. "It sounded better in Latin."

"And why that? What does *eyes open* mean?"

"When you told us about Mingus Avenue being destroyed, Muki, we called some of the people we knew. And you were right. So this message—it was to let people know that yes, we need to start watching and thinking."

"You mean worrying."

"Not worrying," Dad says. "Acting. You'll find that if you take action, you have less time to worry."

"Wait." The questions and answers roll over each other, jump into dog piles. "That's why you were so mad about Tinley being here? You thought Tinley would *spy* on you?"

"You can never be too careful, Muki. And this changes nothing, by the way. You are still forbidden—*forbidden*—from going to her house or bringing her here. Do you understand?"

"I make no promises."

"Muki."

"Okay, fine." I avoid Lee's eyes. "Dad?"

"Yes, Thumbi."

"I'm part of this now, right? You won't keep anything from me anymore, right?"

Dad looks at Amma, who's turned off the sink to listen. "You are part of this now, Muki." He smiles at me, puts a hand on my shoulder. "Welcome to the revolution."

Chapter 16

When Lee leaves, the sky over Oceanview blushes pink. I fall into bed, so exhausted I barely hear Paati's snores. If she tries to snap me awake in the morning, it doesn't work. I don't hear the usual sounds of Mingus Avenue waking up— Mrs. Calderón pulling in the laundry line, Mrs. Demba unlocking her laundromat, Mrs. Wong cranking up the awning of her restaurant.

When I do wake up, the sun beams high in the sky. I wander from my room to the kitchen, where Paati sits, reading a newspaper, her glasses perched at the tip of her nose. I get the strange feeling that the day has moved on without me.

"Good morning, Mingus Mouse," she says.

"What time is it?"

"Eleven thirty. Your amma thought you should sleep."

"*Eleven thirty?* I'm missing school! Why didn't anyone wake me up?"

After breakfast, Paati comes to me with a shallow bowl. The bowl holds a thin layer of water and a small oil lamp, its flame lit and quivering. In Sanskrit, she mutters a prayer and circles the bowl three times around my head. Then she dips her finger into the lamp's well of black, burned soot and presses that finger to my forehead. I must have a look on my face, because she pauses. "Your amma doesn't do this for you?"

"Um . . . no."

She tuts and shakes her head, then snuffs out the light.

"What're you doing?"

"I'm protecting you, Muki. From the evil eye. And everything else."

"Oh. Thanks."

"You're very welcome."

"What about you?"

"Me?"

"Who's going to protect you?"

"No need to protect me," she says, drying off her hands. "I'm just an old lady. They'll leave me alone."

"Who's *they*?"

"I don't know. Maybe the demons. Maybe that Bumburger. Now go get ready for school, somberi."

Sometimes, I don't know when to take Paati seriously. It's lunchtime now at school. If I get on the subway in thirty minutes, I can be there for my last class of the day. Kind of a waste, but it doesn't seem right to just stay home.

"I'll walk with you to the station," she says.

"I'll be safe, Paati. I promise."

"Nonsense. This old goose needs to spread her wings." She does a little chicken dance and goes to put her coat on.

Heading down to the sidewalk, I jump the last six steps. Paati's just behind me. "Just wait," she says. "I want to try."

"What? Jumping? Paati, no!"

"Don't worry, Muki. This old goose can fly, too, you know."

"Paati—"

"Just four steps."

"I don't think—" Before I can stop her, she jumps the steps and falls with a *whump* to the ground. "Are you okay? Paati?!"

She begins to laugh, lifting herself to her hands and knees, clutching her lower back. She starts to say something, but then collapses in another wave of giggles. Finally, she puts a hand up, and I help hoist her to her feet. "Sometimes," she says, "I'm an utter fool."

Out on the street, she holds my hand, her grip as fierce as ever. After last night's storm, the smell of rain rises warm and clean off the sidewalk. From the laundry line above, the butterflies drop and dance around Paati's head. They look more like a shower of blossoms than flying insects. One lands on her shoulder and stays there as she walks.

I touch my finger to my forehead, where the soot still

sits, oily and smelling like medicine. "Paati," I ask her, "do you ever miss home?"

"Of course I do." I didn't expect that answer.

"Don't you want to go back?"

"I miss India. But when I was there, I missed *you*."

"You did?" This surprises me. "But you barely knew me."

She chuckles. "Such is the way of paatis, Muki."

Honestly, I've never missed her. I feel a little bad about that.

I rub the black soot off. "This smells like a temple."

"You were so scared of the temples in Chennai. Do you remember?"

"Yeah. It was the poor people, they were . . . scary." Outside every ancient stone-carved temple in Paati's city, rows of people sat with begging bowls, hoping for a few coins. Young and old, kids with matted hair, men with matted beards, one missing an arm.

"They are difficult to see, Muki, but they aren't ghosts, they're people. They are part of life, part of this world we live in." We get to the subway station. She stops me, looks hard into my face. "Listen to me," she says. "I don't want you to live blindly in this world. I want you to see all of it, beautiful and ugly, good and bad. When you're given the choice to be blissfully blind, I hope you will choose to see. Will you do that for me?"

I nod. "Eyes open," I say.

"Eyes open." She gives me a long, ferocious hug. "Now get to school, Lazybones."

I go down the station stairs. When I look up, she's still there. She sticks her tongue out. Of all the things I expected from Paati, I never expected her to be so unexpected.

I make it to MHP in time for civics. An hour later, school's over. Fabi rides the subway home with me, and she has a hundred questions. "I didn't feel good," I lie. I'm not ready to tell her about Lee or the rebellion or the samosas. Instead, I show her the butterfly diagrams in my sketchbook.

When we step out of the Oceanview station, the afternoon feels strange. It's not the fact that I was just here. There's something in the air—I can't give it words. Something's off, like if the day were a song, its notes would be a little flat. When we turn onto Mingus Avenue, things get stranger.

A black van sits on the curb. On its door is painted a butterfly, with the words *Government of Mariposa* stamped below. A few yards down sits another black van with the same insignia. Here's what else is strange: there's not a person in sight. Mingus Avenue is so quiet, I can hear the buzz of a distant Dragonfly. Fabi and I stop in front of her door. Above us, butterflies crowd our laundry line. One of them, a monarch, is looking down at me. I can see its antennae, sharp against the blue sky. I can see the gleam in its black eyes. It's looking right at me. I'm sure of it.

The door of the shop bangs open. Amma's shouting,

"No! Leave her!" Out come two men in black uniforms—Crickets—dragging Paati by the elbows. Paati kicks at them, twists in their arms. Dad tries talking to them, waving his hands, pleading. Amma chases after them, hitting them with her fists, grabbing at Paati's waist. "Take me instead!" she cries, and grabs the man's arm. He pushes Amma away, and she falls to the pavement. They lift Paati off her feet and force her into the van.

"Paati!" I run at the car. I lunge at one of the men, *this* close to tackling his legs, when Dad grabs me. He wraps his arms around me, restraining me, but I struggle free. I run at the car, but the doors slide shut. On her knees on the sidewalk, Amma claws at the air. "Amma!" she screams. "Amma!" The engine revs up and the van drives away. I crouch next to Dad, who crouches next to Amma, who's bent over, curled into the ground, slamming the sidewalk with the palm of her hand.

A few doors down, the van stops again. Mrs. Demba is dragged from her laundromat, her skinny legs kicking at the sky. We watch the scene like we can't move, like our feet are stuck in the cement of the sidewalk. We watch it like it's a television show, like it isn't happening to us. On the front step stands a woman in an orange tie, just like Buff's. All of us, together, watch Mrs. Demba disappear into the van, the door slide shut. We watch the van start up and drive down Mingus Avenue. We watch it until it's gone.

Chapter 17

What did I do then? What do you do when your grandmother's taken away? If you had a Dragonfly follow me around every second for the next few days, you would know. You'd see me and my parents waking up early every morning to mash a pot of potatoes and onions and peas. You'd see us taking our sadness for Paati and stuffing it into pyramids of samosa dough. You'd see us printing out messages and running them through a laminating machine—a *laminating machine*! I've always wanted one of those, and who knew we had one all along? You'd see me picking up empanadas from the Calderóns, dumplings from the Wongs.

One afternoon, just after lunch, Amma stands gazing out the window. "It was my fault," she says. "I brought her here."

"None of this is your fault, Sindu," Dad says. He hugs her from behind, but she elbows him away, then turns on the sink and starts to rinse our plates.

The resistance courses through Pacific City. Dad lets

me go with him to run packages from our kitchen, from the Calderóns and the Wongs to the staff entrances of restaurants, the back doors of big houses. We watch out for Dragonflies. We try to look casual, like we're just making deliveries, just minding our beeswax. Really, though, we're building alliances. We're spreading the news about who's on our side, whether it's a janitor in the capitol building or the minister of education herself. Day by day, more people join our side. Day by day, news reports seem less charmed by Bamberger. They start to question what he's doing. The revolution is widening. The revolution is deepening. The revolution will be wrapped in flaky dough, poked into steamed dumplings. The revolution will be delicious.

When I ask about Paati, Amma and Dad don't have answers. They barely know more than I do. I ask if Paati being taken was my fault, if I got us in trouble. *Absolutely not, Muki.* That's the one answer they do have. They call a lawyer. The lawyer opens a case. The lawyer says, *We'll see.* Amma moves through the house like a low gray cloud. She is a fog I can't break through. I want to, though. I want to pull the cloud open and step into it with her, but she won't let me.

No one makes me go to school. I spend two days at home drawing butterflies—blue morphos, golden swallowtails, orange-and-black monarchs. They don't exactly help me *forget* about Paati. It's more like I un-remember her, for a few minutes at a time, when I'm drawing. Gliding my pen across paper, tracing the smooth curve of a thorax, the symmetry of a wing—this calms me down.

I think a lot about Tinley Schaedler's butterfly grove, the trees dripping wings. If only butterflies knew how humans were using them. I can only un-remember for so long. When I go to my room at night, Paati's bed—my old bed—lies made and empty, with a little lump under the quilt where her socks must be.

On Thursday afternoon, Flip and Fabi come by after school. Sitting on the floor in my room, we stare at each other for a while. No one knows what to say. So I say the only thing I

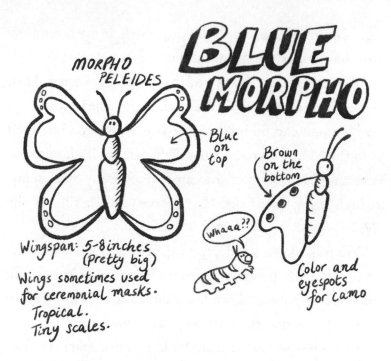

BLUE MORPHO

MORPHO PELEIDES

Blue on top

Brown on the bottom

Whaaa??

Wingspan: 5-8 inches (pretty big)
Wings sometimes used for ceremonial masks.
Tropical.
Tiny scales.

Color and eyespots for camo

---

know is true. "We have to get her back. We have to get her out of that Moth camp."

Fabi stares back, wide-eyed. "I was thinking the exact same thing."

"Me too," says Flip.

I look from Flip to Fabi and back to Flip again. "How do we break her out?"

"We'll have to figure that out," Flip says. "We'll go on reconnaissance, back to the camp."

I nod. I've been thinking about getting Paati back almost nonstop. So far, it's felt complicated and impossible. But now, with Flip and Fabi kneeling on my bedroom floor, light from my desk lamp sparking in their eyes, rescuing Paati only seems *mostly* impossible.

We hop on our bikes and head up Oceanview Hill, toward the soccer fields. We turn right when we should turn left and end up back on the big, empty road that led us to the Moth camp last time. Fabi's in the lead, as usual. When we catch sight of the camp, its faraway black tents, its high fence, Fabi halts. "Let's leave our bikes here," she says.

We walk down the dusty road. It's a warm day, but the air is damp and it smells like rain. Fabi breaks into a run, and so does my heart. I can feel Paati close by. I can feel her somewhere behind those curls of razor wire.

Getting closer to the main building now, there are news vans. No reporters, though. No cameras. They must be inside the camps. Beyond the vans sits a building with a giant moth painted on it. To the right of the main building stands one big black tent, and then two more behind it. I can see the spot in the fence where we snuck in last time. It's been closed off. The camp sits on empty land—no trees or bushes, nothing to hide us. If a guard looks out, they'll have a clear view of three kids who shouldn't be here.

Then I spot a big green metal box, one of those electricity boxes you see on the sidewalk sometimes. I run toward it, knowing that any second I might be spotted. Flip and Fabi follow.

And that's how we find ourselves crouching outside the

Moth camp, behind a big green box, with no idea what to do next.

"I wonder where they keep them," Fabi says. "I guess in those tents. They must sleep there."

"I wonder what they do all day," Flip says. "I wonder if they're even there still. What if they sent them away already?"

I hadn't thought of this. What if they have? The idea of Paati already being gone—it's like a kick in the gut, and the next thing I know, I'm curled up on the ground.

"*Muki*," Fabi hisses. "Flip, you drone! Muki, they haven't sent her away yet. I promise."

"How do you know?" I ask, still holding my stomach.

"They said it in the paper. They're called Elder-Moths because they're old. The Elder-Moths are staying here for a while."

I sit up. "It's in the paper?"

She looks at me, at Flip. "Don't you guys read the newspaper?" We both shrug. Fabi shakes her head and sighs. "Anyway. They're not sending them away yet. They said two weeks."

I curl up into the ball again. Two weeks—and then what? Will Paati end up in a strange country? Alone?

I sense movement somewhere beyond the fence. I can almost feel footsteps through the ground. Paati. Any second, I might see Paati.

"Look!" Fabi whispers. "Look look look!"

From the door of the main building walks a group of people in green uniforms, gold butterfly badges on their chests. People with big news cameras skip around the uniforms, trying to get a good shot. At the back of the group: General Schaedler.

"Tinley's dad!" I whisper. My stomach sinks. No Paati. And then it sinks even further. I knew the general worked for Bamberger. I knew, sure, but now I *know*. I know he's part of this operation that took Paati away. I'm not mad, though. This pit in my gut—it isn't anger. I don't know what it is, exactly.

Just then, woken by the thunder of all those feet, a cloud of little black birds rises from behind the main building. They fly in formation, swirling and swooping, following some invisible leader. It's called a murmuration. Butterflies do it, too. The group doesn't notice, but General Schaedler does. He stops, looks up, and watches the shape-shifting cloud of birds as it rises and falls, a black ghost against the pale sky. Then he breaks into a jog to catch up with the group.

From inside the camp, we hear another drumming of feet, a clatter of voices. A new group has emerged from a tent. "It's them," Fabi whispers, "the Elder-Moths!" With their loose gray clothes, their gray and white hair, they look like a storm rolling through the courtyard. Maybe it's the vast sky, the massive black tents, the nothingness all around, but out here, the Elder-Moths look almost miniature.

And then the crowd parts just a little, and among the small bodies, there's an even smaller one, her chin held high, the sun beaming off her glasses, her mad mop of white hair corralled into a bun. "Fabi, it's her!"

"You're right," Fabi says. "So this is our chance. We've got to do it now. Today. Now."

"Holy mamba," Flip mutters. My heart pounds in my throat.

"If the officers go back into the building," Fabi continues, "that's when we get up and sneak around the fence. That's when we find a way in."

Beyond the fence, the Elder-Moths and officers fall silent. It's like they sense something. It's like they sense us. I hold my breath.

"Oh for Jeebus *Christmas*!"

I spin around. "Lee!" He isn't even trying to hide. "Get down!" I hiss.

He drops to the ground. Fabi flinches and grabs my arm.

"It's okay," I say. Flip stares at Lee, stares at me, then stares at Lee again.

"What are you doing here?" I ask.

"What're *you* doing here?"

"Recon," Flip says, very seriously. "Reconnaissance."

"Shut up, Flip," Fabi says. She gives Lee the Fabi Special—stink eye and side-eye, both at the same time.

"Buddy," Lee says to me. "You can't be out here. Someone

161

might see you. *I* saw you."

"I know."

"You're lucky there are no Dragonflies around," he says. "Come on. Let's get you out of here."

"How? What if someone sees us?"

"I'll wrap you in my invisibility cloak."

"You have one?"

"What? No."

A whistle blows. A Cricket shouts something, and the Elder-Moths turn to him. They're standing differently now, their backs stiff, their arms stick-straight at their sides. The Cricket shouts an order, and the Elder-Moths stamp their heels together. He shouts again and they march in perfect sync. Some of them manage to get their knees high. Paati wobbles in line, half sideways. The camp guards stand around them, batons in hand.

The Cricket blows his whistle again and the Elder-Moths halt. They break off into small groups and stroll around the courtyard. Paati walks arm in arm with Mrs. Demba. Some walk in circles, some in lines. They churn in mixed formations. A murmuration with no leader.

"Hey, Muki," Lee whispers. "It's time." He looks worried. A little sad. Maybe he's sad about the general, too. And that's when I know: I'm not angry to see General Schaedler here. I'm sad. Maybe, if Tinley weren't my friend, I wouldn't be sad. But she is and I am. I'm sad that there are adults in the world who want to keep Paati in a big black tent, then send her away. They look at people like us and see difference and danger and not much else. General Schaedler is one of them. My friend's dad. Dads are supposed to be better than that.

"We'll figure this out, okay?" Lee puts one hand on my shoulder, one hand on Flip's. He nods at Fabi. "You guys ready? We're going to have to run. Quietly." He peers through the fence, where the guards stand facing away from us.

"They might see us," Flip whispers.

"They could be out here for a while, though. We'll have to keep quiet and low to the ground. Can you guys scamper?"

A raindrop lands on my hand. Another on my cheek, and another on the ground next to me. Rain starts falling faster and faster. The people in the yard look up and start shouting and calling up to the sky—like people always do, for some reason, always surprised by the rain. Just then, the sky cracks open to a torrent, and there's water everywhere, sheets and sheets, so much I can hardly see. It's loud, like rocks smashing to the ground. "Go!" Lee shouts. "Go go go!" We run back across the concrete expanse, shielded by the rain, until we reach the main road, and farther down it, our bicycles.

"Follow me!" Lee calls. A little way down, his silver pickup waits. We ride to it, the rain lashing our faces. He throws our bikes in the back and herds us into the passenger seat, where we sit smashed together like the folds of a wet accordion.

Flip groans. "Oh man, we were so *close.*"

"Close to what?" Lee asks.

"Close to Paati!" Flip says. I've never heard another kid call Paati *Paati.*

"That was a big risk you all took," Lee says. "If they found you, I don't know what would have happened. What were you trying to do out there, anyway?"

Fabi turns to Lee, frowns, looks him over. "Who *are* you?"

He turns to her, turns to the road, turns to her.

"That's Lee. He's helping out with the revolution," I say, and it sounds ridiculous. You help out with bake sales, not revolutions.

"There's a revolution?" Flip asks. "I thought we were just trying to get Paati out."

Lee glances at me.

"I'll explain it later, Flip."

"Well, either way," Flip says, "we need a name."

"For who?"

"For what we're doing. We can't just call it *Getting Paati Out,* can we?"

I shrug. "Sounds okay to me."

"Nah, we need a good name. How about Operation Awesome Eagle?"

"Why that?"

"I don't know. It sounds good."

"How about Operation Free Paati?" I say.

"Boring."

"How about Operation Paati Break?" Fabi says.

"I don't think so. Operation Chrysalis?" I offer.

"Operation Vampire Moth!" Flip says.

"Look," Lee cuts in. "How about Operation Go to School and Stop Putting Yourselves in Dangerous Situations?"

"Bad," Flip says.

"Seriously, you guys. This isn't a game, okay? This isn't *Good Night, Gorilla*. You can't just break into the Moth camp and let everyone out. That would make everything worse."

"How?"

"It's complicated."

"Isn't that what you're doing? The grown-ups?" I ask.

"I think we explained all that to you the other night, Muki."

I shrug. "I guess."

"It's hard to see now, I know," Lee says. "But we've got to be patient. And smart. We can't just run around creating chaos."

That's exactly what an adult would say, and Lee's probably right, but to me, it sounds like more of the boring pessimism adults are famous for. I don't see how patience will make anything better.

"We're just trying to do something. Before it's too late."

"Before the adults make it worse again," Fabi adds.

We drive on. "Lee?"

"Sir."

"If we leave Mariposa, will things get better for people here?"

He thinks about this. "Not really, Muki."

"There won't be more nectar for poor people who don't have jobs?"

"The thing is, your families? They're not the ones hogging the money and the jobs. Those hogs are Butterflies, mostly. They'd still be here."

Fabi pipes up, "If they loved this country so much, they wouldn't be hogging all the nectar."

Lee smiles sadly. "You're right. What's your name? Never mind. The point is, you're not the ones making the poor people poor. You're not the ones in mansions, driving Lamborghinis and Bugattis paid for by the government. I mean, they can kick you guys out, sure. But I don't know what's going to change for poor folks if you're gone. Probably not much."

We're quiet the rest of the way home. A few blocks from the shop, Lee sticks his head out the window, looks up and down the street. "No Dragonflies," he says, and hops out. We get back on our bikes and ride home. It's stopped raining, and the sun—what's left of it—peeps up over the buildings.

Flip and Fabi come upstairs with me, and we run through the kitchen, where Dad's chopping something, and settle down in my room. Outside my window, a single butterfly dances around the laundry line. Without Paati's saris, the clothes out there are gray and grayer. They drip with rain.

"That was crazy," Fabi says.

"Yeah."

"Tell me what you were going to tell me," Flip says. "In the car."

So I tell Flip about the samosas, about Tinley's dad, about my parents and Lee. "*Hold it,*" he says. "So the empanadas? That Mamá cooks? And the dumplings from the Wongs? Those have *messages* in them?" I nod. His mouth drops wide open. Like, I can see his molars.

"It's the safest way to communicate."

He shakes his head, still wonder struck. "Empanadas are safer than cell phones."

That's when I hear a voice from down on the street. "*Mingus Mouse!*"

Fabi looks at Flip, who looks at me. Everyone who ever shouts Mingus Mouse is here, in this room. We scramble to the window. Down below, on the sidewalk: Andrew Wong.

"Hi," he calls. Andrew Wong's in high school. He has hair on his legs.

"Hi," I say.

"You're supposed to come to dinner at the restaurant tomorrow night. Can you tell your parents?" I tell Andrew

I'll pass on the message. He lingers for a second, and then turns on his heel and heads back home.

"That was weird."

"Weirdest," Fabi says. "The Wongs' dumplings, though. You can't beat those."

"Dumplings." Flip pulls out his red ball and bounces it once against the wall. "How about Operation Vengeful Dumpling?"

MURMURATION

Chapter 18

I lie awake that night, watching the moon spread its light across Paati's bed. Cars pass below, and so do the scattered voices of people walking by. I start to drift off, but then I hear footsteps on the stairs.

I'm up and dressed in seconds. I don't even think about it. When I walk out of my room, no one's around, but I can feel the echo of a body. In the stairway to the street, the light is on. I take the steps two at a time, hop off the last six.

On the sidewalk, it's misty, but not cold. The moon casts a beam of light down the street. I see Dad. He's crouching down by our Honda, fiddling with the door handle. He doesn't hear me when I walk up behind him.

"Dad."

"Gah!" He jumps and wheels around. He's panting, staring wild-eyed at me, holding a hand to his heart.

"What are you doing?"

"Thumbi! You need to be in bed."

"The revolution doesn't happen in bed, Dad."

"I'm just going to pick something up. Okay?"

"At one in the morning?"

He thinks for a second. "Yes."

"I want to come."

"Absolutely not. *No.*"

"Why?"

"You know why." He sighs and presses his palms to his eyes.

My ears prick up. From a distance, up the quiet street, a Dragonfly whines toward us. Dad hears it, too. "It's coming closer," he says.

"We'd better get out of here."

"Oh god. Fine. Get in. *Get in!*"

He's hugely annoyed with me, I know. But hey, that's okay, because here I am, going on a mission with my dad. We rumble down Mingus Avenue toward the soccer fields.

"You think this is exciting, don't you," he grumbles.

"You said you wouldn't keep me out of anything. You said I'd be part of this now."

"That doesn't mean putting you in danger."

My skin tingles. "Will this be dangerous?"

He glances over, clears his throat. "Maybe I could use you. This time."

"Yes! For what?"

"You'll see." We're both quiet. A few people are out at

this time of night, but mostly the roads are empty. The night world is an in-between world. It's like a dream I can't remember.

Dad clears his throat. "There's this fence lined with razor wire, with a gap under it. I was going to try to get through it myself, wearing three sweaters and a hat. I would be badly cut, I have no doubt." He pats his belly. "Too many samosas."

"But me?"

"You'd get through, no problem."

"I'm a shape-shifter."

"That you are," Dad says.

"What do I do once I'm through?"

"Well, there's a message sitting in the bottom of a drain-pipe. On the western end of the main building."

He reaches between our seats and pulls out a compass. It lights up in the dark, pointing east now.

"Nice." I expect more instructions, but none come. "Is that all? What do I do after I have the paper?"

"Well, I imagine you'd want to make sure no one sees you, and then you will probably run like a maniac back to the car. A silent maniac."

Heat rises up my neck. "Will people be there?"

"Two guards patrol at night."

"That's not very many."

"You're right. But they walk continuously around and around the camp."

"Do they walk in a certain pattern?"

"Actually, yes." I can tell he's impressed I thought of this. "They walk in opposite directions, one clockwise, one counterclockwise, and every two rounds, they walk straight down the middle."

"Wow. Who figured that out?"

He doesn't answer. We're on the big road now, and in the distance, I see a few faint beams of light. The Moth camp. I can't see the black tents, but I can see where the dark thickens, and I know they're there. And inside one of them is Paati.

"Can we see Paati, too?"

"No. You know that."

I have at least seven more questions, but Dad slows to a stop, about a thirty-second run from the camp. For a minute, we sit there, looking at it.

"Couldn't they just text you what's in the note?" The question flies out before I can stop it, and now I'm embarrassed. "No, forget that—"

"Our text messages can be traced," Dad says. "You know that." He rummages in the glove compartment, then pauses and turns to me. "This is something I know you can do, Thumbi. I wouldn't be sending you out there if I didn't think—if I didn't think . . ." He doesn't finish his sentence. Instead, he pulls out a pair of gloves. "Put these on. For the razor wire." He takes off his own black sweater and hands it to me. I put all of this on. The sweater is thick and warmed by Dad; the gloves make my hands look like a gorilla's. It's all too big, but somehow, it makes me feel safer.

He points at the fence. "There's a gap just ahead. Just walk in a straight—"

"I see it."

He lays his bare hand on my gloved hand and looks hard into my face. "I'll be here waiting. You're sure you want to do this?"

"I'm sure."

I am not sure. I step out of the car, close the door. I am *very* not sure. Still, I make my feet move, one in front of the other. As I get closer to the camp, the night's silence sharpens to a thin whine, and I can actually hear the air move past my ears. I find the gap under the fence, its sharp points of razor wire gleaming in the moonlight. Dad's right. This is a very narrow opening. He would have gotten stuck, for sure. On my left, in the distance, is the main building. I pull out the compass and turn it until it points west.

Crickets. They're somewhere around here. Since I don't see them yet, there's a good chance they're both at the far end of the camp, heading back to the main building. I lie down next to the fence, stomach flat against the cold, hard ground, and I wait. I'll have to wait until I see them, wait until they head away from me again. And so I wait. And wait. And wait.

I don't know how long I lie here with no trace of the guards. If they were really doing their rounds, they would have reached the main building by now. The concrete chill is giving me a stomachache. I think of Dad in the car, getting more worried with each passing second. It's time to just do this.

I take a deep breath, suck in my stomach, and slither through the gap. The razor wire bares its fangs. I ease through a little more, a little more, until my shoulders are in. I'm moving through slowly, the razors just barely grazing me. I'm almost through.

My sweater snags. It yanks at my back, just below my left shoulder. I pull forward, but the blade digs deeper. If I move wrong, I'll be stabbed. I shift a little to the side and reach behind my head. I grab a handful of sweater and try to wiggle it free. It doesn't budge. It's stuck on the blade. That's when I hear footsteps. *Dad!* I almost call out. The footsteps draw closer, coming from inside the camp. No. The word throbs in my ears. No. No. No. No.

All I see is the jagged dark. I listen again for footsteps, but my ears are ringing and all I can hear is my own panic. I start to suck at the air. I'm losing control, breathing in weird little hiccups that won't stop. I can't breathe out, just in, in, in. I can't stop gulping. *Breathe*, I tell myself. I remember Paati's exercises. I imagine butterfly wings. Open. Close. Inhale. Exhale. My breath calms.

Silence. The footsteps have faded away, and there's no one in sight. Inhale. Exhale. With a final mad yank, I tug the yarn off the razor wire and break free.

The moonlight has shifted, and it falls now on the main building. On the cinder-block wall closest to me, I can just make out a long metal rod that climbs from ground to roof. The drainpipe.

How does a person sneak across a dark camp with two Crickets prowling around? They don't teach us anything useful at MHP. On my hands and knees, I crawl along the perimeter fence. I figure if the Crickets have flashlights, they'll aim them high. They won't be looking for a kid, definitely not for a kid crawling.

As I near the main building, my hands and knees go numb. This is good. Numb is good. I go even lower now, down on my belly, across a field of sharp gravel, and I'm more grateful than ever for Dad's sweater and his gloves. Now I'm crawling combat style, slithering along like a gecko. The drainpipe is twenty feet away, then ten, then five, then zero.

I reach up into its mouth, and yes. I feel something. A roll of paper, which I slip out. Should I read it? In case I lose it or have to swallow it? I unroll the paper. It's a drawing of a hand, with stars scattered up and down the fingers. The words scrawled around the hand are too small to read in this dim light.

"What in the world," I whisper.

Distant footsteps.

"—mayonnaise—" Mayonnaise?

Voices trail from the other side of the building. Whoever's talking is talking loud.

"The thing about the ham sandwich, see, is the ham

sandwich requires a good slather of mustard. Gives the fatty taste a' the ham a nice acidity."

Two Crickets in puffy dark jackets and wool caps walk out of the main building. One of them is holding a sandwich. He chomps down on it and keeps talking, his mouth full of food. "But the problem, see, with mustard, is that it disappears into the bread, gets absorbed. But the *mayo*. The *mayo*—"

"Hold it." The other guard stops in his tracks and so do I. "I heard something." He swings his flashlight around. I'm in open territory, nothing to hide behind. "You hear something?"

A second flashlight switches on. The beams leap left, right, above me. The Crickets turn around, their eyes trained on the tents. I could run now. Maybe. I could run silently, reach the fence in the next three seconds. A silent maniac, Dad said.

No. Instead I slide around the building—*What are you doing, Muki?*—until the perimeter fence is out of sight. A flashlight beam hits the wall, just a few feet away from me. If I were a real moth, the night wouldn't feel so foreign. I'd flit over this building on luminescent wings, headed for the moon. But I'm not a moth. I'm a sixth grader with big feet.

I press my head flat against the wall, looking away from the guards. That's when I see it: a little red box built into the wall. How many times have I passed the same little box at school? How many times have I gazed at the lever on that box, daring myself to pull it? And what happened that one time when Box Tuttle *did* pull that lever? Fire alarms sounded, students flooded the halls, and the entire school spent the afternoon in the lunch yard. Anyone could have done anything in that mess—and no one would have noticed.

When the beam of light swings away from me, I leap for the box and yank the lever down. And yes! Sirens scream, louder than anything I've ever heard. The noise shreds the sky. The camp erupts in voices, floodlights switch on, and so many bodies fill the yard that I can't see the Crickets anymore. I can't tell prisoner from guard, and no one knows what's happening. I sprint from the wall to the perimeter fence, a silent, boy-shaped riot in the deafening dark.

When I reach the gap in the fence, I slide through too quickly and a blade streaks across my back. The pain is a lightning strike. I've never felt anything like it.

Pounding footsteps. I feel them vibrate across the ground, coming closer. Flashlight beams leap along the fence. They've spotted me. I run.

Back across the concrete stretch, back to the silent car. Dad starts the engine and I leap into my seat and he speeds away, even before I've closed the door. His headlights are off, and we careen through the night, blind and deaf and full of hope.

Dad doesn't stop, doesn't say anything, until we're back home on Mingus Avenue. He stops the car and we just sit there for a while, staring straight ahead. Finally, he turns to me.

"Are you okay?"

I nod. Then I remember the cut across my back and my face crumples with pain. My shirt sticks to my back with blood. Dad turns me around and cries out. "My god," he says. "It was the fence!"

I shake my head. "It's okay. I'm okay." I reach into my shoe, pull out the message, and hand it to him. He looks at it and nods.

"Okay," he says.

"What does it mean?"

"We'll figure it out."

Back in the kitchen, Amma waits, her face streaked with fury. But she's not angry at me. She is one hundred and ten percent angry at Dad. She is *mad*. So mad she hasn't said a word to either of us. Dad sits down next to her, still in a daze.

"Dad?"

He blinks himself back into the room. "I shouldn't have brought you." His voice is hoarse, and I think he might cry.

"Dad, I think they saw me."

He shakes his head. "Don't worry about that. Are you okay? Does it hurt?"

The pain of the scrape is fading, but I can feel a trickle of blood down my back.

Without a word, Amma pulls my shirt off and gasps. She touches the wound gingerly and yanks her hand away. Then she dabs the cut with an alcohol wipe. It stings, and I can't help the tears that roll down my face, even when she smears my back with ointment. She opens my palms and examines them, runs her fingers over the tiny pockmarks left by the concrete. She takes my cheeks in her hands, looks deep into my eyes. She runs her thumb along my forehead. Then she stands up, pulls her robe tightly around her, gives Dad one last, long, shredding glare, and leaves the kitchen.

Dad sighs. "I'm in big trouble."

"Sorry."

"Never again, Thumbi."

"Okay. The message, though."

We unfurl the message on the table. The writing, scrawled along the edges of the hand, is just barely legible now.

> Long years ago we made a tryst with destiny, and now the time comes when we shall redeem our pledge.

"Do you recognize this?" he asks.

"I've read it somewhere."

"It's from Nehru's 'Tryst with Destiny' speech. Delivered on the eve of India's independence—"

"—from the British! We read this! In Miss P.'s class!"

"Very good," Dad says. He gets up and turns the kettle on.

"Who put it there, in the drainpipe?"

"I don't know. I *can't* know. This resistance operates as a team, but the players are blind."

I'm confused. "They're blind?"

"Meaning no one in this operation knows what anyone else is doing, or who's doing what. It's safer that way.

We're less likely to be discovered."

"So what does it mean? The hand and the stars and the quote? Do you know?" I can see it on his face: he knows. "Well?"

He stares at the floor for a few seconds, opens his mouth and closes it. Finally: "No. I'm in enough trouble already. You need to get to bed."

"Dad!"

"I'm serious, Thumbi. Now."

"But—"

"*Now.*"

I roll up the message and stick it in my pocket. I'll figure it out myself if he's not going to help me. He can't stop me from doing that.

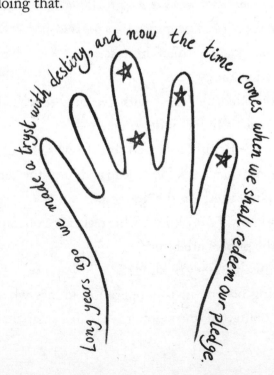

Chapter 19

The next morning, Amma wakes me up with an announcement. "You're going to school." She doesn't say anything about the night before, doesn't mention the fact that I've only had three hours of sleep. I consider pretending I didn't hear her, rolling back into corpse pose for a few more hours. But she stands in the doorway until I'm up, on my feet, and well clear of my warm, soft, heavenly blankets. I'm going to school.

It occurs to me that our civics project is due in a little over a week. "Amma? I might be staying after school to work on my project."

"Okay, Muki."

At school, Tinley finds me at my locker.

"Uh—*hi*. Good to see you're *alive*."

"Hi."

"Were you sick?"

"Yeah," I lie. She doesn't know. No one at school seems to know what happened to Paati. I prefer it that way.

"We should probably work on our project today, right?" she asks.

"Yeah. I guess."

She peers into my face. "Are you okay?"

"I don't really feel like thinking about butterflies." I shove my sketchbook in my locker and shut it.

"Okay. Well, um, maybe come over, and we'll work a little? We'll at least try?"

I find Tinley after school. She's flanked by Tinleys, their hair all in little buns, and normally, seeing Tinley flanked by Tinleys, I'd walk right back the other way. But today, I care less about pretty much everything, so I walk right up to her and say, "Hey. Ready?"

Outside the school, something's happening. Students, teachers, parents—they're gathered in a crowd at the foot of the school steps. Tinley and I push through, and she slips ahead of me. "What is it?" I call.

For a few seconds, I think I've lost her. I squeeze past some eighth graders, get an elbow in the forehead, and finally make my way closer to the front of the crowd, though I still can't see a thing. That's when I hear a growl. It's a hungry, deep growl, but not from an animal.

It can only be one thing. The Bugatti.

Tinley's hand grabs mine and pulls me through a clot

of students, past Mr. Pinto, and down the last few steps. I find myself standing right in front of a Bugatti Divo. The passenger door opens.

"Get in, Muki," Tinley says. "And scootch over." There's no back seat, so Tinley squeezes in next to me, ignoring everyone, even Mr. Pinto.

She sighs. "This happens every time. You'd think they never saw a Bugatti before."

"I think they probably *haven't* seen a Bugatti before."

"Good afternoon, Muki." The general sits with a hand on the wheel, a small smile. "Tinley texted me. She said you could use a distraction. And that you've never been to the beach before."

"Well, I wouldn't say *never*—"

"Let's go."

The Bugatti creeps through the school pickup zone, crammed in by other cars. It grunts and purrs like a wildcat thirsty for prey. The most powerful engine in the world won't do you any good in the MHP pickup zone.

Finally, we're out on the road, then on a highway that's nearly empty, and the wildcats are racing. My heart races with them. My seat thrums and vibrates. We're going way faster than we're supposed to, but I'm not scared. I forget to be scared. I forget everything. Tinley opens our window, and I can smell the ocean now. The water skids by in a blur.

Soon, too soon, we stop in front of a vast beach of white sand. Tinley throws the door open and runs out, sprinting across the sand, pulling her socks and shoes off and stomping straight into the water, moving farther and farther out, until the dark waves soak her to her waist. I follow cautiously. The water is a shock. When a wave comes in, it pools around my feet. And when the wave goes out again, I feel my whole body rushing backward, even though I'm standing still. The sand sinks around my feet, too, and I end up standing in two little ditches, ice-cold froth clinging to my toes. I roll my pants up and venture farther in, just to my knees. Tinley's bobbing around like a seal now. The general's on the shore, walking toward the water, barefoot. When he gets close, he breaks into a run, heads straight to the deep, and dives into a towering green and frothy wave. For a few minutes, he is lost in the ocean. I don't see him anywhere. The waves rise and crash and I start to worry. But then I spot him, a single small head in the distance.

We regroup, eventually, back on the warm sand. All of us are soaked and no one's brought a towel. If Amma were here, she'd have towels and a cooler full of idlis.

Tinley plops down next to me and pours a line of sand over her bare legs, brushes the sand off, does it again. The general looks up at the overcast sky. "Looks like rain," he says. If Mariposa had a national motto, that would be it—it rains all the time here. Today, I can tell, we'll get a warm, soft rain, like the ocean and the sky are reaching for each other, and Mariposa just happens to be in the way.

"See these little dots in the sand?" the general asks.

He points to a scatter of perfectly round pin-sized holes. "If you dig in a little, you'll rout out a ghost crab." He jams his fingers into the ground and burrows a tunnel, using his hand as a kind of excavator, until he finds the crab— small, yellow and white, its claws scrambling against the sand. It takes a dizzy little walk, then digs back down and disappears.

For a while, we sit quietly and watch the ocean, the waves rolling in, gathering foamy white crests, then pulling back and vanishing. "It's amazing to think," he finally says, "that under that water, you'll find entire ecosystems, entire galaxies of life in the sea. And here we are, living our lives, hardly thinking about them at all." He picks up a stick of driftwood and pokes at the sand. "Mariposa's quite a small country, you see. And it's important to many other countries. But out here, by the ocean, it's easy to think we're alone in this world. It's hard to imagine that anything else exists, besides Mariposa and the waves."

"I disagree."

He turns to me. "Explain."

"I don't feel alone in the world, ever. I'll never *just* be Mariposan." It surprises me to say this, but it's true. For most of my life, I've felt nothing *but* Mariposan. Something's changed. "My parents. And India. They're always with me, even when they're not with me."

"You have two homes," Tinley says.

With his piece of wood, the general draws a square in

185

the sand. "Home is relative, Blossom. You can find a home wherever you choose to. Like a crab."

"You compare people to animals a lot," I say.

He looks right at me and my face goes all hot. "Do I?"

Tinley chimes in. "Yup. You do."

"People are animals, aren't they? We're not that different from crabs or zebras or—"

"Butterflies," Tinley says. The word hovers in the air, until the wind picks up and blows it away.

"General?"

"Sir."

"You asked me about moths, last time."

He clears his throat. A sailboat appears on the horizon, inches its way along. Its sails stand high and proud. "I'm sorry about that, Muki. That must have struck you as an aggression."

"I can tell you about moths, though."

"Can you? Go ahead."

"Do you want to know about the insects or the people?"

"Let's start with people."

"Well, there's my dad."

"Sure."

"He used to be a chemist. That's what he studied, and that's what he did when he first moved here. He worked in a lab. But after a while, he quit."

"Why'd he quit?"

"I don't know. He wouldn't really tell me."

"Is he employed now?" The general draws another little square on the ground, right next to the first square.

"He and my mom own a shop. They also make samosas. They're these fried—"

"I've had samosas." He draws a third, neat square in the sand.

"In Pacific City?"

"Sure."

"Then you've probably had our samosas. I can tell you something about moths, the insects."

"Okay."

"They're masters of disguise. Some moths can disguise themselves as bird poop."

"They've always seemed a little . . . unsettling. Ghostly. Strange."

"They're misunderstood. Everyone thinks they're obsessed with light bulbs. But it's just that they use the moon to navigate, and sometimes they think porch lights are the moon."

"You don't say."

"Crazy that they can't tell the difference between a light bulb and the moon."

He thinks about this for a while. He draws square after square in the sand, like he's trying to box up his thoughts.

Then: "You're an only child."

"Yeah. I am." I hesitate. It would be easier not to tell him. "There's also my grandmother."

He turns to me now. "Your grandmother." His eyes flicker. He must know.

"They took her away last week."

"What?" Tinley cuts in. "What do you mean?"

It's hard to say these words, but I force myself to. "Some Crickets showed up at our house," I say. The tremors start in my belly. "They made her get in a car with a butterfly painted on the side and they took her away." My mouth shakes, my voice, my fingers.

"Muki!" Tinley gasps. "Why didn't you say anything?"

"I'm very sorry, Muki. These things can be difficult."

"What will they do with her?"

The general squints out at the sailboat. "Well, they'll keep her for a while. They'll give her a bed and food, like they're doing for everyone, and then they'll send her off."

"Are they coming for us next?" My voice shakes. "For me and my parents?"

The general looks down at me for a few seconds, probably deciding whether to lie or tell the truth. "I'll tell you what I can tell you, Muki. We started with the Elder-Moths first. It just made more sense to apprehend people who probably don't have jobs."

"You know about this, Papa?" Tinley asks.

He looks at Tinley and doesn't say anything.

"You took Muki's grandma away?" She looks terrified.

"No, Blossom, not me pers—"

"But you told them to do it?"

188

"I am an adviser to the president, Tinley. And yes, this is one of my operations."

"You're kidnapping grandmas."

"Tinley—" The general clenches his jaw. His face is perfectly still. But up by his eye, one muscle twitches, tiny and rebellious.

"But you didn't have to do it. You could have said *no* to the president, and stopped everything," she says.

"No. Not quite. The president would find someone else to do it. I work for him, so I do his bidding. Like any job." The general speaks calmly. He isn't angry. He breathes normally. His voice is quiet and almost kind. He's just talking to a kid.

That's when I see it: the Schaedlers move through this world like sailboats over the sea—smooth and sleek, sure that they belong, blind to what swirls below the surface. No matter what happens in Mariposa, the general and Tinley will be fine. They'll keep their home. They'll keep the life they know.

I find my voice. "And this whole thing was your idea, right? The Moths and Butterflies? Did you start that?"

The waves climb and crash and I can hardly hear my own words. Maybe that's what's making me brave. Tinley and I fix our eyes on the general. He looks from me to her and back again.

"The removal plan is a joint effort," he says. It sounds like something he'd say at a press conference. He blinks very fast, and then he looks me right in the eye. "Muki, this country is in a very complicated situation right now. Things aren't as simple—"

"Then why do you act like they're simple?"

He stares down at me. I know I've said more than I should have. "I mean, Butterflies and Moths? We're not butterflies or moths. We're people. You can't stick pins through us and label us like we're insects. It's not that simple."

His dark eyes rest on my forehead, like he's peering inside me, like he's counting every thought, reading every unspoken question. My hands go cold and the wind turns icy. It's scary, sometimes, to say what you know is true. It's even scarier when people listen. But I'm learning this much: if I don't say what I know is true, I may as well be lying.

The general looks down at the sand, at the field of squares he's drawn. With the long end of the driftwood, he wipes the whole thing away.

"I think it's time to go," he says. The sun sinks over the ocean and the wind raises a whorl of stinging sand. He stands up, rolls the bottoms of his pants down, and starts walking back up the beach, back to the car.

Chapter 20

I'm so busy thinking that I don't notice the general's heading in the direction of Oceanview. Before I can stop him, he turns onto Mingus Avenue and rolls to a stop in front of the shop.

He opens his car door.

"Wait," I say, "you don't have to—"

He turns to me. "I'd like to meet this father of yours."

"Why?"

He gets out of the car.

When we walk into the shop, we don't find Dad. Instead, we find Buff, munching on a MegaNut bar he probably didn't pay for, a little dribble of chocolate on his orange tie. Buff looks up, and even though the general's in jeans and a sweatshirt, trailing sand from his sneakers, Buff recognizes him. His mouth drops open and his eyes bug out of his head. He bangs around behind the counter, spits the MegaNut into the trash, straightens everything he can, pats down his tie, and stands a little straighter. He salutes the general. A smudge of chocolate sits on his chin.

"Where's my dad?" I ask.

Buff just stands there, gaping.

"What's wrong with him?" Tinley asks.

"Buff! Where's my dad?"

That's when Amma walks into the room. She screeches to a halt and starts chewing at her cheek. She's twisting inside with questions. And then she straightens up and speaks.

"Hello, Muki." She smiles calmly at me. She gazes at Tinley. "Hello." She walks to the general and offers her hand. "I'm Sindu Krishnan." She smiles, and her eyes crinkle and twinkle, and I see it: my mom can be *charming*. Sindu Krishnan, independent businesswoman, gracious hostess.

"Dogwood Schaedler." The general looks, for a microsecond, the tiniest bit awestruck. He shakes her hand, grasping just the tips of Amma's fingers, like he's scared he might break them.

Outside, a crowd starts to gather around the Bugatti. "Thank you for bringing Muki home, Mr. Schaedler." Amma examines my damp trousers, Tinley's ratty wet hair. "Exciting day at school?"

"We went to the beach," I say. I look Amma in the eye. I'm telling the truth. I really hope I get some credit for telling the truth.

"Tea, Mr. Schaedler?" Her smile slathers him with sunshine. She is furious.

Obediently, the general takes his tea. He sips at it, makes sounds of approval. I wonder if he's pretending, too. "I've heard about your samosas," he says.

The blood drains from her face. She smiles even brighter. "Our samosas!"

That's when the general turns around, sees the crowd gathered around his car, and lets out a string of swear words that can't be repeated here. "Shoo!" he says to no one. "Get away!" Then he tromps out the door and flicks his hand at the people gathered around. "Get away from my car!" he yells. "All of you! Back!"

Tinley and I follow him out.

The crowd backs away—the Wongs are there, and Fabi and Flip. They look scared for a second, then offended, then amused. "Away!" The general's voice cracks. "Step away!"

The crowd does back away, then disperses, people shaking their heads, a few laughing. He turns back around, looking a little scared himself.

"Dude," I hear myself say, "they weren't gonna do anything to your car."

The general stands on the sidewalk, his chest heaving, looking angry, then a little bewildered. I think back a few hours, to the crowd outside our school. The general didn't shoo *them* away. What made people in my neighborhood any different? Amma's standing in the doorway, waiting.

Her charm, the thin mist of it, has evaporated. Now she flashes and crackles like lightning.

She waits for him to turn to her. Finally, he does. "Those people weren't going to hurt your car, General Schaedler."

"I think that's—"

"Let me finish," she says. "I don't know why you brought my son home today, or why you took him to the beach. I don't know what any of this is about, but I plan to find out. As for your car, Muki is perfectly capable of taking the subway. He doesn't need a lift from you, and he certainly doesn't need a lift in this—this monstrosity you drive. But aside from that, I may never have this chance again, so I'm going to tell you something."

The general sinks into the ground a little, the way I sank into the ocean sand.

"I know exactly who you are and what you do for a living. I know what you're planning to do to me and other people in this neighborhood—the people you just shooed away like flies. Maybe you've never met people like us. Maybe you've never been to Oceanview and you don't know how things work here. But I can tell you this much: none of these people would come to your neighborhood and yell at you. We have manners, General Schaedler. We know how to treat people. And one more thing. This Butterfly business? Poppycock. Nonsense. I may be brown. I may be a Moth. But I am Mariposan. So is my son. So is my mother. So is my husband. For ten years, I've kept this shop open until midnight. Every morning, people come through this neighborhood because of this shop. They know my name. I know theirs. Do you understand me, General Schaedler? I am a part of this country. You can't remove me. And your Bambi can't remove me, either. You can give a necktie and a fancy title to my shop boy. You can put me in a camp and send me away. You can take me out of Mariposa, but you can't keep me out. This is my home now." She takes a long, shuddering breath. "This is my home."

Silence. The air buzzes, like lightning's about to strike. The wind flaps through the clothesline. A golden butterfly flits past us and up into the sky.

The general clears his throat and gazes back at Amma. His face hangs heavy. Then he turns to Tinley. "Let's get going, Blossom."

I've never seen Tinley this sad. She gives Amma a long look that I can't read, then turns and climbs into the Bugatti. The car starts up and growls down Mingus Avenue. Amma takes my hand, and I feel her fingers shaking. "Come upstairs, Muki."

In the kitchen, she sits down at the table, waiting for an explanation. I know better than to barrel through to my room.

"Sorry, Amma."

"For what, Muki?"

When they took Paati, Amma became a cloud wrapped in a cloud. Even around me and Dad, she's seemed alone. I can see now that my lying to her has made her even lonelier.

"I lied to you."

"I know."

"I wasn't working on my project at school. I was at Tinley's house."

"I know, Muki."

"How?"

"I have my ways."

"I'm sorry they took Paati."

Her face starts to twist in on itself, like she's trying not to cry. Her fists sit clenched on the table, her fingernails digging into her palms. I've never seen my mom cry, and I've always thought it would be the scariest thing in the world. But as I stand here, it happens. Tears stream down her cheeks. They run in toward her nose. She starts sniffing loudly and biting her lip. It isn't as terrifying as I thought it would be. I walk to her chair and hug her around the shoulders. And then she pulls me onto her lap, like she used to when I was little, only now I'm almost as big as her. She wraps her arms around me and we sit like this until Dad gets home, the two of us caught in her cloud.

Chapter 21

A couple hours later, we're walking down the street to the Wongs' restaurant. The memory of the afternoon pinches at me. I'm looking forward to dumplings. Out on the curb, a couple of doors down from the Wongs, sits a familiar red car. When we walk in, Amma lets out a little cry and rushes forward. It's Sonal Aunty. She sits with Raju and Raj Uncle. Sonal Aunty gets up and wraps her arms around Amma. She's wearing a twinkly sort of peacock feather in her hair, and her cheeks are painted pink, like a doll's.

She releases Amma. "A little surprise, darling. Just to cheer us all up. We booked the table yesterday." She smiles. Then she spots me and grabs my face with her hands, singing her Sonal Aunty warble, peppering my cheek with kisses. Raju looks up from his phone and grimaces. I wonder, now, where Sonal Aunty's been all this time. Amma could have used her best friend. She might have felt less alone.

We order dumplings and soup and noodles, and the food feels hot and good in my belly. Raj Uncle asks about Paati, about the night she was taken, but only briefly. Sonal Aunty tuts and shakes her head and looks like she's going to cry, but then Dad changes the subject, and everyone, I guess, is happy not to talk about Paati for a while. Maybe we're all thinking about her, though. All except Raju. He spends the dinner zapping things on his phone, pausing only to let his mom stuff dumplings in his mouth. I'm so hungry and so happy to be eating that I almost forget that these dumplings, on another day, could have held messages.

When the bill comes, so do the fortune cookies. These are my favorite part. When I pick mine up, though, it's strangely heavy. I look up at Amma. I look at the others. There must be a message in my cookie. I feel it. There has to be.

I crack it open, pull out a piece of paper, and it says: *Be a pebble in the giant's shoe.*

No hidden message. Just a plain old fortune. Everything is pleasant and boring, just like I want it to be, until Andrew Wong comes out of the kitchen, walks over, and gives me a fist bump. "You hear they're cracking down on the rebels?" he asks me, like it's nothing, like he's asking if I saw the basketball game.

The adults stop talking. "So they're coming after *us* next," he tells everyone, rubbing his chin, happy for the attention, "I just saw it on the news. The resistance. Bamberger says he can't ignore it any longer. So they're making arrests now, all over town. They've tracked some people down already." He crosses his arms over his chest. "Pretty intense."

"I'm sorry, Andrew," Dad says. "Where did you hear this?"

"Six o'clock news."

"Do your mother and father know?"

"Yeah. We're closing down for a week, heading to the lake, where my aunt lives."

Amma looks at Dad. Sonal Aunty looks at Raj Uncle, and her eyelids flutter nervously. Amma clears her throat. "Thank you, Andrew. That is helpful to know."

We sit quietly for a few minutes. Amma studies the fortune that's slipped out of her cookie. Dad sips his tea and peers out the window. Then he sits up straight, grips the table with both hands.

"Do you hear that?" He looks at the rest of us. "Listen." Far in the distance, growing louder, we hear the rumble of an approaching engine. A black van crawls past the restaurant window, moving down Mingus Avenue. I spot the yellow butterfly on its door. It doesn't stop in front of the restaurant, though. It pushes on, then slows down, pushes on, then slows down. Finally, it rolls to a stop, right outside our shop.

"My god," Dad whispers. He puts a hand on Amma's. They both look at me.

"It can't be this soon," Sonal Aunty says. "Raj?"

Raj Uncle tosses his napkin on the table. "No. No. This can't be happening now." He turns to Dad. "Are they here for you? For Sindu?"

Amma jumps from her chair and comes around to where I'm sitting. She crouches in front of me. "Muki?" She smooths my hair down, and in her eyes, I see fear. She's breathing so fast now she can hardly speak. "Muki? Everything's okay. Okay? This is what we're going to do."

Dad comes around the table to crouch next to her, both my parents at my feet, their faces clenched with worry. Amma's voice shakes. "You'll go with Raju now, okay? I don't know if they've come for me and Daddy, or if they're just buying something. But just in case, Muki. Just in case, you're going to Raju's house." She turns to Raj Uncle. "Raj, please drive your car to the back of the restaurant. The alley." Raj Uncle bolts to his feet and heads out of the restaurant. Their red car starts up.

"Are you coming with me?" I ask.

Dad shakes his head. He's gripping my arm. It's starting to hurt, and I wriggle in his grasp. "Thumbi, listen to me," he says. He clears his throat. "You may not see us for a few days or hear from us. But we'll be okay. And we'll send word to you as soon as we can."

"But I don't have my toothbrush." It just comes out. I don't know why.

"You'll borrow one." Amma smiles. Tears balance on her lower lids. She straightens the collar of my shirt, picks a bit of dried noodle off the front. She searches my face for something.

Outside the shop, a car door slams. A man in black rings our doorbell.

"Let's go," Dad says, pulling me up by the arm.

Dad and Amma hurry me to the back of the restaurant and through the kitchen door. We push through a puff of steam and find the back exit. Raju and Sonal Aunty follow. The red car waits in the alley. "Muki, keep your head down, out of sight. Just in case."

Dad opens the car door for me, but I stop. "Go on," he says.

"But where will you be?"

"Get in, Muki."

Sonal Aunty and Raju are in the car. The engine hums, waiting.

"Muki, you have to go now," Amma says.

"Why can't you come with me?"

"You're safer without us."

I grab Amma's wrist. "Where will you go?" I ask.

"We'll let you know. You have to go." She looks stern now, almost angry, as she pries my fingers from her wrist. Then she's smoothing down the sleeve of my shirt, rubbing at it and rubbing at it, like that's going to help, like that's going to make things better.

"Amma!" I grab her and hug her, and for a few seconds, she sobs wildly into my neck. I'm breathing too fast, gulping at air. I hold her with every part of me. I won't let go. I won't. But Dad grabs me from behind and clutches me around the shoulders. He kisses me roughly on the cheek and shoves me into the open car door. He slams the door shut. The car jerks forward.

Chapter 22

I'm in Raj Uncle's car, but I may as well be alone in a cave. All I know is the sudden hollow in my chest, the sobs that rock me forward and yank me back, again and again. By the time we get to Raju's house, I feel like a rag that's been soaked and wrung dry.

We sit in the Rajarajans' living room. Nobody speaks for a long time. Raj Uncle turns on the news and I see footage of black vans—the news calls them MothMobiles—prowling Mingus Avenue and other parts of Pacific City.

"Change the channel," Sonal Aunty says. "My goodness. I can't stand this." She squeezes me harder, and Raj Uncle switches to a comedy about people sitting in a café. For maybe the first time in my life, I'm glad for Sonal Aunty's powdered sweetness. I'm glad when she pulls me into a big soft hug and lets me stay there. I don't follow what's happening on the show, but the colors on-screen are bright and easy to watch, and for a few minutes, the tinny laugh track makes this terrifying night feel normal again.

In Raju's room, there's a mattress set up on the floor. Just like home. Up in his own bed, he falls asleep without saying good night. At least I think he does. He doesn't snore like Paati does—his silence just dips a little deeper. I can't sleep. My bones are heavy and sink into the mattress, but my mind is on high alert. I still feel the scratch of Dad's stubble on my cheek, the molten rain of Amma's tears. The general said people are animals, and I can feel now how right he was, because my stomach aches in a way that isn't human. It has nothing to do with camps or restaurants or presidents. My stomach aches like a cave, like fangs and wet fur and dirty wounds. Loneliness is an animal inside me, and it wants to break out. It wants to claw through my skin and into the world. It wants me to scream into that room, scream into my pillow. And I think, why don't I? Why don't I scream? Why do babies get to scream when boys like me have to be quiet, be good, be asleep? I don't scream. I actually try, but I can't. The thought of the sound frightens me. So instead, I cry. I cry and cry into my pillow. I don't care if Raju hears.

A long time passes. It's so dark in here I can't see my own hand. I feel like I'm floating. I feel like I'm nowhere.

"Muki." It's Raju's voice. "*Muki.*"

"What?"

"Are you okay?"

"Yeah."

"Sorry."

"It's okay."

We're quiet for a few minutes again, and I think he may have fallen asleep. "Where do you think your parents are?"

"I'm not sure. Hiding somewhere."

"Do you think my parents will have to go into hiding?"

"I don't think your parents are doing what my parents did. I think they'll be okay."

"They won't get into trouble?"

I sigh. "I don't know. I don't think so."

"Do you think it's helping? What your mom and dad did?"

"I don't know."

I hear a shuffling and his lamp switches on, blinding me for a few seconds. The clock on the wall reads 1:17 a.m. "Want to play *BB*?"

BB is *Ballistic Bagpipes*, this video game that every kid at school has, that every kid in the *world* has. Every kid but me.

He turns on his big screen and hands me a controller. "You be Archibald," he says. He's always Hamish.

In the game, you're from a country called Highlandia, and your bagpipes are loaded with weapons and fireballs and your goal is to blast the bejesus out of everything you see and eventually get to this mountain, which is full of treasure. If you get caught, a droopy little bagpipe plays, and your bagpiper steps up to a guillotine, looking very sorry.

But everyone knows that. It's impossible to be a kid alive in the world and not know every detail of *Ballistic Bagpipes*.

So we play *BB* and I get pretty good at scaling walls and commando crawling across the hills in my little skirt—a *kilt*, Raju tells me—with bagpipes on my back and a hunting dagger in my mouth. I don't tell Raju that I've real-life commando crawled, that I've excavated drainpipes and cut myself on razor wire. I don't tell him how your heart pounds, how your lungs and throat fall out of sync and you find yourself sucking in air so fast your body forgets how to breathe, how everything starts to feel wrong. No one panics in *Ballistic Bagpipes*.

The soft drone of bagpipes wakes me at dawn. I'm on the carpet of Raju's bedroom, my controller next to me. Raju's conked out on the floor, too. On-screen, *BB* has gone into screen saver mode, and there's a silhouetted bagpiper, standing on a mountain at sunrise. It's not the worst thing to wake up to, but it's weird. For a second or two, I forget why I'm here. I forget what happened yesterday. But then it comes to me. The questions tap me on the shoulder. They don't want to bother me, but they have to. They have to know: Will I be okay? Will I see Amma and Dad again? How did the MothMobile find my parents? How did they know where we live? Did Buff report us? Will they come for me next? I don't have answers.

By Monday, I'm desperate to get to school, to push away

the questions, to find Fabi. She'll know what to do. But for now, I'm hungry. It's morning. *Oculi aperti.*

The good thing about an aunty who makes everything into muffins is that sometimes, she makes actual muffins. I eat three blueberry ones, dipped in a bowl of melted butter, before climbing into Raj Uncle's car and heading to school. It takes about five minutes from Raju's door to the school gates, which beats my hour-long subway ride. I find Fabi before first period begins. When I tell her what happened, she reaches right out and hugs me, and doesn't let go.

"I saw the MothMobile on Mingus last night," she says, when I finally push away. "Did you know they went into the shop, and then into your house?"

"How'd they get into our house?"

"I don't know. Someone must know the code. Are you okay? You're staying at Raju's?"

"How'd you know?"

"Word gets around."

"Wait. Do people know about my parents?"

"People think they were put in a camp. That's the rumor, anyway. I don't think anyone knows about—anything else." She glances over her shoulder, then lowers her voice. "I think you should just pretend that everything's okay. You want to come over after school?"

"Let me think. I need to figure some stuff out."

We walk to her locker, which isn't far from Tinley Schaedler's. The other Tinleys stand in a slouchy circle, and for some reason they're looking at me. Fabi sees, too.

"I guess you're on their radar now," she says. "Congratulations."

"I don't think so. They're probably just wondering what my deal is. Why Tinley's actually nice to me."

"Hm," Fabi says.

"What?"

"I guess I've been wondering the same thing."

"Wondering why Tinley's nice to me?"

"Yes. No. I know why she's nice to you. It's because *you're* nice."

I'm not sure if I get what she's talking about, so I don't respond. Sometimes Fabi says more than she's saying.

The first bell rings, and we head to class. It's easy to swim along and pretend things are okay in this middle school ocean, where I'm just another fish. But what I want to be is that ghost crab, with its tunnel in the sand, hidden from the world and safe.

Chapter 23

Here's what's happening these days: all is not peaceful in Mariposa. Not every Butterfly wants to be a Butterfly. Not everyone wants the Moths out. I think it's maybe this, more than anything else, that keeps me from losing hope. On the news at night, I hear that people—first just Moths, then the Butterflies who support them—are walking off their jobs, to protest what's happening in Mariposa. Tonight, the news is frantic with reports that government workers have started striking. They're refusing to work for a president like Bamberger. They're going to get fired, the news is saying. So maybe they'll get fired, and Bamberger will keep doing what Bamberger does. None of that changes the fact that my parents are gone.

The next day, in civics, Miss Pistachio greets us at the classroom door. "Have a seat, but don't get too comfy," she says. "Keep your sweaters on." Closing the door, she turns to us. "As you probably know, today is an international walkout day for schools. To protest Mariposa's treatment of Moths. I'm sure you've heard about it?" Blank stares. Her faces falls. "Civil disobedience, my friends, is a cornerstone of civil society. It is the right of citizens in Mariposa, and in much of the world, to practice nonviolent protest against their governments."

Box Tuttle raises his hand. "What if you agree with your government?"

She blinks at him. "Then you don't protest." She claps her hands. "Chop, chop! Let's get a move on. Backpacks on! We're going out to the courtyard."

"We're doing the walkout?" Fabi asks.

"You got it, Fabiana." To the rest of the class, she says, "Civil disobedience means we're *civil*. Single-file, please. No talking in the hallway."

Out in the schoolyard, we sit in a circle. Miss P. looks around the group. "I know not all of you agree with this act of protest. But here is my wish for you: one day, each of you will believe passionately in something. So passionately that you will put your body on the line for it. That means going to a march, a sit-in, a community meeting, a fundraiser, a food drive. There are many ways to demonstrate what is important to us, class. And so *many* things to believe in."

With that, she pulls out her phone, and we gather around her in a tight circle. She scrolls through video footage of other students, from elementary to high school, even the biggest universities, all around the world. We see a college, halfway across the world, whose students swarm the street, shouting and marching. Reporters stick microphones in their faces. The students hold up signs that say *Moths are Mariposan* and *Bambi doesn't speak for me.*

They're all doing it for Mariposa. They're all doing it for people like me. Looking at this, something inside me unclenches, and I can feel, suddenly, the warm concrete beneath me, a kiss of heat from the sun. A monarch floats by. Those faraway college students probably don't know it, but they've made me feel less alone.

After school, I go to Tinley's. I drink my chocolate milk in the kitchen and wait for Lee. No Lee.

"Where's your butler today?"

She gazes at me for a few seconds but doesn't answer.

"Muki? Did they take your parents, too?"

"I can't really talk about it."

"Where'd they take your grandma?"

"There's a place outside the city. The Moth camp."

"Have you been there?"

I nod. Her mouth drops open. "Wow. What's it like?"

"It's like . . . how I imagine the surface of the moon to be. There's nothing out there except some big black tents. And there's always this weird wind blowing. I don't know. It's like a different planet."

"I want to see it," she whispers.

"Tinley?"

"Yeah."

"Butterflies."

She holds her stomach. "Me too."

"No, I mean we have the project to do. It's due in a week. Remember?"

She looks offended, then sighs and says, "Fine. What do you have so far?" I pull out my notebook. I've been drawing—not just the butterflies in our report, but every butterfly I come across. I've been inventing butterflies, making my own.

"Wow!" Tinley says. "You drew these? By yourself?"

"I guess."

"With your hands?"

"No, with my nose. Of course with my hands. How about you?"

"Well," she says, "I've combined all our notes and started writing the first section. The thing is . . . Remember what Miss P. said?"

"What?"

"We have to commit to a lens."

"Yeah. I think I get that."

"We can't just spill out a bunch of information about butterflies. We need to talk about what they have to do with Mariposa. And what they have to do with us. What they really say about the country."

"Why *did* we choose butterflies?" I ask.

"I don't really remember."

"I think it was pretty much because one of them flew in

through the window and landed on my desk. And you got excited. Remember?"

"That's why we chose them? Because I got excited?"

I shrug.

"We should have had a better reason than that."

"I don't know. You were excited. I was scared of you."

She laughs and belts me on the arm.

"We'll come up with something," I say.

That's when the kitchen door opens and Lee walks in. I'm so happy to see him I almost jump up. He does a double take when he sees me, but he doesn't say anything. Instead, he goes to the pantry, comes out with two fortune cookies, and puts one on the table for each of us.

"Fortune cookies!" Tinley squeals. "Lee, where'd you get these?"

Lee clears his throat. "Oceanview," he says. "A restaurant there." He shoots me a sidelong glance.

"Lee, where's George?" Tinley asks, cracking her cookie open.

"Out front, Miss Tinley. Would you like me to summon him?"

"Yes, please, Lee. I want him to take us somewhere." Lee walks to the door but pauses to give me a look. It says *Don't do anything stupid.* He glances at the cookies cracked open on the table.

Tinley slips the fortune from her cookie. My own hands tremble as I snap mine open.

"What does yours say?" she asks.

"'Every Animal Senses Treachery.'" The words are stark black against the white slip of paper. "You?"

"'We are all right.' Hm. Yeah. I guess we are." She tosses the fortune on the table, and I pick it up.

Tinley's fortune doesn't sound like a fortune. *We are all right.* Could this be a message from Amma and Dad? Lee walks back in. "Everything all right?" he asks.

"Yup." I pick up the fortune. I give him a pointed look. *"We are all right."*

He looks back just as deliberately. "That's a good fortune," he says. "You should hold on to that." He juts his chin at the other slip of paper, but I don't read it aloud. *Every Animal Senses Treachery.* What if it really is a secret code? We're in the general's kitchen—there might be recording devices all over this house. Just because we don't see Dragonflies doesn't mean no one's listening.

Still, the messages make me feel better. Something's opened in my chest. My head and hands have grown lighter.

That's when George walks into the kitchen. Tinley jumps to her feet.

"George! We need to go somewhere. Please."

I catch Lee's eye again. "Tinley wants to go to the Moth camp. She wants to see it."

"Miss Tinley," Lee says, "I don't think you have clearance for that, do you?"

"Lee's right, Tinley kid," George says. "I don't think

your daddy would like that. It's no place for kids."

"Except for Moth kids," Tinley says, looking each man in the eye. "It's a place for Moth kids, I guess."

George and Lee glance at each other.

"Muki got to go," she says. "How come Muki got to go?"

George shakes his head and walks out of the kitchen. "George!" Tinley yells after him. Her voice lowers to a growl. "I can't believe he just walked out." She turns her glare on Lee.

He sips his coffee. "Looks like you're out of luck, Miss Tinley. You should probably get back to your project, right?"

Tinley sits back and crosses her arms over her chest. She stares at Lee until he leaves the kitchen.

"There's not much to see," I tell her, when we're alone. "It's not, like, a tourist attraction."

She leans in and whispers, "I want to be part of the rebellion, Muki."

"Shush, Tinley!"

Her whisper gets even softer, almost inaudible. "You're part of it. I know you are. Right? Is that why your parents ran away?"

My heart thrums in my chest. Panic, like a windup toy, buzzes around my brain. If she knows—if she tells her dad—

"I won't tell my dad," she says, as if she heard me.

"How do you know my parents ran away?"

"Maple told me." Maple is one of the Tinleys. "I don't know how she knows."

"Fabi wouldn't have told."

"So it's true?"

I nod.

"Where do you think they went?"

"I bet it's Raju. I bet stupid Raju told Box Tuttle." I shake my head. "What a bag of hammers."

"Let me help, Muki," Tinley pleads.

"Help to what?"

"To stop all this. I don't want you to get taken away. I don't want your grandma in there."

"But your dad. What if he finds out?"

"He won't. We'll be okay."

"*You'll* be okay," I say. "*You* will always be okay. What if I get found out? Or Lee?"

Her eyes pop wide. "What? Lee?"

"Oh, poop." I drop my head to the table.

"*Lee?*" she whispers. "*Lee's* part of it?"

"Tinley." I look up again. "You can't tell anyone. Not your friends. Not your dad. No one. It'll ruin everything. I'll be in the biggest trouble. I really *will* get sent away. Do you get that?"

She nods. "I won't tell anyone, Muki. I want to help."

I zip my lips tight and shake my head. Tinley. This house. I pull out my binder and flip to my project notes. "We need to do this project. Okay? That's all we're doing today. That's all."

She sighs, deflated. "Okay." We work for three hours straight, until our chapters are outlined. It's amazing what you can finish when you're trying not to talk.

When it's time to go—Sonal Aunty wants me back before dinner—George is on his dinner break, so Lee drives me home. He's quiet as we make our way down the winding drive. He sips at a mug of coffee, his eyes fixed on the road ahead. I've outed him to Tinley, and the guilt of this overtakes me. But I can't tell him. I can't tell him that I've maybe jeopardized the resistance. I decide just to tell him something else. "Tinley wants to join the rebellion."

He spits out his coffee. "Jesus in blue jeans," he says, wiping coffee from his chin and his pants. "That kid. She thinks she can do anything."

"I think she probably can do anything."

"Just another day at Daddy's office. Another day of giggles. That's all this is to her."

I get a little annoyed. Something—loyalty?—sits up inside me. "I don't think that's all it is to her. I think she really cares."

"Well. Maybe. But what's she going to do? Change her dad's mind?"

We're back at the Rajarajans' now. As I get out, Lee stops me. "Hey," he says. "Sorry about your parents. They know what they're doing, you know."

I shrug.

"You all right?"

I pick up my backpack and slide out the door. I think for a second. *"We are all right,"* I answer.

Lee gives me a little salute and pulls away.

The next day at school, Fabi studies the fortune. "We are all right." The lunch yard swarms around us. "You really think it's from them? Where do you think they are?" She looks up at the sky, like maybe my parents are in the clouds. "They'd have to be somewhere hidden."

"Duh."

"No. I mean away from the Dragonflies, away from everything. Someplace really hidden."

"They'll tell me when they can."

"You think they'd really want you to know?"

"They know me. They know I'd want to know."

"Huh."

We watch the lunch yard for a while. Box Tuttle has Raju in an armlock, and Raju's kicking uselessly at Box Tuttle's legs. "Box Tuttle's such a drone."

"Hey," Fabi says. "You were with Tinley Schaedler, right? When you got the fortune cookie?"

"Yeah."

"So how would Lee know which one you were going to open? If there were two?"

"I don't know. I mean, this one wasn't even mine. It was Tinley's."

"Wait. So *you* got a different one? What did yours say?"

"Nothing. Something about animals."

"Really? Do you have it?"

I feel around in my pocket and find the other fortune, crumpled into a ball. I unroll it. "Every Animal Senses Treachery."

"What does it mean?"

"I guess it means what it says."

"It must be a message from them, Muki."

"You think?"

"I mean, your parents sent it. Right? Just like the other one?"

"You think it's a warning? Every animal senses treachery. Is someone being treacherous?"

"Who could be treacherous?" she asks. She peers into my eyes. "Is there someone you can't trust?"

To be honest, I wasn't totally sure what *treachery* even meant. It's one of those words you memorize for a vocab test and then forget. But I get it now. Context.

"Maybe they're warning me," I say. "Maybe there's someone around me . . ."

"Weird that every word is capitalized on this fortune, but not on the other one."

"That's what I thought." We hold them up side by side.

"And look," she says. "The *e* dips down a little. It's not totally lined up with the other letters. You know what that means?"

"It means it wasn't printed from a computer."

We say it at the same time: "Typewriter." That's why the ink is so black. That's why the letters, from the very first time I saw them, looked a little unusual to me. The bell rings, and Fabi hops to her feet. My stomach growls. Sonal Aunty packed mushroom muffins, and I couldn't stomach them.

"Do you have food?"

She rummages in her lunch bag and hands me a banana. We head to fourth period. Strange things are afoot, but at least I have Fabi.

Chapter 24

Tonight, I help Sonal Aunty set the table. I do this most nights, thinking of Amma. *Always leave a place a little bit better than you found it.* It was one of those Amma lectures I thought I could ignore. As I lay the napkins and forks, Raj Uncle leans back in his chair to give me space, but he doesn't put down his newspaper. Sonal Aunty flits around and fusses, unfolds a napkin and stuffs it in Raju's collar. When I sit down, she tries to do the same for me, but I take the napkin from her before she can. Tonight, she's made actual chicken curry—not a muffin in sight—and I am grateful. There's something about the spicy, soupy curry, the way it wraps itself around the rice, the way it dissolves in my mouth, that makes me feel like I'm at home. I could sink into this feeling, if not for Raju. Raju, who told someone—probably Box Tuttle—about my parents. Is he the treacherous one? No. He's just dumb. I glare at him across the table, and he glares back, but I can tell he doesn't know why we're glaring.

"How was school today?" Sonal Aunty asks.

"Fine," we mumble at the same time.

"You have your big projects due soon, no?"

"Yeah," we say, again at the same time. Raju pulls his glare from mine at last, and turns to his mother. "Box's dad found his old soccer jerseys." Raju and Box are researching Mariposan soccer. I think they're just bringing in old junk from Box's basement. Not that butterflies feel very important anymore.

"Muki, how is your project coming?"

"Great. We're researching butterflies."

"No surprise, your choice of entomology," Raj Uncle says, looking up from his paper. "You have scientific research in your blood. Your father was a great scientist, you know." His face is big and square like Raju's. When he smiles at me, his eyes crinkle at the corners. I miss my dad.

"*Is*," Sonal Aunty says. "Your daddy *is* the greatest scientist in Mariposa, Muki."

Raj Uncle puts his paper down. "My wife has a tendency to exaggerate," he says. "But she's not exaggerating about this. Your father was very promising."

"So what did he do? Why did he stop?"

"Well, these things happen, don't they?"

"But what happened?"

Raj Uncle and Sonal Aunty exchange the *should we tell him?* look. Sonal Aunty begins. "There was a scientist, a very successful one. He was your father's superior. His boss.

And—let me back up. Every project has a budget. You know what a budget is, Cookie?"

I nod. Raju smirks.

"It seems your father's boss was stealing bits of money from your father's budget, to use for his own project, because he had run out of his own money."

"So he was stealing from Dad?"

"From Dad's project. Yes. And so, soon enough, your daddy's project ran out of money. Of course, he should have been keeping track of this, but you know your father, head in the clouds. So trusting. Anyway, his budget went almost to zero. And people wondered, *What did Vikram do with all that money?* Of course, his boss had been stealing it."

"So his boss got in trouble."

"That's what should have happened," Raj Uncle cuts in. "But you see, the boss came from an old Mariposa family. He had been at the lab for a very long time. He had influence and friends and no one was going to get rid of him."

"So they punished my dad instead?"

"That's the way it works in this country, I'm afraid. We've all paid the price, in some way or other, for the color of our skin, for the country we were born in."

I'm not sure what Raj Uncle means, but Sonal Aunty goes on: "They accused your daddy of leaking the money into his own bank account. They did an investigation. They treated the poor man like he was a criminal, automatically guilty. And maybe he actually felt like a criminal by the end of it, even though he'd done nothing wrong."

"So they fired him?"

"No. He was too valuable—cheap labor, hard worker. The investigation was to punish him, not fire him. It was to show him how things worked, who was in charge. To teach him not to—to—"

"To rat out his boss," I say. Dad was the pebble in the giant's shoe.

"Yes. It was a lesson in keeping his mouth shut and being invisible. And so he quit."

"He's a kind man," Sonal Aunty says, "but he's very proud. He wouldn't let them push him around."

"And you were just born. He wanted to be close to home, not working all hours in a laboratory far away. So he and your amma joined forces, and they opened their shop."

Raju seems to wake up a little. "Who's running the shop now?" he asks.

"The shop assistant," Sonal Aunty says. "Biff?"

"Buff." I haven't thought about Buff or the shop.

Raj Uncle burps, pats his stomach, and picks up his newspaper again.

"So where are Muki's parents now?" Raju asks.

"No one knows," I snap.

"Yes, Cookie," Sonal Aunty says. "Nobody knows." She rests her gaze on me. "Muki? Do you know where your parents are?"

Raj Uncle lowers his paper and stares at me.

"I don't know," I say. Sonal Aunty touches her napkin to the corners of her mouth and gives me a quiet smile.

After dinner, I follow Raju to our room.

"Dude." ·

"What?" He starts up his game console. "You want to be Archibald again?"

"You can't tell Box Tuttle anything about me. Or my parents."

He blinks at me. "What?"

"Box Tuttle. You told him my parents went into hiding. Right?"

Raju shrugs. "Box won't tell."

"He *will*. He *did*."

"Okay, well, choose your weapons." I watch Hamish lower the bagpipes over his shoulders and Raju calmly load them with grenades and fireballs. Sitting here on this soft carpet, the truth settles on me. Kids—us—we are the keepers of the revolution. I used to think it belonged to our moms and dads, but where are they? Where's Dad? And Amma? I wish Fabi were here. I decide to shut up and play *Ballistic Bagpipes* and pretend my name is Archibald. Better Archibald than Muki. Better Highlandia's freedom than my own messed-up life. Better a fantasy set of bagpipes than my real-life bag of hammers.

Chapter 25

The next day at school, I open my locker after lunch, expecting to see my poster of the West City soccer team, the gym socks I keep forgetting to take home, my butterfly notebook, and nothing more. But what I find is another fortune cookie. I crack it open, stuff half a cookie in my mouth, and unfurl the message. It's typed in black ink, just like the others. *Heroes Inevitably Locate Love in Strength.*

We're one day away from the Butterfly Day Parade, and Marble Hill Prep is starting to break out in color, like a rain forest in bloom, or a kid with a zitty face, depending on how you look at it. All through the hallways, red and yellow paper flowers hang from the ceilings and pop from the walls. A huge monarch butterfly is painted across the middle of the lunch yard, with the words *MHP Takes Flight!* painted below.

Fabi and I sit with our lunches. She's brought me two empanadas. "From my mom." I unwrap them carefully, take a bite of the flaky, warm crust, and peer inside the dough.

"No messages," she says.

I pull the fortune from my pocket and hand it to her. Fabi stares hard at the words, typed just like the other two fortunes. "Heroes Inevitably Locate Love in Strength." She sighs, exasperated. "Why can't they just say what they mean?" The lunch bell rings, and kids stampede to fourth period. I take the fortune back and stuff it in my pocket. It means something. It has to.

After school, in Tinley's kitchen, Lee turns the fortune over in his hands. He looks up at me, uncertain about something, I can tell.

"Do you know what it means?"

"I think it could mean a few things," he says.

I lower my voice. "It's code."

He nods. "In case it gets intercepted."

I study the message. "They want me to feel loved, maybe. Or they want me to look for love. Why didn't they just say that?"

The kitchen is empty, except for me and Lee. He's making me a sandwich. Outside, it's cloudy again. There's a lot of mumbling about the weather, about whether it's going to rain during the Butterfly Day Parade.

When Tinley walks in, I slip the fortune in my pocket.

"You think the parade'll get rained out?" she asks as she spreads peanut butter over a piece of bread.

"I'm sure the parade will happen, Miss Tinley. People just like worrying about stuff like this. You know what Mariposa's like. We plan a huge parade, we get excited about it, and then we remember why we don't plan huge parades."

"That doesn't make me feel better Lee," Tinley says.

There's a strange something hanging over the kitchen today. I'm pretty sure it's my guilt. Thanks to me, Tinley knows that Lee's in the rebellion—that he's working *against* her dad while he's working *for* her dad. And here stands Lee, totally innocent, acting like a butler still. He doesn't have a clue about what I've done. I've never felt guilty for much before. Guilt is heavier than knowledge. You tell one lie, and then you tell another, and soon you're hiding so much you don't know what you're hiding anymore. Maybe *I'm* the treacherous one.

"Lee," I say. The sound of his name rings loud in that kitchen, louder than I intended.

He cocks an eyebrow.

"Can I talk to you?"

"Sure thing."

"In the library?"

"I'm real busy, Muki." He frowns meaningfully at me.

"Just for a minute? Please?"

"I don't think so. No."

Tinley plops her sandwich on a plate. "He just wants to tell you I know, Lee."

"Excuse me?" His eyes dart around the room.

She speaks slowly, like she's speaking to a little kid. "He wants you to know that I *know*."

Lee looks like someone's walked up and punched him in the stomach. I clutch my own stomach. He asks, "And what—what do you know?"

She speaks through a mouth full of peanut butter. "That you're *in the rebellion*—"

"*SHHHHHHHHHH.*" We both lunge at Tinley and she freezes.

Lee stares at Tinley, digesting what just happened. Then he starts stomping around the kitchen, sticks his fist in his mouth. He stops, holds a finger up, like he's about to announce something. Then he shakes his head and keeps stomping. "Nope," he says. "Nope, nope, nope." He stops again, gazes at Tinley, like he's here, but not here. Then he turns to me. And then he flops into a chair and puts his head in his arms.

"Lee," Tinley says, and taps him, with a single finger, on the shoulder. "It's okay. I promise—" She lowers her voice to a whisper. "I promise I won't say anything. You're safe."

Slowly, Lee sits up. His face is red. His hair is matted to one side. He looks like an old dishrag that's fallen from the laundry line and been run over by a truck. "You're killing me." He lifts a hand, lets it fall. "Both of you. You're killing me."

"I want to help, Lee," Tinley whispers. "What can I do?"

He looks from me to Tinley. "You want to help. Is that

right? You want to help." He lets out a deep sigh. "Luke and Leia want to help."

I don't know what he's talking about. I wonder if we've somehow broken him. We sit there, the three of us, not saying anything for a while. Then—it's almost imperceptible, but it's there—a little spark. "You really want to help?" he asks. This time, he asks the question calmly.

"You thought of something."

"I sure did."

Lee pulls us into the pantry. "Okay," he whispers. "Listen up, you two. The general—"

"Papa?" Tinley cuts in.

"I'm just gonna call him the general. Okay?"

She nods.

"The general is out until dinner, so we should be okay here. We've been searching for a code. It's ten digits, and we're pretty sure the general has it written down. We've been through his files, his computer, through everything digital. We can't find it." He looks out, slightly panicked, like someone could be lurking in the kitchen. His voice gets even quieter. "We've been inside his office, but we haven't found it there, either. But look, one of our guys inside the camp? Said the general keeps the code in a box."

"A box? What kind of box?"

"Just—I don't know. Someone who works for Bamberger said he used the code one time—just once—and he pulled the number from a little black box. That's all the guy could tell me." He pulls us in closer. "I think I know where it might be. He has a safe hidden under his desk. It's in a tiny, narrow space. An adult couldn't get in there. I think the general must be able to turn the combination, just by touch."

"But a kid could fit."

Lee nods. "How'd you guess?"

"It helps to be small. That's the only way kids get to do anything in this rebellion."

"Easy, Skywalker. Let's keep the R-word out of this, okay?"

"What's the code for?"

"Nope," Lee says.

"Then nope, I won't get it for you." I'm pretty sure this isn't going to work. But Lee gazes at me for a few seconds, then says, "Fine. It's for a munitions locker. Weapons. If we're going to take over the Moth camp, if we're going to follow through on all this and take control? We'll need weapons."

"Weapons," I whisper.

"Weapons," Tinley whispers.

Lee nods at her, then at me. "It's getting real, kiddos. We have every entry code we need. To the camp gates. To the main building. This is the last piece of the puzzle. Are you ready? You sure you want to do this?"

"How come Muki gets to do everything?" Tinley asks. "He's *my* dad."

"Miss Tinley. You're on L and D. Lookout and diversion.

Your dad comes home early, you distract him, you lead him away from the office. You're the only person in the world who can do that job."

She sniffs and considers this.

"Ready? We don't have a lot of time."

"Where will you be?" Tinley asks.

"Kitchen."

Lee leads us down a hallway to a door of heavy, dark wood. He punches a code into a little console, and the door whirs unlocked. It's so heavy he has to push it open with his shoulder.

Then he turns to me and pulls something from his pocket. A slip of paper with numbers on it, left turns and right turns. "Just like your locker at school, right?"

"Yeah."

"Memorize that," he says.

"Why?"

"Trust me."

So I say the combination to myself again and again, until it's locked in my head.

He pulls something else from his pocket. A headlamp.

"Cool."

He loops it onto my head. "Now, go," he says.

I slip through the open door.

"Okay. See the big desk?"

"Yeah?"

"Crawl under it."

The desk is as big as my bed. I turn on the headlamp and crawl, like this is nothing but a game of hide-and-seek. Down here, the smell of wood resin shoots straight into my nose and fills my head. "Now face out, toward me," Lee whispers. "On your left is a little knob. Pull at it, and that whole wood panel should open up."

I do. It does.

Inside is a narrow opening, big enough for me to stick my head and torso into. Tucked into the opening is a big silver box. There should be a combination dial, like on my school locker, but I can't see it from here. It must be on the other side of the box. How does the general do this? I'm going to have to slide into the opening. Somehow.

Pigeon pose. It comes to me, clear as Paati's voice at dawn. *Giddy-up, somberi!* I find I'm more flexible than I thought I was as I fold my right foot close to my body and slide farther into the opening. I can just about reach the dial—and then I can't. I twist and bend even more. *Are you a cobra or a kitty cat?* Cobra pose, boat pose, child's pose. I manage, finally, to wedge my shoulders and head right in front of the dial. I wonder if Lee's still out there. I imagine the general approaching, his straight-backed march down the hallway, his hand on the door. A hot wave of panic surges through me and I let out a yelp.

"Are you okay?" Tinley calls, faintly, from the hallway.

"Yes," I whimper.

"Did you find anything?"

"Shush." I'm closer than ever now. I bring my knee up by my chin, and I twist into the lord of the fishes pose, just barely getting my hand on the dial. The headlamp lights it up.

I can see now why I had to memorize the combination. I would never have been able to hold up a slip of paper in this cramped space. I turn the knob left, right, left. The door clicks, and like a hand, it opens.

Inside the safe: papers and more papers. I'm looking for a box. A box . . .

It's pitch-black down here. I move my lamp-lit head around, trying to slice through the gloom. The only box I see is a small jewelry box, the kind rings come in. *Take it*, says a voice inside.

I clutch the box, close the safe, and child's pose backward. Out of the hole, I open the box. It's a diamond ring. No numbers. Just a lousy diamond ring. I snap the box shut.

"Papa!" It's Tinley. "I missed you!"

She's practically yelling. "Would you play with me? Please? Would you look at my project?"

I hear the general's heavy step in the doorway, and my mind goes blank. He can't see me—not yet. I scoot back into the gap. I'm trying to breathe, but I can't. I'm gulping again, breathing in frantic little hiccups. They're getting louder and louder, and all I can do is wait for them to pass, try to still my breath, try not to cry out. I hear him walk into the office, walk into the middle of the room. He stops. A few seconds of silence, and then he turns back around.

"Tinley?" he asks. "Why was this door unlocked?"

I hear a faint stammer from Tinley, but I can't make out the words. Then the general enters the room and closes the door. He's followed by a second set of footsteps, too heavy to be Tinley's.

"Charming," a voice says. It's eerily familiar, but I can't pin it down. "I've always wondered what it's like to have kids." Bamberger!

The two men settle into the armchairs on either side of this desk. The toes of their shoes rest just inches from mine. Bamberger spins his chair around once, then twice. The general waits, then clears his throat. "You wanted to talk, Bambi?"

"I've been thinking, Dogwood. I've been having . . . thoughts." Bamberger taps his foot in the silence that follows. "The camps are losing support. With the walkouts, sympathy for the resistance . . ."

My heart punches at its cage. The resistance. That's us. That's me!

The general clears his throat. "What is it you're thinking?"

"I need you to call a press conference. Make it seem impromptu, unplanned. I need you to issue an urgent warning about some new findings. Crime statistics. Crimes committed by Moths. The numbers are soaring and the crimes are violent. Moth crime is through the roof."

"It is?" No answer. "Is it really—"

"Well, *no*," Bamberger snaps. He stage-whispers, "But no one needs to know that."

"Bambi—"

"Look, Doggy. People trust you. Must be those big brown eyes. Whatever it is—you say something? People believe it. General Schaedler says *Moth crime is rising*? Mariposa will say *Round up all the Moths*."

"There's a difference between people believing something, and it being true."

"You're getting philosophical."

"You want me to lie for you."

"Well, gee whiz, yes, I suppose I do." A pause. "Oh, don't look at me like that. You're no angel, Schaedler."

The general goes quiet. "I understand what you want, Mr. President."

"Mr. President," Bamberger scoffs. "Now I'm *Mr. President*."

"I wonder if you're as loved as you think you are, Bambi." The general pushes his chair back and stands. Bamberger stays put.

"Listen, Schaedler. I have Congress on my side. The vice president supports me. The media *loves* me. If you don't do this, someone else will."

The general falls silent, like he's thinking through something. I wait for his answer. It doesn't come.

"Doggy," Bamberger mutters. "Doggy, Doggy . . ." His

chair rolls back. He stands. "So I can count on you? We'll need the press conference to happen soon, maybe after the parade."

"I'll see you out."

When they get to the office door, the general stops. "You want to know what it's like to have kids, Bambi? They ask a lot of questions. They want to know why we do the things we do." He goes quiet again. "Don't worry. Your plans are on track. Let's talk tomorrow."

The door clicks shut.

I cross my legs and wrap my arms around my knees. I squeeze my eyes shut. I'm in my kitchen, I tell myself. I'm safe at home. Amma's there, and Dad. Paati's there. Paati's doing a headstand in the living room. I can smell the sour warmth of idlis, the peppery sting of sambar, the rich hot oil of the samosas, the milky cardamom chai. For a second, I'm really there. For a second, I'm honest and good. I am not a boy who breaks into safes. I am not here, under this desk, alone and scared, having just stolen, of all things, a diamond ring.

Their footsteps fade back down the hall. I scoot out again, the box in my pants pocket. This is me, I guess. I'm a boy who steals things. Who eavesdrops. I'm a boy without his parents. I'm a boy in the dark, alone.

And now I am a boy in the kitchen. Tinley sits at the table, wide-eyed, holding a glass of milk. She grips the glass tightly, like it's the only thing holding her still. Before either of us can say a word, the general walks in. When he sees me, he hesitates for just a moment.

"Well, hello, Muki," he says, and moves to the sink, as if seeing me in his kitchen were the most normal thing in the world. It might have been normal, if he hadn't just come after my parents, if I hadn't just been in his office, stealing a diamond ring.

"Hi, General Schaedler."

He pours himself a glass of water. "Nice headlamp." I whip it off. "How's the project going?"

"Fine."

He takes a sip and fixes his eyes on me. "Fine," he says. "Just fine?"

"I think we're doing a really great job, Papa," Tinley pipes up. "Aren't we, Muki?"

"Yeah. We're almost done. Almost ready for next week."

The general switches his gaze to Tinley. "That's wonderful, Blossom. And how go the preparations for the Butterfly Day Parade?"

Now Tinley seems genuinely excited. "*Oh*, well, the school's all decked out. It looks *beautiful*. The hallways? They're lined in these giant flowers. That was Willow and Fava's idea." Willow and Fava are two of the Tinleys. I can't decide if Tinley really is as excited as she seems, or if she's putting it on her for her dad. Can she really be excited for Butterfly Day when she's part of the rebellion? A sudden, sinking dread moves through me. Her dad's an interrogator. If he interrogates *her*, will she crack? Will she rat us out?

"Where's Lee?" I ask. They both turn to me, Tinley's eyebrows arched with genuine surprise. "I—I was wondering if he'd get a book down from the library. From a high shelf." In my head, I kick myself. I kick myself again.

"Funny you should ask about Lee," the general says. "I was just wondering the same thing." He stares at me, takes a sip of water, says nothing more.

Tinley says nothing.

I say nothing.

I try to search behind his gaze, but it's like being in the dark under his desk, trying to sift through the shadows.

Just then, I hear shouts in the hallway. Heavy footsteps, and Lee's voice, yelling words I don't understand. Something heavy—a person?—slams against the hallway wall.

"Well," the general says calmly, "that must be him now."

I run to the kitchen door and open it. And yes, there's Lee, his wrists handcuffed behind his back, kicking at the two Crickets dragging him down the hallway. He manages to kick one in the stomach, but the man shoves him to the ground. One soldier grabs his ankles and the other digs a knee into Lee's back until he cries out and pleads with him to stop. When they yank him to his feet, he stands still for a second. Then he turns to look at me. I've never seen him look like this—hunched, sad, and hopeless, like he's finally seen his end.

The house door opens. Lee is a silhouette against the blinding sun, and then he's gone. The door clangs shut.

I hear a voice at my ear. Tinley's crouched at my side. I've crumpled to the floor, and now I lie curled into a ball, staring at the spot where I last saw Lee.

Tinley puts a hand on my back. "What just happened?"

I turn to her. "Don't you know?" Somehow, I find the strength to wrench myself to my feet and walk back into the kitchen. There stands the general, still leaning against the counter, glass in hand, like nothing at all has changed.

Again, we stare at each other. "Well, you didn't expect me to keep him in my employ, did you, Muki?"

"How—?" *How did you know?* I almost ask. Luckily, the questions are smarter than I am, and this one stops itself before I ask it.

"You must know." He answers the question I couldn't ask. "You must have known what Lee was up to. Arm in arm with your mom and dad," he says, raising his glass, like he's toasting me. "Three peas in a pod. Or should I say three peas in a samosa?"

He knows. He knows about the samosas. He's going to get rid of me now.

The general gazes out the kitchen window. "Any idea where I might find your parents?"

"What's going to happen to Lee?"

He lifts his glass to the light, peers into its water. "Not

sure yet. All I know is that I found my office door open. Only Lee knows the code, and he isn't allowed in there when I'm not there. He knows that. For all I know, he was looking through classified government files. You know what that's called?"

"What?"

"Espionage."

The word whips up a little storm in my chest. Espionage.

"And you . . ." The general turns to me. "The great shoe thrower. Oceanview's very own Dragonfly slayer."

My mouth goes dry. "You saw that—"

"You didn't think the Dragonflies were just for kicks, did you?" The tiniest laugh rattles out of him. "I've been watching you, Muki Krishnan. Your soccer games. Your charming habit of yelling at the neighbors from your window. Your little trips to the camp. You and your parents went to dim sum at the Great Wall that night. They went in—but they never came out. And *that*, Muki, is what's been bugging the heck out of me." He shakes his head.

The room swims around me, tilting one way, then the other. "This whole time? This whole time—"

"Tinley's new friend. Of course I've kept an eye on my daughter's new friend. And knowing what I know about your mom and dad? I'd be perfectly justified arresting you. Right now. How'd you like to see your grandma again?"

The room stops moving. My heart sits up and listens,

but then I get what he's saying. He's threatening to put me in the camp.

"I could arrest you before dinner. I could have your parents hunted down and put in the camp before dessert. I could send all three of you out of the country, if I wanted, before bedtime. Did you know that?"

My heart's beating like crazy and the words thrash around my head, but I rein them in. I breathe. "I don't believe you. You can't find them. You can't just send us away."

"Oh, but I can."

"Are you going to?"

"Should I?"

"Papa," Tinley speaks up. "Stop it. You can't send Muki away."

The general turns to Tinley, then looks away, like he's forgotten what she said.

"I have a question," I say. And I do. I have a big question. It's been there, in my head, all along, sleeping like a giant, growling awake at last.

The general nods.

"Why are you doing this to us?"

"Doing what? To whom?"

"You know what. You know . . . whom."

"He means why are you trying to kick the Moths out of Mariposa, Papa."

The general turns sharply to Tinley.

Her question is like an ocean wave, lifting my flailing

little boat. "Yeah," I say. "Why are you blaming us for everything that's wrong with Mariposa?" I ask. "And don't say you're doing it because Bamberger told you to. That doesn't work for *me* when I do something bad. And don't say *nectar*. Nectar is just money. And jobs and houses. The Moths aren't taking those." I look around at the cavernous kitchen, at the ceiling that rises as high as our entire building. "You have more house than everyone in Oceanview, combined. And you're not a Moth."

He opens his mouth to speak.

"And don't say it's complicated. And don't say I don't understand. Because I do. I do understand." I'm close to crying now. "Buff, this guy who works in our store? He says that Moths are freeloaders. That we just take and don't give anything back. Now, *that* I know is wrong. Just look around my neighborhood. Just look at every Moth I know."

He sits down and rests his chin on his hand, listening.

I go on. "But you know why some Butterflies are poor? Not because of Moths. They're poor because of other Butterflies." My voice starts to tremble and I hate it for doing that. "Butterflies like you. And Bambi. And the people all over Marble Hill with way more money than they need. You take and take. You're the ones taking."

Something changes. He sighs and rubs his forehead. "*You* take after your mother, clearly. What precisely was your point?"

"That *is* my point. All of that."

"Well. Thank you for sharing."

"What're you going to do about it?"

"I suppose I'll finish drinking my water," he says. "And then I'll call Bambi and tell him to cancel all of it. To take down the camps, to set everyone free, to call off every multinational trade and migration deal we've set up with presidents and prime ministers across four continents."

I stand there, completely still. "Really?" Then I realize he's joking, in that way adults do.

"You have a real talent for wearing a man down, Muki."

I feel for the floor beneath my feet—something to ground me—but I feel nothing.

"Tell you what I'll do," the general goes on. "I'll call George and ask him to drive you home. I'll pretend you weren't here today. Hell, I'll pretend I never even met you. You'll leave my home, and I'll never have to deal with you again. But I won't arrest you. I won't put you in a camp. I'll just let you go. Okay?"

I look at Tinley, who has tears streaming down her face.

"Okay," I say. "I'm ready to go." Now that Lee's gone, I'm done with the general, done with Tinley, done with this house.

I walk out of the kitchen and down the hall. I don't need George. I don't need a ride. It takes all my strength, but I heave open the front door and leave. I can feel the guard's eyes on me as I walk away. All alone, for the first time, I walk down the long, winding driveway. That's when the tears come. I let them. I cry and walk through the dappled shadows of the trees above, along an endless green lawn, sprinkled here and there with dandelion buds.

In the distance, thunder rumbles. A cold wind picks up and snipes at my ears.

"Muki!" It's Tinley. Her voice seems to be coming from the trees. "Muki!"

Finally, she rounds the corner, running. One of her cinnamon bun braids has come undone and swings like a rope from the side of her head.

We stand there, the two of us, on the driveway, saying nothing. She's too busy catching her breath to get anything out. I have nothing to say.

Finally, she shakes her head. "I don't know why I ran out here," she says.

"Okay." I turn to leave.

"Wait! I just didn't want you to leave alone."

"Oh."

We stand there again, saying nothing.

"Can I walk with you to the gate?"

"Sure."

We make our way over the little bridge. "Hey," Tinley says. "What did you find in the safe? Anything?"

I take the box from my pocket. "Just this. Lee said to look for a box. But it was just this." I pop the box open and Tinley gasps. The diamond sparkles and spangles in the sunlight, so brilliant it's almost blinding.

"What are you doing with this?" Tinley asks. "This was my mom's."

"Yeah, I figured. That's all it is—no numbers. Lee must have been wrong." It strikes me now that I failed in my mission, that Lee was caught and taken away for nothing.

She picks the ring out of the box, where it's been wedged, for who knows how long, in its cushiony satin bed. She holds it up to the sun, then slips it on her finger. It's too big for her, and the stone lolls from side to side. "My mom used to wear this," she says again. "Every day."

"Do you remember her wearing it?"

She nods and takes off the ring.

"It's pretty," I say. "But useless. You keep it." Tinley pulls the satin cushion out of the box and examines it, examines the box beneath it, examines the underside of the box. Nothing. Then she pushes the ring into its bed and shuts the box, curls it away in her palm.

I remember my worry from earlier. Will she know to hide the ring? Will she end up telling her dad about all this?

She frowns at me. "What?"

I frown back. We give each other a suspicious stink eye for a few seconds. I figure if she's guilty, and if I squint my eyes and stare at her just right, she'll break and confess everything.

"*What.*"

"What'll you do with the box?" I ask.

"I don't know. I can't give it back to my dad. I can't get it back in the safe."

"That's for sure. Unless you're a contortionist."

"I'll have to keep it for myself, for now. Forever, maybe. Maybe Papa won't notice it's gone."

"Do you think he ever takes it out and looks at it?"

She turns the box over in her hands.

"Well, look. Just keep the ring hidden. You're not—you're not going to say anything. Right?"

"Muki!" She punches me in the arm, and her loose braid dances around her ear. "Cheez-Its. How stupid do you think I am?"

We walk on to the end of the drive, where we find the high iron gates. Tinley pushes a big black button and the gates begin to open, slowly.

"I guess you'll be in the parade tomorrow."

Her face lights up. "Yes!" Again, a far rumble of thunder.

"I'm sure it won't rain."

"Will you be there?"

"I don't know. I might just be at school."

"Oh. Okay. See you the day after, I guess."

I leave her at the gate and walk back to Raju's.

Chapter 26

Yesterday's thunder was nothing but the sky thumping its chest. Friday's sky is dense blue, with a few perfect cumulus clouds. The parade will happen. When I get to school, the halls are empty.

Fabi finds us. "No one's here."

"I guess they're all home, getting ready for the parade."

"Well," Fabi says. "I'm here. I may as well learn something."

As we pass the principal's office, we see Mr. Pinto, Miss Pistachio, and the school secretary, all of whom turn to us and smile, like they've been expecting us all along.

"Well, good morning, soldiers," Mr. Pinto says.

Miss P. marches brightly toward us. "Just in time!" she calls.

In the hallway, she puts one hand on my shoulder, one hand on Raju's. Fabi walks ahead of us, like she knows where to go. "Straight through to my classroom, Fabiana."

Fabi, never one to follow orders, stops in her tracks and turns to face us. "Where're the other kids? How come no one's here?"

"Oh. They're here." Miss P. clears her throat. "Finishing the float."

"Can we see?" Raju asks. Fabi glares at him, but really, I want to see it, too. And so, I'm pretty sure, does she.

Miss Pistachio gazes at us. Are we the only three Moths in the whole school? "Follow me," she says quietly.

She throws the yard doors open. The students of Marble Hill Prep scurry around the float, which looks like a giant, glorious birthday cake. It's bright orange, the color of a monarch butterfly, and trimmed in black. A giant curled proboscis rises from the front, like the figurehead of a ship. On top of it is a 3D sculpture of green butterflies (they look like swallowtails), six of them taking flight, at different heights, each rising a little farther into the sky. I have to admit, it's beautiful.

"So I guess that's it," Fabi says, her voice flat. "Can we go in now?"

I take a last look back. They look so happy, all of them. Happy and busy and flitting and fluttering, like real butterflies, leaping leaf to leaf. They belong in this city, under this blue sky, and they know they do. They've never had to question it.

We walk, without speaking, to Miss Pistachio's classroom. "Will you be our teacher all day?" Raju asks.

The smile springs back to her face. "I'll do better than that," she says. "You're going to the parade. With me!"

We stare at her. I think she was expecting a better reaction. Her smile drops.

"Will we be sitting in the Moth section?" I ask.

"No, Muki, you'll be joining me in the teachers' section. It's all been arranged." Maybe this is supposed to make me feel better. And maybe I do feel better. Just not better enough to actually feel good. I turn to Fabi, who squints skeptically back at me.

Miss P. drops us off in the school library and says she'll be back to get us at two. The librarian glances over at us, then back to the tiny TV behind her desk. On-screen is Bambi, his face red, talking into the camera. He's been on TV every night for the last couple of weeks, and each time he inches closer to a big screamy tantrum.

Raju pulls out his phone and loads up *Ballistic Bagpipes*.

"What does she expect us to do here all day?" I ask.

Fabi sighs and pulls out her binder. It's massive. It's almost as big as she is. When she opens it, she looks like a wizard opening a book of spells.

She looks up. "What're you looking at?"

"Nothing." I open my own backpack and pull out my butterfly book.

"Hey," she says. "Any more fortune cookies?"

I want to tell her everything. I want to spill it all, but

there's so much I can't say in here, this library, where even the smallest whisper echoes like a drum.

I pull out a piece of paper. *They took Lee*, I write.

Who did???????????

I don't know. Soldiers. Crickets. General Scha Shadel Sch

TELL ME!!!

Gen S had him arrested. In Tinley's house. We were trying to get something from the Gen's office and the Gen found out and they took Lee away.

WHEN???? WHO??? WHERE???

Yesterday. Crickets.

WHAT?????????????????

I stop her hand with mine. The question marks will go on forever if I don't.

"What were you doing there?" she whispers.

Working on our project. Don't think he suspected me. Bambi there and I hid.

At this point, the paper is covered in crazy scrawls. Fabi gets up. "Come with me," she says aloud. The librarian looks up and follows us with her eyes.

"Just going to the bathroom," Fabi says sweetly.

Raju barely looks up from his video game as we exit the library. In the hall, Fabi breaks into a run. I've never run down these halls, and now that I can, now that they're empty and I can move my legs and pump my arms and hear the solid thump of my feet on the ground, I don't want to stop. Fabi runs into the lunchroom, which looks huge now that it's empty, and scoots under a table.

I join her, half excited, half terrified, half confused.

"I've been thinking about the fortunes," she says.

"Yeah. Me too."

"What have you figured out?"

"Nothing."

"Okay." She pulls out a ballpoint pen and grabs me by the arm. "Every," she says, and digs into my wrist with the pen.

"Ow! Stop it!"

"Shush." She lets up on the pen but doesn't let go of my hand. "Animal." She writes an *A*.

"Senses." *S*.

"Treachery," I say. *T*. I look down at my arm.

E

A

S

T

"East. You think that's it? Just *east*? What about the treachery?"

"Wait," she says, and grabs my other arm. "Heroes Inevitably Locate Love in Strength."

H

I

L

L

S

We stare at each other. She's right. Of course she's right. We both look toward the East Hills, though we can't see through the walls of the school. Still, we know they're out there, and somewhere in those hills, hidden and safe—I hope—are Amma and Dad.

I stand up. "I have to go."

"To the hills?"

"Not yet. I don't know. I just have to go." I can't sit in this school. Not for another four hours. Not for another second. I run back down the hall and I don't care who sees me. And guess what? No one does. I bust out the doors of Marble Hill Prep and leap down the steps two and three at a time, and soon I'm on the sidewalk, running free. All I can do is run. A Dragonfly detects my movement and starts to follow me, but I don't care. Let it follow me.

I don't think about where I'm going. I just follow my feet, until they lead me through the gates of Raju's neighborhood, where the security guy recognizes me and waves me through.

All I want now is to be alone. All I want is to sit on my bed and think of Amma and Dad, alone in those hills. Or maybe not alone? Where are they living? In a shelter of branches and leaves, like two foxes?

Before I turn into Raju's driveway, I hear a rumble behind me. I turn to see the gullwing car. Tinley. What's she doing here? The car pulls up next to me, and I peer into the back seat. No Tinley. The driver's window slides open.

George. "Hey, kid." George picks something up from the dashboard and hands it to me. It's a gold coin.

"What's this?" I ask.

"I'm just the messenger, Muki kid," he says, before sliding the window shut and driving off. When I look closer, I see the coin isn't gold—it's chocolate covered in gold foil. Someone's drawn a black *X* across its face.

"Hellooo?" I hear Sonal Aunty's high whine from the other side of the house, then her footsteps in the hall, getting closer. "Cookie?" she calls, her voice tight with worry. "Is somebody there? Cookie-boo-boo?"

She squeals and jumps back, a frying pan in hand. "*Muki!*" She lowers the pan and gives me a little slap on the arm. "I thought you were a burglar!" I think about the fact that Sonal Aunty calls burglars *Cookie-boo-boo*. "What are you doing home?" she demands. "Did they let you out early? Where's Raju?"

"He's not—they didn't let us out. I just needed to come home."

Her face softens. She puts the frying pan—the massive kind that Paati uses for dosas—on the entryway table. Then she comes at me with both hands. I back away, but she gets me, her palms on my cheeks, my face smooshed in on itself so that when she says, "Tell me, Cookie, what's happening?" I'm unable to answer. She lets go. "Come to the kitchen. Have some juice."

"It's the parade today. So no one's really in class. They're all getting ready."

She sits down at the table with me. "And they didn't tell us this? No note for the parents?"

"There are only three of us. Moth kids. In the whole school."

Her face is close to mine now, and up this close, I can almost hear the whir of her thoughts. Her eyebrows, painted on with black pencil, dive in and reach for each other. She peers at me.

"Muki? Do you know where your mummy and daddy are?"

"Why?"

"We need to know, Cookie. They're in danger, you see. Raj Uncle"—her eyes shift to the empty hallway—"Raj Uncle needs to communicate with them. He needs to let them know."

"How are they in danger? How do you know?"

She wraps her fingers tightly around my wrist. "Don't worry about how we know. We know." A flicker in her eyes. "We want to bring them back to you. Wouldn't you like that?"

I would like that. I would like that a lot. I look at Sonal Aunty, her bright eyes, her painted eyebrows. I can see powder, like fine white sugar, on the tiny hairs of her face. I think of how much Amma loves Sonal Aunty, how long I've known Sonal Aunty, how much Sonal Aunty seems to love me.

"Okay," I answer. Her grip relaxes. "They're in the East Hills. I think. That's all I know. But what's going to happen to them?"

She sighs. Her smile deepens; her lips quiver at their corners. She lets go of me to bustle back to the stove. "Get ready for lunch, Muki! I made macaroni muffins!"

I go to Raju's room and stand there, fingering the gold coin in my pocket. Raju forgot to turn his game off this morning, and on the screen saver, the serene bagpiper stands silhouetted in the twilight, his little skirt flapping in a breeze, overlooking the hills of his homeland. I hear pots clanging in the kitchen. I hear Sonal Aunty's voice on the phone.

The macaroni muffins are surprisingly good. They look like little bundles of worms, but I eat three of them. Sonal Aunty packs me two more for Raju. "I'll drive you back, Muki. You've been very naughty, skipping school like this." She pinches my arm lightly. "But I won't tell. I promise."

On the short drive back to school, Sonal Aunty goes quiet. We pull up to the school. She turns to me, puts a hand on mine. "You be a good boy, Cookie," she says. "Be strong."

Back in the library, no one seems to remember I was gone. Even Fabi's lost in the book she's reading. She looks up, briefly. "They left," she says, her eyes dull. "All the kids with the float."

"Miss P., too?"

As if on cue, the library door opens and Miss P. walks in, a great big earnest smile stamped across her face. "Ready, Freddies?"

We hear the parade before we see it—the dull clamor swells as we draw closer to downtown Pacific City. Miss P. makes us walk. "Parking? Uh-uh," she says.

Fabi and I walk a few feet behind Miss P., and Raju drops back to join us. "Hey, where'd you go?"

"Your mama's house."

He punches me on the shoulder and it hurts. That's when I remember the macaroni muffins in my pocket, smashed into a sort of wormy pudding when I pull them out. "These are for you," I tell him. "From your mom. With love."

"Drone," he mutters. He grabs them and runs ahead to catch up with Miss P.

"Why'd you go there?" Fabi asks.

"I don't know. I ate lunch."

"Oh."

"Fabi?"

She waits.

"I told Raju's mom . . ." I lower my voice. "I told her that my parents are in the hills."

"Why'd you do *that*?"

"She's their friend. She said they were in trouble up there."

"What does she mean?"

"I don't know."

Heat rises off the sidewalk like steam from a shower. My shirt's getting itchy at the neck and pinching at my armpits. Miss P. stops walking and waits for us. "Almost there, troops," she says, then reaches into her shoulder bag and pulls something out. Masks. They're orange and black, with eyeholes cut into them and elastic bands. I've seen these around town, hanging off newsstands, hawked by street vendors. "Sweet!" Raju says. He puts his on right away.

Miss P. turns to Fabi and me. We're not convinced. "I thought you might enjoy them," she says, with a cheerfulness as forced and garish as these masks. "Go ahead! Put 'em on!" I obey. I don't know why, I just do. To my astonishment, Fabi listens, too. We stare at each other, masked by butterfly wings. We stare up at Miss P., and her big smile wilts.

As we get closer to the edge of downtown, the first thing I see is a line of Crickets. "Why all the guards?" I ask. "I thought this was a parade." I think about the East-West soccer game, the fights in the streets.

"Well, you know. A lot of people to watch over," Miss P. says. "Nothing to worry about, Muki."

Fabi's mask is down around her neck now. I take mine off, too. Soon, we're at the back of the crowd, where the hum grows to a roar. A drumbeat throbs and horns blare. The noise is everywhere—not just in my ears, but in my eyes and mouth and blanketing every inch of skin. The parade has started, but I can't see anything from here, just people's backs and legs.

"Right here!" Miss P. hustles us to the front of the MHP tent. "Make way, people," she calls. "I got kids here." Soon, we're at the edge of the crowd, just a few feet from the street.

The first float rolls toward us, and with it, a swell of sound like an ocean wave.

"Hey, Muki."

I turn around. "Flip!" He's come out of nowhere, and I haven't seen him in so long that I throw my arms around him. He hugs me back.

"How'd you find us, Flip?" I ask. "Fabi, he found us out here, in the middle of all these people!"

She shrugs. "He does that. Where are Mamá and Papi?"

"Moth tent."

"Where's that?"

Flip points, and that's when I see, across the street, a white tent. Sure enough, Mr. and Mrs. Calderón stand at the front of it, surrounded by a small crowd of other Moths. Like Fabi, they watch with calm curiosity. But now, Fabi's dropping the cool act, jumping up and down to see.

"Look at all those guards," she says, pointing to the phalanx of Crickets surrounding the Moth tent. "Why do they need all those guards? What're Mamá and Papi gonna do that's so dangerous?"

Raju's by my side now. "They're keeping them safe."

"Pssh. Yeah, right. Where are *your* parents, Raju?"

He shrugs.

Flip yawns and scratches his cheek. "Way too many floats in this parade. Like, literally every fool in Mariposa has a float in this parade."

"I don't think that's *literally* true," Fabi says.

"Hey, look . . ." I point at the float coming up. I'd know that orange tie anywhere. "There's Buff. And the other Buffs."

The ambassadors of commerce float rolls by, piled high with people wearing orange neckties. "Buff," Fabi mutters. She sticks her tongue out as he passes, and I thumb my nose at him, wrenching my nostrils up as high as they'll go. Flip snorts like a pig.

"Flip!" Fabi cries. "They see us! Look!" She points across the way, to the Moth tent, where Mr. and Mrs. Calderón are waving wildly, laughing and blowing kisses at their kids. Fabi and Flip jump up and down and wave their arms, laughing. Mrs. Calderón spots me, her smile falls, and she blows me a single kiss.

"Look who's next," Fabi says. "It's your girlfriend."

Fabi's right. Not that Tinley's my girlfriend. But here she is, on a float littered with Butterfly flags and government emblems, standing hand in hand with the general. Fabi hisses.

"Hey." I elbow her. "Don't do that. Not here."

"Look at her, though. Daddy's girl. Where's your revolution today, Tinley?"

I watch Tinley approach. Her dad wears a staid, official sort of smile. Tinley's smile has fallen. Her wave's gone limp, like she hardly knows she's in a parade. She's spotted the Moth tent, and she stares at it now, looking more distraught with each passing second. Something's happening. Across the way, a tremor passes through the Moth tent. People turn to each other, talking. Some pull out their phones, pressing one finger to an ear, trying to hear over all the noise.

On his float, General Schaedler pulls out his own phone. He holds it to his ear, yells into it. Then he does something wacky. He gets down on his hands and knees and jumps off the float while it's moving. Tinley calls to him. He holds his arms out and swings her down.

"Muki," Fabi says. She points to the Moth tent. The circle of guards moves in now, tight around the tent. We watch, frozen in place, as the black batons come out. The guards cross arms, batons in hand, forming a fence with their bodies. Those Crickets, put there to keep the Moths safe? They weren't there to keep the Moths safe. Mr. and Mrs. Calderón look around, realize what's happening, and wrap their arms around each other.

Around the Moth tent, other spectators notice what's happening, too. A buzz moves through that crowd of Butterflies, and the next thing I know, they're surrounding the Moth tent themselves. What are they doing? Are they attacking the Moths?

No. They're attacking the Crickets, pulling at their arms. I hear screams. Three Butterflies jump on one Cricket, pulling him away from the tent. More Butterflies try to break the Cricket line, and soon all I see are bodies thrashing and flailing, falling and lunging. The parade halts. Parade watchers flood the street and I can't see the Moth tent anymore.

Fabi shrieks. "Where are they? Where are my parents?"

Through a gap in the crowd I glimpse the tent. It's empty. Completely empty. The Calderóns—they're gone.

"We need to find them," I tell Fabi. "If we find them now, we can follow them!"

But a hand grabs my arm. I turn to see Raju with Box Tuttle, his face painted orange and black, with two bloody gashes on his knees. "Muki," Box pants, "they're coming for you. You've all got to hide."

"What? Who's coming for us?"

"The Crickets! They came to our waiting station looking for you. Get out of here! Please!"

Fabi and I look at each other. We look back at the empty Moth tent. Raju stares at Box. No one moves.

"Please!" Box says again. He's red-faced, sweat or tears running down his cheeks. "You gotta believe me. They swept all the schools in the city. They're moving through town and picking up Moths. Taking them—" His voice breaks. "Just get out of here."

"Let's go," Raju says. He yanks his mask over his face. I

do the same, and so does Fabi.

"Where'd our parents go?" Flip asks, just now realizing.
"Fabi, where are they?" Fabi pulls him by the arm, and the
four of us ram into the crowd, masks on, pushing in and out
of adult bodies. I don't know where we're going. I can barely
see the road ahead.

"Muki!" I hear my name again. I'm not going to stop.
"Muki, wait!"

"It's her!" Fabi calls from behind. "It's Tinley!"

I turn. Tinley Schaedler: just a few steps behind Flip.
She waves frantically. "Wait!"

"Stop," I call to Fabi.

Tinley catches up. "Muki, I have to tell you something,"
she says, catching her breath. She reaches for a chain at her
neck. Just then, I sense a ripple in the crowd, a poisonous
wave. Behind Tinley, a trio of black helmets pushes through.
Crickets. They've spotted us.

"Run!" I shout. I forget Tinley. I forget everything. I
push against bodies and I move forward and forward and
forward. Finally, I crack through the edge of the crowd and
break into a sprint.

I run forever. I run until I can't see. I run until I trip
on a bump and crash to the ground. Raju, Fabi, Flip, and
Tinley—they're still with me. They gather around and pull
me up. We stand there for a minute, catching our breath.
We're deep in Marble Hill now. I can't even hear the parade
anymore.

"Now what?" Fabi asks.

"We need a safe place. To figure out what we're doing."

"My house," Raju says.

We start walking. "And then what?" Flip asks.

"And then, after dark, the camp," I answer.

"Are you crazy?" Fabi snaps. "That's the last place we should be."

"No, Fabi. It's happening. They're going to take us—it's all happening. This is our only chance."

"For what?" Raju asks.

"To fight back. To stop what they're doing to us."

"I'm in," Flip says.

"Me too," Tinley says.

"Okay," Fabi says. "Me too."

Raju shakes his head. "I still don't know what's happening."

"Let's just get back to your house."

As we walk, the air calms. No Crickets, no Dragonflies. I can see the hills to the east, where Amma and Dad are hiding. *Where are you?* I whisper. *I need you here.*

Raju falls into step with me. I pull the gold coin from my jacket. It's gone mushy from my body heat. "What's that?" he asks. The rest of the group presses in to get a look at the coin.

"George gave it to me outside your house. I don't know what it means."

"It's a clue," Flip whispers.

"To what, though?"

"To treasure?" Fabi says. "*X* marks the spot?"

"What's gold?"

"Jewels are gold," Tinley says.

"The sun."

"Apple juice," Flip adds. "And why an *X*?"

"*X* can mean *Don't go there*, right? It can mean danger."

"Gold is money. It's wealth," Fabi says.

Raju grabs the coin from me. "Hey!" I grab for it, but he pulls away, looks closely at it.

"I mean, it's just a regular chocolate coin," he mutters, "unless it's poisoned. But also, it's my mom's name."

"What?"

"Sonal. It means gold."

"Your mom's name with an *X* on it? You think your mom's in danger?"

He stares back at me. "Why would she be in danger?"

I'm sorry I brought it up. There's nothing we can do now, and Raju's chest has started to heave up and down with fear. "She's probably fine," I say. "She's probably at your house right now, waiting for us. With muffins. Why would she be in danger?" I try to sound sure of myself, but the possibilities continue to roll and tumble, like clothes in a Dembubbles dryer.

Chapter 27

By the time we get to Raju's house, the sun is starting to dim. Night isn't far.

The house is empty. No Sonal Aunty, no Raj Uncle. It's colder than usual. Something has changed, but I don't know what. My stomach rumbles.

"Let's eat," I say. The fridge is muffins. The freezer is muffins.

"I have never, ever seen this many muffins before," Flip says. "This. Is. Incredible."

"They're all yours." I find an actual blueberry muffin and grab that. I take a macaroni muffin, too. They really weren't that bad.

"Where's your mom?" I ask.

"What do you mean?"

"Do you think—" Fabi stops herself. I know what she means. Could Raju's parents be in the camp now, too? Have they been taken?

His eyes cloud with worry, but he says nothing, just gazes into the kitchen, blinking, thinking.

"So we get to the camp," Fabi says. "Then what?"

"We carry out the resistance plan, to infiltrate the camp. And we have codes," I answer. "Let's sort out what we know, and what we don't."

"Well, for codes, we have the hand with the stars," Fabi says. "We never solved that one."

From my pocket I pull the crumpled bit of paper. "Someone—someone at the camp, maybe, has star-shaped scars on their knuckles. And maybe they have the code we need. We just have to find them."

"But how?" Flip asks.

"I don't know. I have a feeling we'll know them when we see them."

"There's a quote," he says, and reads it aloud. "What's a tryst?"

"It's from a speech by Nehru, the first prime minister of India."

"Look," Raju cuts in. "I don't think this is helping. I don't think we're figuring anything out here."

"We *are* figuring it out, drone," Fabi says. "That's what we're *trying* to do."

"Okay," he says, "so let's say we do find the guy—"

"Or woman—"

"Or woman, with the star-shaped scars on her knuckles. And she gives us a code or whatever. What's it the code to?"

"The main building," I answer.

"And you have another code from Papa's safe," Tinley chimes in.

"There *was* no code in the safe."

"Ha! But there *was*." Tinley steps forward, her eyes glinting. "Are you going to listen to me now? I've been trying to tell you." She slips the chain off her neck. Looped over it is her mother's ring, the one from the box. "Look inside the ring," she orders.

"Look inside?" I hold it to my eye. "How do you look inside a ring?"

"No, Muki." Fabi steps forward. "She means look *on* the inside. The inside of the ring." She takes the ring from me and peers at its inner edge. "I see numbers."

"Give me!" I grab for it, but Fabi pulls away. "Calm *down*, please." She peers into the ring. "Three four seven . . . four two four . . ."

"One six nine two," Tinley says. "There's our number. Ten digits!"

Of course. I can't believe I didn't think of it myself. The inside of the ring! "What is this, your phone number?"

"No, I don't know what it is. But it'll get us into the munitions room, right?"

We look at each other, each of us silently weighing the options. "Two codes. Maybe that's all we need."

"But what are we going to *do*?" Flip asks.

"Okay. So, we go to the camp tonight, when it's dark.

We'll let ourselves in through the gap in the fence. I'll show you where it is. We'll go to the munitions locker, pick up as many weapons as we can—"

"Sweet!" Flip whispers.

"And then we take those weapons, and we go to each tent, and we set everyone free."

"That's it?" Tinley asks.

"That's it."

"But what if they come after us?" Raju says. "They have weapons, right?" He looks worried. Mr. *Ballistic Bagpipes* isn't so hot on weapons now.

"Lee said setting everyone free would make things worse," Flip says.

"Do you have a better idea, Flip?" He's right, but I glare down at him like a bullying big brother.

"No," he says, staring at his feet. Now I feel bad. He's just asking the questions that need to be asked.

"We don't know what we're doing, do we?" Fabi asks.

"Not really. We just have to show up and—and do it."

"Whatever *it* is," Flip says.

"Whatever *it* is," I repeat, and pat him on the back. I look around at the four of them. Now I really wish we had a name for this operation.

"Tonight," Flip says.

"Tonight," I answer.

Raju shakes his head. "We're kids, though. They have actual *guns* in there. Do you have guns, Muki?"

He's right.

"Listen up, Cookie." Fabi steps right up to him. "We got this far without you. Do you want to be part of this? Or do you want stay home?"

"Um. Well. I guess I'd *prefer* to think about *reality*, Fabi."

Fabi leans even closer to Raju, whose face is getting pink now, and the next thing I know their voices get louder and louder until both of them are shouting and Fabi pushes Raju in the chest.

"HOLD IT!" I shout.

"You . . ." I point to Fabi. "Stand next to Flip. And *you*, Raju, stand next to Tinley. Nobody touch each other. Nobody talk!"

Raju heaves a sigh. Then he mumbles something about *Ballistic Bagpipes* and disappears up the stairs. Flip runs after him. I'm too full of thoughts to play *BB*.

A few minutes later, Tinley's walking back and forth through the beaded curtain, letting the waterfall of glass beads slip over her face and hands. Fabi's sitting straight and stiff on the white sofa, not talking. I decide not to tell her that I threw up exactly where she's sitting.

"Flip's playing video games," she says, to no one in particular.

"Yup. *BB*. Raju's got it in his room."

She puts a hand out, like she's holding a piece of evidence. "So our parents," she says, "our *mom* and *dad* are in the Moth camp, doing who knows what, and my *brother*"—she holds out her other hand—"is playing video games."

I shrug. "Maybe he doesn't want to think about it. Raju's probably the same."

"He doesn't seem worried, though," Tinley says, wrapping a strand of beads around her wrist, examining the play of light on glass.

"Maybe not everyone shows it the same way."

Fabi looks up at me, and I can tell she's both in the room and not in the room. "You think my parents are out there? At the camp?"

I nod.

"You think your grandma's still in there? And the Wongs and Mrs. Demba?"

"I think they're all there, Fabi."

Fabi turns to Tinley. "Until when? When do they get sent away?"

Tinley freezes, a strand of beads wrapped over her forehead. "Why are you asking me?"

"You would know, wouldn't you? Hasn't your daddy told you?"

"Fabi," I mutter.

"What?"

"You know what."

I'm sure I'm in for a Fabi verbal smackdown, but when she turns to me, she's blinking back tears. "Maybe you can forget what her dad does, Muki, but I can't. I think it's crazy that we go to school with these people. Even crazier that you're friends with her. That you go to her *house*."

Tinley lets go of the beads. "What's wrong with my house?"

"You mean your castle?"

Tinley's eyes narrow to two quivering little slits. "It's a castillo."

Fabi leans in, glaring just as hard. "That's just Spanish for *castle*."

"It's a *small* castle."

"A small castle? Ha! Big enough for you and your mom and dad, though, right? And all your servants?"

Tinley sighs.

Fabi crosses her arms, satisfied. "See? No answer. You give one little piece of truth to these people and—"

"I don't see what's wrong with being friends with me," Tinley says. "I'm not a bad person. I don't know what *these people* means. I know you all think I'm some kind of spoiled princess, but *Muki* . . ." She takes a deep breath. "Muki got to know me. He gave me a chance." She peeks shyly at me. "I think he knows I'm not a bad person."

"Your father kidnapped my parents and put them in a camp," Fabi says.

"Well, that was—"

"Your father kidnapped my parents and put them in a camp."

"But that wasn't me!"

"Your father kidnapped my mother and father and put

them in a camp. Your father did that to my parents. *Your family* did that to *my* family." Tears stream down Fabi's face. "And you say you're not bad people? Then what are you? How can you be good when you do that to my family?"

Tinley lets go of the glass beads. They clack and swing around her. She gazes at Fabi and me, like she's watching us from another dimension. I don't know what to do. Fabi's right.

She goes on. "The thing that bugs me most about you, Tinley Schaedler, is that you don't even have to *think* about what it's like for Moths. The things happening to us? They don't even *touch* you."

"Well, they do," Tinley says. "They do touch me. I have to think about them."

"Wrong."

"Not wrong! Muki's my friend and his parents are gone. I think about that! I have to! And now your mom and dad. They're in the camps, too!"

Fabi crosses her arms and shoots a subarctic glare at Tinley. Tinley stomps over to the sofa and plops down next to Fabi. "I'm here. I'm on your team. So let's get them out."

"Yeah!" I jump up, practically shouting. "Let's get them out! Let's stop fighting and get them all out!"

Both girls stare at me like they forgot I was here.

It would have been easy to forget what we were doing, to let go completely and lose ourselves in the pillow-soft world of the Rajarajan house. Raju and Flip play video games. Every so often someone gets up and wanders to the kitchen and comes back with more muffins.

Fabi turns on the television, and the first thing on is Bambi, still talking to the camera, his talking head intercut with images of the parade, the ruckus around the Moth tent. Bambi's on mute, so all we see is his snarled and twisted face, his lips wet with spit. Even without sound, I can see it: Bambi is panicking, like an overwhelmed defensive line. The resistance is a wall of strikers rushing his goal, passing from player to player. Bambi's thrashing around the field and hoping to bring someone down, anyone down.

Fabi changes the channel. All I want is to forget this afternoon, and for a little while, I do. We spend two hours watching television, stretched out in our socks on the white sofa, like three ordinary kids on a Friday afternoon.

But this isn't just any Friday.

On this Friday, as the house around us dips deeper into night, Fabi, Flip, Raju, Tinley, and I gather around the long, black dining room table. It's so polished I can see our faces in it. Raju squints into the room, adjusting to real-world light. In Oceanview, on laundry lines and power lines, butterflies gather, measuring their wingbeats, but here, all I see are five revolutionaries, each more scared than the other.

"Okay," I begin. "Everyone ready?"

"You really think this will work?" Raju says. "How are we going to fight the Crickets? There's just five of us." He's right. My plan is barely a plan.

"Let's just get there. And keep our eyes open."

"Oculi aperti," Tinley says.

Eyes open. And then it comes to me. Paati, that last day I saw her: *I hope you will choose to see.* "If people can *see* what we're doing, then maybe the Crickets won't hurt us." It's time to open people's eyes, to show them what happens when kids fight back. I can see it now—rows and rows of round glass eyes, watching, recording. Cameras. "They won't hurt us if we have news cameras on us!"

"News cameras?" Fabi asks.

"Yeah." I turn to her. "Do you have your phone? Do you still have Miss Pistachio's number?"

She perks up, slides her phone from her sweater. This wasn't my plan until I said it aloud. "When we get to the camp—not before, 'cause she'll try to stop us—when we get to the camp, you need to call Miss Pistachio and tell her what we're doing. Tell her we're staging a standoff with the Crickets and she needs to call every newspaper and television station she can. She'll do that for us."

"But why the news cameras?" Flip asks.

"You were right, Flip. *Just* letting the Moths out? That won't help anything, not in the long run. We need to actually change something for the Moths. With reporters there, watching, Bamberger can't ignore us. And the cameras will watch the Crickets, too. To protect us. We need the whole world to see what happens."

"Like a protest," Tinley says. "We'll stand there until they let the Moths out." The group falls quiet and thinks about that for a minute.

"Well, are we doing this or not?" Fabi stands up. "Come on!"

The four of us leave Raju's house with nothing but a flashlight and a phone. We walk in silence for a while, when Raju speaks up. "Why Nehru?" he asks. "Why that quote?"

"On the star-knuckles clue? I don't know. I've been thinking about that all day."

"Maybe for inspiration. Maybe whoever made the clue knows we're Indian."

"It's got to be more than that. It *has* to." I can feel the answer. It's in my head, skulking in the alleys of my memory.

We cross a little creek toward Marble Hill Prep and start to cut across the school fields. That's when I hear a car engine gunning in the distance. It's dark out, but as it gets closer, I can see that it's a red SUV. It roars toward us. Raju peers into the dark. "I think that's our car. What's it doing here?"

The car speeds up to the field, then screeches to a halt beneath a floodlight. The passenger window opens. It's Sonal Aunty. "Raju! Why aren't you home? Get in the car. Now!"

Raju gapes at his mother, then slowly shakes his head.

"Raju! This is no time—"

"Where are we going?" he asks. "What about Muki?"

Sonal Aunty looks at me. Her gaze is unreadable. "We're going away, Raju. Muki can stay here."

Sometimes, I don't understand things until all the pieces stop moving—like looking into a kaleidoscope, when all the pieces stop turning and settle into a pattern. Here's what I suddenly see:

That first night at the Rajarajans, Raju's question: *If they take you away, Mama. . . .* And Sonal Aunty's response: *We'll be fine. I promise.*

Sonal Aunty, this afternoon, asking again if I knew where my parents were. *The East Hills*, I answered. Her smile. It was sweet, yes. But at the end of it, like a bite of old apple, the sweet turned to mealy mush. There was something rotten in that smile.

The fortune cookie: Every animal senses treachery. Amma was warning me, but I didn't see it in time.

The night Dad and Amma went into hiding: Had Sonal Aunty ratted them out?

The gold coin: *Sonal* means "gold." An *X* means danger. Sonal Aunty wasn't in danger. Sonal Aunty *was* danger.

"Raju! Enough!" Sonal Aunty shrieks. She jumps from the passenger seat and lunges at her kid. He leaps away and runs into a thick grove of trees behind the school, out of sight.

That's all I need to know. "You told them," I say to her, quietly at first. Then I shout. I shout and I don't care who hears. "You told the Crickets where my parents were hiding! You told them!"

"Don't be ridiculous, Muki!" Sonal Aunty hisses. But I see it in her eyes—a lightning flash of guilt. She gets down from the car and starts to chase Raju, but she slips on the muddy grass and catches herself, her hair baubles wobbling.

"What did they give you for it?" I ask her. "Are they letting you go? Are you escaping? Where are *you* going?"

For a second, I stand frozen, unsure of everything I thought I knew. Sonal Aunty glares at me. "I can't tell you where we're going." Her face softens. Her lip quivers. "We had to protect our family, Muki. Raj Uncle and me. We had to make sure we were safe, that our Raju was safe. So we told them. It was all we could do. Okay? Okay?"

It isn't okay. I'm trying hard not to cry, but it's not working. Nothing about this is okay.

Raj Uncle calls from the car. "Sonu! Get in and close the door. They'll send Raju to us on his own. We have to go now. *Now!*"

She flaps her hands and lets out a long, high screech. Then she skids and slides back to the car, throws herself into the front seat, and shuts the door, her hands covering her face. Raj Uncle revs the engine, and in a soft spray of mud, they're gone.

After a few minutes, Raju emerges from the trees, his face streaked with mud, his hair wet. He looks like a squirrel that's been chased to its den, his fur frayed, every nerve on high alert. He gazes down the barren, hazy road at the ghost of his parents. They were the treacherous ones. I walk over to him. "They'll be okay, Raju. We will, too." I'm sure of the first thing, but not the second.

He wakes up a little and nods. Then he turns to the East Hills. "Your parents, now my parents." He looks stricken again. "Did my parents turn your parents in?"

Fabi takes my hand. Tinley takes my other hand. Flip puts a hand on my shoulder. We all look up at the East Hills. "They're okay up there," Flip says. "In those hills? Finding two little ol' brown people? That's like finding a needle in a—I don't know what. Wherever you find needles."

"Haystack," Fabi says.

"What?"

"Haystack. Needle in a haystack."

"What're you *talking* about?"

She groans.

The road to the Moth camp is desolate. There are no streetlights out here, but the moon pours over the East Hills and lights the road ahead. Fabi leads us, flashlight in hand, Tinley by her side and Flip just behind. Raju sticks close to my side. I'm sure he's never, in all his muffin-shaped life, walked alone in the dark before. He winces at every sound. "What's that?" he whispers.

"Probably just an animal."

"An animal? What animal?"

"Something small."

"How'd you know?"

"I don't think we have tigers on the island, Raju."

"Tigers?"

"Hey, look, we're almost there," Fabi calls. The sight of floodlights in the distance kicks my feet into higher gear. All of us speed up.

"Muki?" Raju says, a little out of breath.

"Yeah?"

"Are you scared?"

"No."

"Really?"

"Really."

Raju says nothing.

"Okay," I admit. "I'm scared."

"Yeah. Me too." And for the first time, I feel sorry for the guy. Yes, his parents might have put my parents in even more danger. But they're still his parents. They left him behind, all alone.

"Where do you think they're going?" I ask. "Your mom and dad?"

He shakes his head and keeps walking, pumping his arms, his head thrust forward like a battering ram against the night. A few seconds later, I hear him sniff, then sniff again. He jams his palms into his eyes but keeps walking.

"Sorry," I say. "I didn't—"

"I'm not."

"Okay."

He stops walking. I stop with him. The rest of the group keeps going, but I let them go.

He just stands there, looking at the ground. His sniffles get snottier, more complicated.

"I don't know what to do," he says.

"Now that your parents left?"

He nods. I wish I had an answer. "My parents left, too. You just figure it out. Every day. You figure it out."

He stares down the road.

"Think about *BB*. Right? Think about Hamish. You don't really know what to do when you're Hamish, right? You just do what seems right. You just level up, try stuff out, and level up again." I don't mention that Hamish gets killed every five minutes.

"But this is real life."

"I'll be here. Okay? We're all here with you."

He nods.

"Just think Hamish," I say.

"Hamish." He smiles a little. Raju. I would never have expected him here, now, with us. But here he is. I wouldn't expect to be glad to see him, but I am.

Together, we break into a run, our breath steaming in clouds, until we catch up with the rest of the group. We can see the fence around the camp now. The border fence is unguarded. Pathetic. If I were turning a country on its head,

I'd do a much better job of it than Bamberger.

"There you are," Fabi says as we join the group. The five of us look out over the camp. The main building is dark, but the three tents sit bathed in overhead light. "First, we go to the main building. But not till we're all in. We do everything together." I look from face to face. "Okay? No one gets left behind."

When we reach the gap in the fence, I stop. "This is where we sneak in."

Raju's first on the ground. "They do this in *BB*!" He flops to the ground by the fence, lies flat on his back, and looks up at me.

"Hamish," I say.

"Hamish," he says, and wiggles, feet-first, under the fence. The secret to the *BB* shimmy is that you go feet-first. It's crazy how much he actually looks like Hamish when he does it. Fabi does it, too, then Tinley.

Flip goes next, slides his feet under, but then he stops. "I can't move," he whimpers. "I'm stuck." His tummy's pushed out against the bottom of the fence, just a millimeter from a razored spike. If he moves wrong, it'll slice into him. He starts to panic. He breathes hard and fast and his belly grazes the blade.

"Flip! You've got to calm down."

He shakes his head wildly. "I can't make it. I'm too fat. They're gonna find me—"

Fabi drops to her knees beside him. "Hey, Felipe, look

at me." She starts talking quietly to him—too quietly for me to hear. His eyes focus on hers and he calms a little. Still, he doesn't move.

"Flip," I whisper. "You need to slide under. You can do it, I promise."

He starts to gulp at the air, unable to catch a breath, his stomach jumping up and down, closer and closer to the bladed wire.

"Okay, look." I think of Paati, of the early mornings, of the breathing exercises she made me do. "Try this. Breathe in for three counts, hold it for one, and let it out in three counts, slow. Do it with me." Flip trains his eyes on my mouth. I count the way Paati does, touching the top, middle, and bottom pads of each finger. We do it two times. I try not to think of the seconds ticking by, of the growing chance that someone will see us. Instead, I breathe. He breathes. He calms down, his breathing slows.

Now Raju's kneeling next to Flip and before I can tell him to back off, he says, "Flip, remember Archibald? Under the Wall of Ballantine?" Flip nods. "Here," Raju says, and guides Flip's foot a little farther into the camp. "Bear down on your heel, 'kay? And use it to pull yourself over a little. Just a tiny bit. Try moving one centimeter and then stop."

Flip's face scrunches with the effort. He strains, wiggles a little, and stops, panting. "Good," Raju says. "Do it again, and this time we'll count with you."

"One, two, three," I count. Flip's face stays placid as he

breathes out, and this time he budges noticeably.

"Again," Raju says.

We all count together, and Flip slides under a little more. A tiny dagger of razor wire hangs right at his ribs. I can feel how close it is. "He's gonna get cut," I whisper. "If he moves."

"Hold it, guys," Tinley says. She kneels down and takes off her school sweater. She wraps the fabric around her hand. "Give me a second, Flip," she says. With her hand wrapped in the sweater, she clutches the razor wire and wrenches it up. It lifts an inch, then two. "*Quick*," Tinley whispers. Her arms shake with the strain of holding up the stiff, heavy wire.

"Breathe, Flip. Remember to use your foot."

Flip sucks in one big breath, and like a pro, like the baddest ballistic bagpiper, he slides beneath the razor wire, and he's free. The others cheer, in whispers, and Raju slings an arm around him. Now I shimmy under, my eyes fixed on the camp yard. Crickets prowl, but I can't see them. They must be everywhere, as black as the night beyond the floodlights.

"Take your shoes off," I tell the group. "We need to be totally silent."

"I can't believe I did it," Flip says as we walk, heel-toe, heel-toe, along the shadowy border fence. He's proud of himself, and I'm proud of him, too. But there's not much time to be proud, because the main building's getting closer and closer, and with it, the realization that we have a job to do, a big job, and almost no idea how to do it.

"I see one," Fabi says, and points to a Cricket standing by the main building.

"He's right by the front door," I whisper. "Now what?"

The group looks at me like I'm the one with the answer. "We need to get him away from there," I say. "We need a distraction."

"I could yell for help," Tinley says.

"But then he'd come over *here*."

"I could throw my voice."

"You can do that?"

"I don't know. I've never tried."

"Okay. No. What else?"

"If this were *BB*, we could throw a hand grenade," Raju offers.

"Wait!" Flip whispers. "I've got something." From his pocket, he pulls his little red ball. Before anyone can stop him, he tosses it up in the air and kicks it in a colossal arc. It disappears in the gleam of the floodlights, and lands with a distant thump on the pavement. The Cricket stands up straighter and takes something from his pocket—a flashlight, which he switches on. From where I stand, he looks barely older than us. He lobs his light over the nearest tent, where Flip's ball landed, and jogs into the yard. He disappears behind the tent.

"Flip!" Fabi whispers. "That was amazing!"

"Let's go," I say. "Now. Now!"

The five of us run alongside the main building, quiet as socks, until we reach the entrance. A keypad glows out at us, letters and numbers, and my stomach plummets. "This is the code we don't know. This is star-knuckles."

"We didn't find star-knuckles," Fabi whispers.

"What should we do?"

"We'll have to find him," Raju says. "He must be obvious, right? We'll have to get close to the Crickets without them seeing us. Close enough to see their knuckles."

"No," I answer. "That just doesn't seem right. It can't be that complicated."

I search my brain. It's there. The answer is there, so close, that to give up now—I can't give up now. Not after all our missions, after making it to the camp, after getting Flip under the fence, those breathing exercises, that tiny, sharp blade hanging over him—

"Wait." It's coming to me. It's getting close. "I've almost got it."

"You do?"

"There's something . . ." There's something about the breathing exercises. The scene at the fence comes back to me in flashes. Flip. The blade. The breathing. The counting. The counting. Yes!

"The counting!" I reach into my pocket and pull out the crumpled star-knuckles clue. "Fabi. Flashlight."

My hand is shaking so badly I can hardly see the

diagram in the flashlight's glow. I hold up my hand. "We were thinking of this all wrong. There's no guard with stars on his knuckles. There are no knuckles. It isn't the *outside* of a hand. It's the *inside* of a hand. Like Paati's," I whisper. "Her counting method." I reconstruct it, touching my thumb to the top third of my pinkie, the middle third, the bottom third. I count down each pad of each finger—twelve counts on one hand.

"Oh," Raju says. "Wait. Is that—?"

"Look at the diagram," I whisper. "A star on the top of the pinkie. That's the number one. Top of the ring finger. Four."

"Seven," Raju says, pointing to the next finger.

"And nine!" we whisper together.

"One four seven nine."

"What the heck is that?" Fabi asks. "What did you just do?"

"Indian counting. It's how my paati counts."

"And the Nehru quote—"

"—was to tell us it was the Indian counting method."

"Wow," Raju says. "I mean, they could have just put an Indian flag on there. Or just the word *India*. Why—"

"Can we *please* get going?" Tinley whispers. "I hear the Crickets."

"Okay." I take a deep breath. "Here goes nothing."

I punch in the numbers. One, four, seven, nine. I hold my breath.

Nothing.

"What happened?"

I hear footsteps.

"Try again."

"Did you do it hard enough?"

"Is it a different order?"

"I knew this wouldn't work."

The footsteps draw closer.

"Wait!" I hiss. "Nehru. Independence. The 'tryst with destiny' speech happened on the eve of Indian independence. What year was that?"

"Oh jeez," Fabi groans. "I don't know."

"Neither do I. But look. I know it was the 1900s. And these are the numbers we have. If we just shuffle them around, we get a year in the 1900s. 1947."

"One nine four seven!" Fabi whispers. Before I can stop her, she shoves me over and punches the numbers in.

The keypad lights up. The door starts to whir, deep and metallic. It clicks open. We slip into complete darkness. It worked!

I don't know what to do, now that we're here. Fabi points her flashlight down a cramped hallway. Farther down, there's a lit room. I hear talk and laughter. Now I wish there weren't five of us here. It's a lot easier to spot five kids than one. But what can I do about that now?

The door closest to us is heavy and metal and has another keypad next to it. "Maybe that's it," I whisper. "The munitions room."

I take the flashlight from Fabi and move toward it. She grabs the back of my shirt, sticks close to me. I glance back and see Tinley stuck close behind her, Raju right behind Tinley, and Flip bringing up the rear. We're like a top secret choo-choo train.

The keypad glows green. The code. The code. What's the next code? My mind goes blank. "Code. Tinley, code!"

Tinley recites the ten digits. My finger shakes as I press the final numbers. One. Six. Nine. Two. I expect nothing. I expect a helpless blink from the keypad. Instead, it flashes three times and the door clicks open.

"It worked!" I feel a little jiggle of excitement from the group behind me. Their bodies push into mine, and I stumble through the door. I run my hand against the wall and flip a switch.

Light. Blinding. A buzzing sound. I blink into the bright room and wait for my eyes to adjust. First, I see a bare floor. I see high shelves that rise to the ceiling. I see strange gray machinery. And then I hear a voice.

"Well, holy coconuts, am I glad to see you."

Wedged into the corner, sitting on a folding chair, almost hidden by a mountain of crates, is Lee.

"Lee!" I step forward and trip over something low and heavy, and the rest of the group topples after me. We sit there, a pile of us, gaping at Lee. His arm sits in a sling, a big square bandage on his forehead.

"It's the truck guy!" Flip says.

"Lee, what are you doing here?"

"Living the dream."

Tinley pushes past me and rushes over to Lee. She kneels in front of him, lays a hand on his sling.

"Hello, Miss Tinley."

She stares up at him, speechless.

"What did they do to you?" I ask. "Why are you here?"

"I guess they didn't know where else to put me." He nods to a crusty bowl of food by his side. "I'd offer you something, but it's all pretty gross."

"Did they hurt you? What happened to your head?" Tinley asks. I can't pull my eyes from the bandage above his eye. It's clean, with a perfect circle of blood at its center.

Lee beams at us. "It really is good to see you kids."

"Why were you sitting in the dark?" Fabi asks.

"Easier on the old noggin," he says, pointing to the bandage. "What're you doing here anyway?"

"Exactly what you told us not to," Fabi says.

"Good for you."

"We almost didn't make it. My brother got stuck at the fence. He almost couldn't squeeze through."

Flip pats himself on the tummy. "I put the *belly* in *rebellion*."

"Nice one," Lee says.

We look at him and he looks at us, and no one knows exactly what to say. That's when I glance in the corner and see a small cannon—barely bigger than a dog—and remember where we are. "This is the munitions room."

"That's right," Lee says. "And these are the munitions. If you can call them that." He struggles to his feet, takes a second to steady himself, and limps over to the high shelves. "I did a re-org in here the other day, just to pass the time." He reaches for the nearest shelf. "This one's cool. Ever see a trench club?" He holds up a gnarled wooden stick, its head covered in metal spikes. "Looks like something you'd use to beat up a troll." He picks up a heavy black thing. "This here's a gauntlet dagger. Goes over your arm." He hands it to me. "That's for hand-to-hand combat."

"It looks like a narwhal." The gauntlet dagger is a heavy metal glove that covers my whole hand, without finger holes. From its tip juts a long metal spike. I slip it over my arm and point it at Lee.

Lee nods. "Ideal for the poking out of the eye."

Flip stands by a far shelf, wearing a round hood—it's white with two eyeholes and a little screen over his mouth. It looks like a little kid's drawing of a ghost. "Gas mask," Lee says. "To protect you from poisonous gas in the trenches."

Lee watches us like it's the most normal thing in the world to see five kids in a munitions locker trying on gauntlet daggers and gas masks.

"These are the weirdest weapons I've ever seen," Raju says.

"Crickets took all the newer stuff."

Raju drags something from the back of a low shelf. "Bagpipes!" he calls. "Sweet!"

"Why are there bagpipes in a munitions locker?" I ask.

"Bagpipes can be used in battle," Raju answers. "To sound the battle cry."

"We got training grenades, too," Lee adds. "A whole bag of 'em." He dips into a big canvas sack by his side and tosses up a grenade, green and dusty.

"Careful," I say.

"Nothing to worry about," he answers. "They're inactive. See?" He pulls the pin out and the room erupts with shuffling and screeching.

"Lee," I shout. "What are you *doing*? Are you insane?"

"Shhh! They'll hear you. They're all dead, all these grenades. I promise." He picks another one out of the sack and pulls out its pin. "See? Nothing." He's grinning all big and toothy, and I wonder if maybe he's lost his mind in here. He pulls out another pin, and another.

"I think that's enough," I say. The group falls silent. Raju's bagpipes let out a nasal sigh.

Lee tosses a grenade back into the sack. "So now what?" he asks.

I look to Flip, to Fabi, to Raju and Tinley. "So now we head out to the tent."

"With these?" Flip asks. He's holding a stick with a ball and chain hanging from it.

"It's all we've got."

Finally, Lee gets very serious. "Muki? What are you planning?"

I think about his question. I think about answering it. I think about what he might say.

"I'm not going to tell you. But do you want to come along?"

He nods and sticks a couple of hand grenades in his pockets. "Lead the way."

Chapter 28

Outside the storeroom door, we hear a sudden thunder of boots on the ground.

"Uh-oh. Dinnertime," Lee says.

"What does that mean?"

"It means you hide. All of you!" He springs into action. "You—*there*." He slides Raju onto a low shelf, crams Flip in beside him, uses his good arm to cover them up with crates. Tinley and Fabi, he sweeps into a narrow broom closet.

"What about me?" I won't fit in the closet. There's no room left on the shelves.

He looks around. He looks back at me. In the distance, a door bangs open.

"In here." He opens the mouth of the grenade bag.

"No!"

"It's *fine*."

The footsteps get louder, louder still, until they stop in front of the door.

"*In!*" Lee hisses.

I step one foot in the bag. I have no choice. I stick the other foot in. I cringe for the explosion. Nothing. I hear the beep of the keypad, the whir of the lock, and I sink into the bag. Lee pulls the drawstring, and it closes around me. The door clicks open.

All I can see now is the room's light, but like a chick in an egg, I listen to the world around me. The scrape of a chair. Heavy boots on the cement floor. A gruff, low voice: "Dinner is served."

"Thank you," Lee says. The Cricket grunts. I hear his feet move around the room. And then the feet stop.

"You move things around again?" the Cricket asks.

"Just a little," he says. "Passing the time."

"Something's different." I can sense the guard peering around the room, sniffing the air. "Something's off."

"Oh—that'll be lunch. Didn't quite sit right with me."

It's hard to breathe in this bag, the smell of paint heavy and chemical in my head.

"I do love grits, though," Lee says.

"Don't push it, butler."

More scraping metal, more heavy boots, a jolt and clang, and the guard is gone. The room, the entire room, lets out an audible sigh.

"Can we come out?" It's Flip.

"You can come out," Lee mutters. "That was terrifying." Flip and Raju crawl out from their shelf, Fabi and

Tinley from their closet.

"Fabi," I say, "we forgot to call Miss P. about the news people."

"Done. I have the TV news coming."

The other four turn to her. "You *do*?"

"You've got the *what* now?" Lee asks.

"The TV news. Miss Pistachio texted me. They're on their way." She shrugs, like it's no big deal.

TV news. And here I am, with no idea what I'm doing. I close my eyes and try to envision it: each of us sitting in the dark, in front of a tent. That's all we have to do, right? Just sit. Sit and be kids. Kids with weapons. And wait for the cameras. "Is everyone ready?" I look around at every face, and we're all ready and we're all not ready.

When we slip into the hallway, the cold from the stone floor shoots through my socks and up my spine. Farther down the hall, I hear the Crickets at dinner. "Perfect timing," Lee whispers.

I'm wearing my gauntlet dagger. The others have cudgels and clubs. That's when I hear a low, reedy whine. "Raju! I told you to leave those!" He straightens up, bagpipes strapped across his chest, their four rods rising proudly into the air.

"But I wanted them," he says, looking guilty.

"I can't believe you."

"Quiet, you two," Lee says. "It's dinner, but they'll have a couple guards still on duty." Outside, the moon is stuck behind a cloud bank. The sky glows silver, but here on earth, the dark is iron clad.

"Which tent?" Fabi whispers.

"The first tent." I can feel Paati in there. I can feel something pulling me in, like invisible fishing line.

I'm the first to reach the tent. My socks are already wet, so sitting on the cold, damp ground doesn't matter much. Lee sits on one side of me. He's stopped asking questions, stopped telling us what to do. I think he's just happy to be out. There's a steady murmur from inside the tent, and maybe we're not as safe as I think we are. In that tent—anyone could be in there. They could have a whole troop of Crickets in there, waiting to capture us. My plan seemed so simple back at Raju's house. Now it's gone all wobbly.

On my other side sits Fabi, with Tinley next to her, then Flip, then Raju. We're each holding a rusty old weapon. We're each wondering what happens next. "This is stupid," Raju says.

"Shut it, Bagpipes."

"Why aren't we just going inside and letting them out?"

"Because."

Tinley jumps to her knees. "What's that sound?" A few seconds later, I hear it, too: a high, staticky whine, followed by a rapid drumbeat. It's getting louder, closer.

"It's a helicopter!" Flip yells, and it doesn't matter anymore that he's yelling, that he's giving us away, because the helicopter has sunk in the sky and there it is now, right above us, blades thrashing, bobbing and bouncing on air, like the loudest, angriest wasp. On its side: NewsCopter 10. From the open door of NewsCopter 10, a cameraperson points a giant eye at us. By instinct, we wave. By instinct, a thrill runs through me.

What happens next feels like a dream, like reality whipped into a milkshake by the dark and the noise of the chopper blades. First, the door of the main building opens and a mob of Crickets run toward us. Then I hear Fabi's voice in my ear. "Raju! Come back!" Raju pauses at the mouth of the tent, his doofy bagpipes splayed across his chest, and waits for me to say something. He's going to do it. He's going to set them free.

"Do it, Raju. But don't come out until I tell you."

"Are you sure?"

"Hamish," I yell. He disappears into the tent, and Lee goes with him.

When the first Crickets reach me, I raise my gauntlet dagger, and they rear back. One of them—the one closest—raises a rifle. He points it at me, peers into its viewfinder. I raise my gauntlet dagger and lunge to the side: warrior pose. That's when the cameraman jumps from the door of the helicopter, which hovers just a few feet off the ground. He moves in closer, his lens trained on me, then on the Cricket with the gun. The Cricket scowls at the cameraman and lowers his weapon. He yells something. Just then, another helicopter appears. It swoops down and spits out three reporters, another camera. From who knows where, another reporter appears, this one holding out a giant microphone. And another. And another. My friends stand like paper dolls, stock-still, their arms frozen at their sides. If anyone does anything, it'll have to be me.

The helicopters have landed now. Their engines idle, their blades slow, and then it's quiet again. A horde of Crickets stand before me, guns raised. I punch my fist into the air, the gauntlet dagger piercing the sky. "Let these people go!"

A reporter moves in, holds her mike to my face. "Can you repeat your demand?"

I swallow against my dry throat. I remember to breathe. I think of Paati. "Let these—let these people go."

"What's your name?" the reporter asks.

All I can do is stare at her. Tinley steps up. "His name is Muki Krishnan. He's here to free the Moth camp."

"What's *your* name?"

Tinley hesitates. And then, from a distance, we hear the answer. "Tinley! Tinley!"

"Papa!" Tinley cries. I feel her bones jolt, like she's about to run to him, but she doesn't. Instead, she takes my hand. Fabi takes her other hand. Flip joins hands with Fabi.

General Schaedler sprints toward us. He cups his hands around his mouth. "Desist!" he yells. "Troops desist! Weapons down!" The entire group of Crickets turns to the general's voice. One lowers his weapons, then another and another.

The general halts at my side. He's out of breath, panting. "Muki," he says. "What in the world?" He turns to Tinley. "What's going on here, Tinley?"

"You have to tell us we're safe," I say. "Tell us we're safe and we'll answer your questions."

"Okay," he says. "You're safe."

I take a chance now. I step over to the tent, open the door, and call into it. "Raju! Lee! You can all come out now."

When I step back out, Lee's by my side. Raju emerges a second later, followed by a trail of people, blinking into the lights. These are the Moths we've come to liberate. They trickle out in a single line, until they stand behind us, an army of faces. They don't look scared, though. They look ready. When their eyes start to adjust, they focus on the general. They look him in the face—every single one of them. *Oculi aperti.*

Just then, the ground begins to vibrate. A new horde of soldiers jog into the camp, each with a gun the size of me. They stand in formation around us, at attention. Some are not much older than me. They wait for the general's orders.

"Papa." Tinley looks up at him. "You didn't need to do this. You didn't need to call an army in to fight us."

"I didn't," the general answers, gaping at the new crowd of soldiers. "I didn't summon them."

"Then who did?"

From the far side of the camp, a rumble. The entire gathering—every soldier, every reporter, every Moth—

turns to the main building, where the roar of an engine grows louder. From around the corner, a humongous metal insect churns forward through the night: a tank. The Crickets split to let it through. When it reaches us, the tank halts. Its engine grumbles, turns over, grumbles some more.

"What is that?" Tinley asks. "Papa?"

The general shakes his head. Then he seems to remember that he's in charge. He stands up straighter, cups his hands around his mouth, and yells, "Attention!" The Crickets, hundreds of them, click their heels together, their weapons at their sides.

That's when the tank spits and coughs and turns its engine off. Its hatch opens, and from it rises a head, a pair of shoulders—a man. Bamberger.

A small riot ripples through the journalists and camerapeople as they scramble to get close to the tank. Soon, they're clustered around him, waiting for him to speak. And for once, he ignores them.

"Schaedler," he calls. "Get these prisoners back to their tent. Tie them to their bunks for the night." A murmur passes through the crowd of Moths, and a few charge forward, but others hold them back. This isn't the time to attack.

The floodlights and camera beams set Bambi's eyes aglow. He trains them like lasers on General Schaedler. He's speaking to him, I can tell, without uttering a word. The general—he's listening. He's thinking. And then he turns to me, as if I have the answer. "Muki?"

"Let these people go. Please. They don't belong in this camp."

The general nods, but he doesn't move. He looks at me for a long time. He's deciding what to do. He is thinking—about what? About the things I've said to him? About Amma, that day outside the shop? About the hundreds of people behind me who've been treated like criminals? About the office workers walking off their jobs, about the teachers walking out of their classrooms? The camp holds its breath. Even Bamberger seems to be waiting. At last, the general raises his chin, turns to his troops, and shouts, "Evacuations will commence tonight. Transport units! We'll need every van and bus on-site."

"Are you letting them go? Or sending them to other countries?" I ask.

The general looks down at me. He doesn't look sorry or worried or scared. He looks, for the first time, like he's sure of what he's doing. Tinley squeezes my arm, and I know it's true.

"I'm letting them go, Muki. They're all going back to their homes, here in Pacific City."

From his tank, Bamberger watches calmly. "Well, Schaedler. I guess I saw this coming. You against me. Do you have any idea what's going to happen to you now? Any idea at all?"

Nobody answers him.

He speaks again, his gaze locked on the general. "Never trust a pair of puppy-dog eyes, right, Schaedler?" He turns to the few Crickets closest to him. "Handcuff the general, please. Bring him to my quarters."

The Crickets turn to each other, confused.

"*Hello,*" Bamberger snaps. "Did I not say that out loud?"

Finally, one Cricket moves toward the general. From his vest pocket, he pulls a pair of handcuffs.

"This isn't the solution, Bambi. You can't just send these people away. They belong here," the general says as the soldier pulls his wrists behind his back. "This plan of yours is ending. I'll make sure of it myself."

"Gag him, too," Bamberger says. The Cricket looks up, a shadow of confusion passing over his face. Bamberger growls with frustration, pulls a handkerchief from his pocket and throws it at the soldier. "Use that." Cautiously, the Cricket places the handkerchief, bright white, over the general's mouth. Next to me, Tinley inhales sharply.

"That's right," Bamberger says, a smirk creeping across his face. "Time to get things back on track. Right, soldier? Time to get this country back on track."

The Cricket glances up at Bamberger. The camera lights bounce off his dark eyes, and he doesn't look convinced. With great care, he ties the cloth over the general's mouth.

And then the Cricket does something strange. He pivots on his heel to face Bamberger. He nods to the soldier beside him. That soldier pivots on his heel. And the one next to him. And the one next to *him*. And then it's like they've all caught a bug. Every soldier turns to face Bamberger. Bamberger's grinning, watching all this like it's his own television show. He surveys the field of Crickets, his helmet a little crooked. He looks, suddenly, like a little kid playing war.

Eventually, bizarrely, miraculously, every single soldier turns to face Bamberger. General Schaedler barks a muffled order. In a single, swift motion, the soldiers raise their weapons, all of them—hundreds of them—pointing at Bamberger. Bambi's smile vanishes.

The truth begins to settle on the president. This isn't Bamberger's army—it's General Schaedler's. The general earned their trust. Even bound by a handkerchief, the general's jaw is clenched and determined. They are speaking without speaking, these two men, and it looks like the general gets the last word.

Paati's words come back to me again. *When you're given the choice to be blissfully blind* . . . the general, even the Crickets— they're choosing to see. They're taking that risk for me, for all us Moths.

Without a word, Bamberger sinks back into his tank. The lid shuts over his head. For a few seconds, the entire camp falls quiet.

"Papa!" Tinley calls. Hundreds of Cricket heads whip in her direction.

The general jerks his head around, searching for her voice. Through his gag he shouts back to her. A Cricket unties the gag and snaps the metal chain on the handcuffs. Tinley runs at her dad. "Tinley, stay there!" She halts.

"Soldiers," the general calls. "Weapons on the tank. Don't move." Then he turns back to Tinley. "Come here, Blossom."

Tinley runs to the general and leaps into his arms. The rest of us watch. Fabi, I know, is looking for her parents in the crowd. I'm looking for Paati.

"Muki!"

I think, for a second, that I must be imagining it. But then I hear it again.

"Muki! Dey, somberi!" And there she is, all at once, parting the crowd like a human plow.

"Paati!"

She grins at me, holds out her arms, and I run to her.

When I throw my arms around Paati, I almost knock her over. The people behind her catch her and hold her upright. She's frail now. She feels hollow compared to before, like she could get picked up and blown away by a strong wind. Her smile pushes out against her cheeks and a teardrop inches down her face.

"You're here, Paati. You're really here."

"I've been waiting for you, Muki." She puts a hand on my cheek and frowns. "Have you been eating? Are you okay? Where are your shoes?"

"I'm fine."

She shakes her head. "You haven't been eating."

"I've eaten more muffins in the last week than I have in my whole life."

Before we can argue any more, Mrs. Demba steps forward and pulls me into a hug. And then I hear a cry behind me. "Mamá! Papi!" The Calieróns emerge from the crowd and Flip and Fabi push past me to jump into their father's arms. Mr. Calderón sobs openly into the tops of his children's heads. Mrs. Calderón joins him. The Calderón family is a bundle of arms, squeezing itself tight, unwilling to ever let go.

I turn to Paati. The same question sits on both our faces: Where are my parents?

Raju's by my side now, and Paati holds him around the waist. I take Paati by the hand and lead her and Raju to where the general now stands. He and Tinley stand hand in hand, staring at the tank. It hasn't moved. Bamberger's still in there. Fabi joins me now, and Flip.

"What's he doing in there?" she whispers.

"No idea. Thinking?"

"Playing checkers," Fabi says.

"Calling his mama," Flip says.

"Peeing his pants," Raju says.

Fabi calls out to the guards, "He probably won't come out on his own, you know!"

But Bamberger does come out. He pops his head out of

the tank, like a groundhog searching for his shadow. Like he just has to see, one last time, the hundreds of people waiting on his word. That's when he turns and sees me, and it sends my blood roller-coastering through my veins. He frowns. "Who the heck are you?" he asks.

"I'm Muki Krishnan."

He tilts his head to the side. "Krishnan." He glances at the general. "Krishnan, as in—" The general sighs and closes his eyes. That's enough of an answer for Bamberger. "So you're the rebel's kid."

"Yeah." I stand a little straighter, puff out my chest. "My parents are in the revolution."

"Your parents?" He considers this. "Yeah, okay, I guess your dad's in on it, too. Really, though, your mom's the real rebel. Did you ever know that? Your *mom*, kid. She looks like a nice lady and all, but *she's* the one to watch out for."

"Where is she? Where's my mom?"

Bamberger shoots me a smile that zaps right through me. My blood turns ice-cold.

Two Crickets have climbed to the top of the tank now. They're pulling Bamberger from the hatch. His time is up. He doesn't resist. Instead, he grins wide, holds his hands out for handcuffs, and calls out to me. "Your parents are in the hills, Muki Krishnan. But you probably knew that. What you *didn't* know, though, is that we're smoking 'em out. All the rebels. Getting them outta those hills." The Crickets lead him away, but his voice rings clear: "The fires should be starting . . . oh, I'd say right . . . about . . . *now*."

All of us, every single person in that camp, turn to the East Hills. Like a tree hung with Christmas lights, the hills begin to sparkle. The orange flames are tiny from where we stand but growing and spreading. A few seconds pass, and two points of light connect. It happens again and again, fire spreading, sprinting like jackals through those hills.

"Dad!" I yell. As if he can hear me. "Amma!" Lee, all at once, is by my side. "They're in those hills, Lee."

"I know."

I don't even have to ask him. He grabs my hand and we go.

Chapter 29

We charge up the empty forest roads. Neither of us thought twice about grabbing the first unmanned van we could find and speeding straight into the fiery hills. Neither of us wondered how we'd find my parents in all that forest, all that fire. I have to do this. And Lee understands. Maybe the days alone in that little room have made him just as crazy as he needs to be.

"I know where they set up camp," he says. Smoke spills down from the fires above.

"It's close?"

He nods. "Let's just hope we get to them before the fire does."

We drive up the hill for another minute, but then he jolts to a stop. A fallen tree blocks the road. The entire road. We can't get past it. Lee stares at the tree. "This is crazy," he says. "There's a fire up there. I can't take you into a fire."

"But they're up there, Lee." I open my door.

"Hold up," he says, and grabs my arm. "You're not going out there."

"Yes, I am. If they're up there, yes, I am!"

I break from his grasp and jump out. I run, climb over the tree trunk, and charge farther up the hill. A hot, dry wind fills my mouth and throat and lungs. I can hear footsteps crunching behind me, but I can't see anything. A wall of smoke blocks everything. I'll do this alone. I push on, calling out for Amma and Dad. I'm sure they'll hear me, because they have to. They *have* to.

Lee grabs my arm and yanks me crashing to the ground. I'm flat on my back, coughing like crazy. Lee's knee is on my chest, his eyes wild. "We're turning back," he growls. "Muki!"

"No, we're not!" The smoke and heat are thick and getting thicker. "Lee! We're the only ones. Only *we* can find them!"

He stares at me for a few seconds. Doesn't move. Then his head snaps to attention. He stands up and hollers, "Sindu!" Over and over, he calls Amma's name. He tromps around the trees, each call a shot that gets lost in the dark. I join him, yelling for both my parents. We do our best to build a wall with our voices, something solid that Amma and Dad can reach for.

Nothing.

And then a deafening crack. The sound shatters the night. The forest explodes with noise—birds cawing, animals screeching.

"Oh god." Lee twists to look at the sky. He grabs my hand and pulls me down the path. "Run, Muki. RUN!" Close behind, I hear a thunderous boom. "Tree down!" he shouts. The air swirls with leaves and ash. My lungs burn, but I can't stop running. The heat gets closer, stroking its ghostly fingers down my back. My foot hits a snag and I go flying. I fly through the air and land, face-first, on the stony ground. "Muki!" Lee stops. He's pulling at my arms, shouting all the bad words. And I'm up again, sprinting down the hill, hunted by some invisible monster, until I hear it: another echoing boom, another tree hitting the ground.

Finally, the hill starts to level out and we're on the outskirts of town, where the air is thinner and cooler. Smoke still sits heavy in my chest, my nose, my mouth. My eyes water, and I'm not sure if I'm crying or not. I don't want to cry. I want to shout. I want to scream for my parents.

We're back at the Moth camp now. No Amma, no Dad. I've failed.

Fire engines howl up the hill, their lights painting the sky red. Outside the camp, I see an ambulance. Above us, more helicopters.

Paati. Suddenly, she's the only person I want to see.

Lee pushes his way through the crowd, and we slip through an open gate. There are so many people around that no one's in charge of stopping us. The tank is gone. I head for Paati's tent. They're all still there, the Moths, milling around, sitting on their cots. I feel like I'm at summer camp. There's a feeling of celebration in the air. People are smiling, for once. People are talking and laughing, busily, happily.

That's when I spot Paati. She's standing by a cot, the overhead lights bouncing off her glasses. She's looking down at the cot. There's a person lying down, looking up at her.

"Dad!"

It's Dad on the cot. Dad raising his hand up, Dad smiling weakly in my direction. I throw myself on top of him. "Dad!" I say, over and over. Dad wraps his arms around me, and I climb onto the cot with him. I let the tears spill from my eyes. Dad, Dad, Dad.

"Dad," I say, one last time, peering into his face. His cheeks and lips are smudged black. His eyes are bright red. He's grown a beard, scraggly and scratchy. I might not have recognized him at all, if I didn't know him in my bones.

"Muki," he says, and grins wide. His voice is hoarse. He coughs.

"Dad?" He's lying on his back. "You can't get up. What's wrong with you?" I shake him by the shoulders. "Get up!"

He coughs, whispers something I can't hear.

"What? *What?*"

"You're pinning me down, Muki. Get off me and I'll sit up."

Slowly, he lowers his feet to the ground and pulls himself up. He's coughing hard now, doubled over. Paati sits beside him and whacks at his back. I hold his hand.

"Dad?"

"Yes," he manages.

"Where's Amma?"

He goes very quiet. Paati avoids my eyes.

"I'm not sure, Muki," he says.

"What do you mean?"

"Captain's orders. She was in charge up there. She told me to go," he says. "She had to stay in the hills to make sure everyone escaped." He drops his face to his hands, presses his palms into his eyes. "My god," he says, his shoulders slumping. "She is so stubborn. So stubborn."

"You left her there? In the fire?"

He looks up at me and I know this was the wrong thing to say.

The Moths will be released at daybreak. For the rest of that night, we sit with Paati and Mrs. Demba in the big tent, all of us waiting for something. All of us waiting, I guess, for Amma to return. A few people wander in from the fires, covered in ash and soot, looking dazed. We ask them about Amma, and they just shake their heads. They don't know any more than we do.

Dad does his best to distract me. He asks about school. Paati and Mrs. Demba tell us about the camp, the few Crickets who treated them like their grandmothers, about the innovations she and Mrs. Demba thought up to make the terrible food less terrible. Did you know that ketchup plus black pepper makes a pretty decent hot sauce?

What we do know is that by five in the morning, as sunlight starts to nuzzle the edges of the tent, Amma should be back. If she were safe, she'd be here by now. Even without looking at them, we know what's happened to those hills. We can smell the charred earth.

Alive. We don't ask ourselves if Amma is alive. That word is too big a question. The flip side of that word— what's the opposite of alive? It's a ruthless current that could pick us up and carry us off forever. So we sit together, the four of us, as the night grows colder, then lighter, and we push away the question of Amma, because we can't let ourselves think that she might be the opposite of alive.

The hours pass, and we hear that the fire has been controlled. It's still burning, but it won't spread. This is what we talk about. We talk about the air, the smoke, whether we should get masks to wear, whether the ocean winds will clear the air. And then the talk turns into a drone, far off, and I crawl into a deep cave of sleep.

Chapter 30

Snap.

Snap snap.

Voices trail into my ears before I remember where I am. *Checked the hospitals.* Slowly, I blink back into the world. *Lee will let us know.*

I'm in the tent still. I have fallen asleep on Paati's lap. *Hope.* With a jerk, I sit up. The room spins. It's loud and hot and crowded in here. My tongue is dry and glued to the top of my mouth. My mind is muddled and staticky, like a radio that won't tune. In my chest, a single sound echoes: Amma, Amma, Amma. If I open my mouth, the sound will fly into the room and crash around like a frantic moth. A memory flares up from deep inside me: Amma wrenching my fingers from her sleeve. That was the last time I saw her. I can still feel the fabric, even now.

A Cricket with a clipboard comes over to us. He finds Mrs. Demba's and Paati's names on his list, and then he writes something on a little piece of paper, rips it off its stack, and hands it to Paati. "That's your exit ticket," he says. "For all of you. Show that to the guard at the gate."

"We're free to go?" Mrs. Demba asks.

He nods. "You're free."

We gaze at the exit ticket. You'd think we'd want to race out of this place and not stop until we were home. But I'm not sure I want to leave. Leaving will mean accepting, finally, that Amma won't sashay through the tent door. Going home will mean walking into a world without her.

Dad seems to know this, but like most grown-ups, he gets up and does what he doesn't want to do. "It's time," he says. "Mrs. Demba, we'll get you home, too."

When the taxi pulls up to Dembubbles, Mrs. Demba lets out a little cry. Standing at her door, wiggling a key in its lock, is Michael Demba, her son, the one who used to play with me. He looks like a man now, grown all the way up. When Mrs. Demba rises from the car, slow on creaky knees, he shouts and bounds over. He pulls her from the car and into his arms, lifting her off the ground. She laughs and whacks him on the shoulder. "Let me down, you crazy boy!"

Dad gives me a nudge, and we get out of the taxi. Michael Demba lowers his mother to the ground and she whacks him on the arm again. "Give me those keys, now," she says. "You'll never figure them out, will you?"

We leave Mrs. Demba to open her own door, and head

home to ours. I wonder what lies beyond it. I wonder if we'll see Buff in the shop. Or worse. I wonder if we'll see Buff in our *house*.

The shop is closed and empty, its metal grating pulled closed. Dad shields his eyes and looks through the grating for a long time. He sighs.

"Well, come on," Paati says. "Let's go see."

"Thumbi," Dad says, still peering into the shop, "go ahead. Do the code." I don't want to do the code, but I do the code. Just like a grown-up.

The inside of the stairwell smells musty and damp, like no one's opened the door for a long time. At the top of the stairs, the lock is broken. Dad stands with his hand on the doorknob. It's official. We're going home without Amma. I pause for a minute and remember how it used to be, coming home. Amma would be in the shop. I'd wave to her through the window. She'd usually have some task for me, and I'd usually be annoyed. If she were in the shop today, I'd do anything she asked. Sometimes, when I get home from school, she's already in the house, stirring onions in a pan or sitting at the kitchen table, sipping tea, as Dad makes dinner. I remind myself that the kitchen today won't be bright and warm and full of food. I won't see Amma. This is day one of our life without her. Dad looks at me, at Paati. "Ready to go home?"

I don't answer.

Dad opens the door. Inside, the shades are drawn and the kitchen is almost pitch-black. I feel for the wall, to orient myself. Paati finds the light switch and flicks it up and down, up and down. "The current is out," she says.

"They must have turned off our electricity," Dad says. "Muki, where are the candles? Go get them."

And then, a voice from the shadows: "We only have birthday candles."

I must be imagining things. "Who was that?"

My heart thumps at my chest like it's banging on a door. *It's her, you idiot*, my heart yells. *It's her!*

I fumble past the kitchen counter, to where the voice has come from. A flashlight switches on, blinding me. Then the beam shifts and I can see again. There, at the kitchen table, sits Amma.

She gapes at me like she can't believe I'm standing there, like I've turned into some kind of a dream. And she smiles. She smiles wide. She laughs and she holds her arms out. I run to her.

I don't know if I'm crying or Amma is. Soon, I'm covered in tears. We don't say any words. She just hugs me and hugs me.

Finally, she lets go a little. "Let me look at you," she says.

That's when I realize Dad and Paati are right there. They've wrapped their arms around Amma, around me. Altogether we're a bundle of arms and legs and faces. When

I untangle my own limbs from theirs, Amma runs a hand through my hair. "You need a haircut."

She looks smaller than I remember her, her body lost in the folds of her pajama shirt.

"Why are you in pajamas?"

"Well, I came home, and I thought, *I have just spent a week in a forest and survived a wildfire. Why don't I take a shower?* And so I did. And then I thought, *Who wants to put on pants? After all that?* So pajamas it is."

Dad gets up and rummages in a drawer. A second later, he strikes a match and holds it to a birthday candle. He brings it back to the table.

"Happy birthday to us," Amma says. We sit there for a minute, Amma pointing her flashlight beam at the ceiling, and Dad with his candle, its tiny flame.

"Why not open these curtains?" Paati asks, moving to the windows.

"Make a wish, Thumbi."

I do.

I blow out the candle and watch the smoke rise into the dark room. When Paati pulls back the curtains, the morning shouts hello. A butterfly, a spotted blue morpho, lands on the windowsill.

I turn to Amma. "Why didn't you come find us? We were waiting for you!"

"Where?"

"At the Moth camp."

Her eyes flit down to her hands. She chews at her cheek. "If they saw me . . . They know who I am. They know I've been in charge all this time. They might have arrested me. And then?"

"You did the right thing," Dad says. "We're safe here."

I search his eyes. "We are?"

"We are now."

Chapter 31

In the bathroom, the shower floor is black with soot. Amma's charcoal footprints trail from the tub back into the hallway. I follow them from the shower to my parents' room, and that's where I see Paati and Amma sitting side by side, Paati's arms wrapped around Amma, Amma's head on her shoulder. I wasn't the only one who almost lost her.

The hours pass, and I spend them shuffling around the house, watching through my bedroom window to see if Flip and Fabi are back. The house feels strange, at first. I have to get to know it again—its walls, its smells, the feel of the floorboards through my socks.

Downstairs, the shop is smelly and dark. I wonder how quickly Buff abandoned it. The milk in the fridge is curdled, the ice cream all melted. Puddles of sticky, melted red goo pool around the slushee machine. We throw out the old stuff, clean everything we can, and it takes us all day.

That evening, my parents and Paati sit in the kitchen

with cups of tea, Amma in a freshly pressed blue sari, Paati in a yellow one. Butterflies dance outside the kitchen window, as if they've heard that Paati's home.

The doorbell rings. Amma whips her head around to look at Dad. Nobody expects visitors. Nobody knows what to do with this sudden arrival. "Maybe it's Fabi and Flip!" I run to the door. As the grown-ups shout *Muki! No! Wait!* I'm already pressing the buzzer. I hear the downstairs door open and clang shut. I hear shoes—many pairs of shoes— clomping up the stairs.

A heavy knock at the kitchen door.

"Stand back, Muki." Dad picks up a spatula and opens the door himself.

It's General Schaedler. Behind him stands Tinley, and behind her, Raju.

"Hi!" Tinley's the first to speak. She smiles hopefully at Dad.

"Hello," Dad says, lowering the spatula. Amma stands up but says nothing.

"I'm sorry to arrive without warning," the general begins. He peeks into the kitchen and seems to lose his train of thought. "I have Raju here. His parents—"

"Yes." Amma's voice is stern. "We know about Raju's parents." Then she looks at Raju, his eyes wide, hovering in the stairwell. She softens. "Raju. Come. Come inside."

"He wanted to stay with you," the general says.

"Of course," Amma says. She steps forward and takes

322

Raju's hand, pulling him close. "Of course," she says again.

The general shifts from one foot to the other, looks down at the floor. "I'm glad you're safe, Mrs. Krishnan. I didn't know they were planning the fires. If I—I would have—"

"I know," she says.

"Well," the general says. "I suppose we should go—"

"Stay for tea. Please."

The general starts to protest but stops himself. "Certainly."

We shuffle awkwardly from the kitchen to the living room. Dad and Amma start making tea, rummaging in the cupboards to see what we have to offer. It's strange—stranger than strange—seeing General Dogwood Schaedler perched on our little green sofa, his hands folded on his knees. Tinley sits on one side of him, Raju on the other. Paati sits across from them and doesn't say a word. For a minute, it's quiet. Then the general turns to me.

"How are you, Muki?"

He's asking about five questions wrapped up in one, but I just say, "Fine." Then: "What's happening at the camp?"

"We're disbanding it. We're using the Cricket vehicles to get people home."

"And what's happening to the president?"

"That's a good question. I don't know myself. I don't even know where he is."

"Really?"

"He vanished in the night."

"And?" Paati says. "Now what? Who will be the president now?"

"The vice president, for now. And then, an election."

I flash back to that day in the general's office, how sure Bambi was that the vice president had his back. "Last night, when you turned on the president. How did you know that other people would support you? Like the vice president? And Congress?"

"I didn't. But I had to do what I thought was right."

Dad and Amma walk into the room with a tea tray.

"This country," Dad says gruffly, sitting down, "has a long way to go."

"It does," says the general. "But we've come a long way in a short time, thanks to you. And Mrs. Krishnan. And the others."

"And us," Tinley says.

"And you, Blossom. And Raju and Muki. Muki, most of all. How does it feel to be a revolutionary, Muki?"

I shrug and look at the ground and my face goes all hot. "I'm not sure." I think about last night, when the general stood staring at Bambi, when all those soldiers turned from one man to the other. "I don't really feel like a revolutionary," I say.

"Well, listen, you talked and I listened. I mean—I always knew better. I always knew the right thing to do. I was just ignoring it. I guess you made the right thing impossible to ignore."

"I did?"

"You changed my mind, Muki. You may have changed the course of history. That's powerful stuff."

I think about this for a second.

"Remember that day on the beach?" the general continues. "I said that if I didn't follow Bambi's orders, someone else would do the job instead. And that might have been true. But it was still important to say no. It took me a while to realize that."

I'm good at saying no. Maybe *that's* my anti-power. Maybe saying *no* is all the power a person needs.

Tinley turns to Amma, who sits next to her, sipping her tea. "What happened to you? Where were you?"

Amma looks a little startled, like she forgot we were all here. "I was up in the hills. In hiding."

"How did you eat? Did you hunt?"

Amma smiles. "No. For the first couple of days, we were on our own. And then people brought us food. Even your father, a few days ago. He brought us a case of water and some food."

I turn to the general. "You *did*?"

Tinley goes on: "And you were up there when the fires started?"

"I was," Amma says, and puts her tea down. "But now I'm here. I'm all right."

"Was Muki worried? Did he know you were okay?"

"We thought she died," I say.

Amma stares at me like I've screamed at her. Then she collects herself, clears her throat. "Well, I didn't die. I'm here." She turns to Tinley, blinking rapidly. "Now. Would you like a cookie?" Tinley smiles so brightly it's like Amma's just swept her up and spun her in a circle.

"I'll take that as a yes." She comes back with three cups of milk and a plate of chocolate chip cookies, the kind from the shop, packed with preservatives. When she sits down, she stares into nothing for a few seconds. Then she looks at Tinley again, more closely this time. She cradles Tinley's ponytail in her hand, and lightly combs her fingers through it. Tinley gazes back at her. Then Amma picks up a cookie for herself. When she bites into it, she sits back and closes her eyes, like she's never tasted anything so delicious. She lets out a deep sigh. "Raju, kanna, you'll be sharing Muki's room with him. Paati will live in the living room."

"Living in the living room," Paati says. She sits back, folds her hands over her belly, and has a good laugh.

When the general gets up to leave, Tinley pulls me aside. "I asked my dad about it. It was my mom's phone number," she says.

"What was?"

"On the ring. The ten digits. It was the number my dad called my mom on when they first met."

"So he knows you have the ring?"

She nods.

"Oh. Wow. Weird."

"Yeah." Tinley pulls her chain out and gazes at the ring. "Weird."

Following Tinley down the stairs, the general calls, "Have a good week at school, Muki."

"See you later, Doggy." He spins around to look at me and I slam the door shut.

I turn to Amma. "I'm going to school?"

"Of course you're going to school. What did you think?"

I shrug. "I thought things were different now."

Amma guffaws. "Mr. Revolutionary, you're going to school."

Chapter 32

Here's what I used to think about revolutions: I used to think they happened mostly in paintings, with people holding torches and storming castles. I used to think revolutions happened in a day. Like the day Martin Luther King Jr. marched on Washington or the French stormed the Bastille. But revolutions don't happen in a day. They're slow. They happen for a long time, with peaks and valleys. Sometimes they're quiet, sometimes loud. Sometimes they're violent, sometimes not. Kids make the best revolutionaries, because rebellion runs in our veins. We have crazy ideas that sometimes actually work, and nobody cares about stuff more than we do.

The next morning, I look across my bedroom and Raju's squirming in his sleep, stuck in a dream. Ghoulish slivers of white peek out from under his eyelids. He's probably dreaming of Hamish and the Highlandian revolution. Something inside me wants, more than anything, to bug him. This must be what it's like to have a brother. I ball up my sock and throw it at him. He scowls and scratches his cheek and then, slowly, his eyes flicker open. I watch him start to wake up and realize where he is. He looks around my room, his eyes moving from the low ceiling to the narrow, dark hallway outside my door. He's hardly ever been here, and I can tell he's not sure what to make of this place, this tiny little apartment.

"Raju?"

"What."

"Never mind."

"*What?*"

"Where do you think your parents are?"

He stares up at the ceiling, and for a long time, he says nothing. Then he turns to me. "You have everything now. Everything's okay for you."

"I know." And that's all we say about it.

From the kitchen comes the tinging of Paati's prayer bell and the distant bang of pans. Outside, a delivery truck rolls by, clatters against a pothole. Oceanview is waking up, like it does every day, like it did every morning we were gone. When I get up, I see butterflies: three fat monarchs on the clothesline. They lift off and away.

Down on the sidewalk, the shop's metal grating is closed. Normally, it would be open by now. I wonder where Buff is, if he'll ever be back. Big changes mean that some things go away forever.

"Mingus Mouse!"

I look up. At the other end of the clothesline: Fabi and Flip, two heads in a window.

I race through the kitchen and down our steps, three at a time, leap the last six, and bang through the stairway door. I throw my arms around Fabi. Flip rams into us, and we let him into the hug.

Fabi shoves a stack of papers into my arms. "Take a look." We're all over the Sunday papers—Fabi, Flip, Raju, Tinley, and me. The headlines go a little overboard with the alliterations, calling us *Preteen Patriots! Middle School Moth Mavericks! The Runty Resistance!* Dad sits at the kitchen table and reads through every paper. Sometimes, he smiles quietly to himself. Other times, he shakes his head. He reads out loud. "'Not only did these four young activists take enormous risks to stand up for the country they loved, they may have also turned the tide of Mariposan history.'" A lump jumps into my throat when he reads that. He looks up at me, and his smile reaches all the way up to his eyes. "It's like the general said, Thumbi. You changed history."

"So did you. Does it mention you and Amma anywhere?"

"No."

"But that's not fair."

"Well, that's how we want it. It's for the best."

"But we couldn't have done all that without you."

"And we," Dad says, squeezing my hand, "couldn't have done it without *you*."

Later that afternoon, Dad drives us to Marble Hill. We have the keys to Raju's house, but we won't be moving in. We're here now to fill a suitcase with his clothes. When we walk through the front door, the curtain of glass beads sways and glimmers, but the rest of the house has sunk into wintry sleep. In his room, Raju opens his dresser, sullenly pulls out T-shirts, and lets them drop to the floor.

I head to the kitchen, where Dad boils water for tea. Amma's clearing out the fridge, tutting and sighing. "How many muffins . . . ," she mutters. Before she can give me a job to do, I ask, "Can't we just live here?"

She frowns. "Absolutely not."

"But Mom!"

She clicks her tongue.

"Amma. There's so much room here. And don't you think Raju—"

"Imagine, Muki, if Raju's parents moved into our house, started living in it like it was theirs. How would you feel?"

I try to imagine Sonal Aunty with her twinkly hair baubles, her powdered cheeks, and her muffin everything, bumping around our little apartment. I can't. "So what are we going to do? What's going to happen to this house?"

"They have plants," she says, picking up a dish towel.

"What?"

"They'll need someone to water their plants." I look around the kitchen. It's filled with plants. Plants hanging from the ceiling, lining the windowsills. I've never noticed them before. "They'll need someone to dust, to keep this house up until—until they come back."

"You would do that for them?"

"Sonal Aunty was my first friend in this country, Muki. She was there when I needed her."

"But she double-crossed you!"

She considers this, running the dish towel through her hands. "I can only think—I can only think that maybe she was trying to survive. Maybe she saw all that she had to lose—"

Maybe that's what Raj Uncle was talking about. The price they had to pay for their skin color. They had all that money, but maybe they had to rat out their friends to have it.

Amma gazes around the kitchen and gets lost for a few seconds. "Did you know, when you were born, she brought me to this house to take care of me? She made me every meal, all the healing foods your paati would have made back home. She changed your diapers. She held you and played with you so I could nap. She made her home my home. And she was pregnant, too. Belly out to here. She must have been exhausted. But she was like a sister . . ." Amma trails off. She goes back to cleaning the fridge. I wait for her to say more, but she doesn't. I don't know if I'll ever understand my mom.

Before we leave Raju's house, Dad gathers the mail piled up at the door. From the top of the stack, he takes a gray envelope. "Raju," he says, "this is for you." Raju sits with the envelope at the long, polished dining table. I guess, before he opens it, that it's from his parents. We watch his eyes move over the page.

Amma clears her throat. "Are they safe?"

"They're okay," he answers, and stares down at the page again. Suddenly, he looks alone—very alone at the big, empty table. I want to hug him, but I don't, because we just don't do that kind of thing, Raju and me. But I do put my hand on his shoulder and he looks up, and I can see in his face that he needs a friend.

"Are they in Mariposa?" Dad asks.

"I'm not supposed to say. They're asking if I want to go join them." He bites his lip and stares at the letter. "But I'd rather stay with you guys, if that's okay."

Amma sits down next to him. "Your school is here. We are here," she says. "You can always stay with us, Raju. Forever, if that's what you want." She wraps her arm around one of his shoulders. I sit down, too, and wrap an arm around his other shoulder. His cheeks go a little pink, and he smiles down at the letter. He's never been my friend, really, but now he's like a brother, and that seems all right to me.

Chapter 33

Monday morning, I wake up to a dark sky. I hear the shop grate opening. I look across the room. Raju's gone. I spring out of bed, my heart racing. He's been taken. His parents came for him. He left without saying goodbye.

"Raju?" I call. No answer. The bathroom is empty. The kitchen is empty. "Raju! Dad? Where is everyone?"

That's when I turn to the living room and see, in the half-light of morning, Paati doing a shoulder stand. Beside her, Raju's doing a shoulder stand, too—his back on a yoga mat, his feet high in the air, his chin scrunched into his chest. They don't see me at first, so I watch them. Raju's hands grip his hips, and he focuses hard on his feet, frowning. He's putting everything he has into this shoulder stand, almost like he's stuck in it. So naturally, I do the only thing I *can* do. I find a black marker in the kitchen drawer, bound into the living room, uncap the pen, and draw a big *X* on his forehead.

"Hey!" he grunts. He swats at me and his legs crash to the ground. He's up now, chasing me down the hall until he gets me with a tackle and a headlock and punches at my ribs until I cry out for him to stop. He drops me to the ground, and for a second I'm mad, but also, I'm laughing. Then I look at his forehead, the big black *X*, and I laugh even harder.

In the kitchen, we eat cereal. Raju shoves enormous spoonfuls into his mouth. He's barely able to chew, crunching laboriously, but still he scowls at me. With a mouth full of food, he says, "You're a slob."

"You're the one talking with your mouth full."

He finally manages to swallow. "You spilled milk all over the table. Look—all around your bowl. What's wrong with you?"

He's right. The table around my bowl is spattered with milk puddles. "Okay," I say. "We're both slobs."

He shakes his head. "Mucus."

When we get to school, no one pretends that nothing happened. When Fabi, Raju, and I walk onto campus, we're swarmed. Suddenly, every student at Marble Hill Prep knows who Muki Krishnan is. Everyone has a question. Everyone wants to hear our story. I'm okay with it, surprisingly. I'm okay standing out a little.

Raju starts out quiet and lets Fabi and me do most of the talking. But as the day wears on, he picks up the story and runs with it. He holds court in the lunchroom, comes up with his own dramatic flourishes. *And then I BB-rolled under the perimeter fence, and I got cut up pretty seriously.* He points to the X on his forehead. *Oh, this? War paint. Yeah.* The Tinleys gather around him, their matching ponytails swaying as they listen. *And the munitions room. Mostly, the weapons were medieval, but there were grenades in there, too. One wrong move and* BOOM.

After lunch, I open my locker and find a note inside. "Ooh!" Fabi says. "Somebody *likes* you!"

My mouth goes dry. "Not so fast, Fabiana," I manage to say. I unfold the note, trying to ignore the possibilities. It's typed. *Muki*, it reads, *You should be so proud of yourself. —Miss Pistachio.*

"Oh. It's just Miss P." I don't know who I was hoping for, but my civics teacher was not in my top five.

"Look!" Fabi gasps. "The *e* in *be*! It drops!"

She's right. The *e* from Miss P.'s typewriter dips just below the line, just like it did in the fortune cookies.

"Do you think?"

"It was her," I whisper. She was part of this all along.

By fifth period, the rumors put Tinley, Fabi, Raju, and me in hand-to-hand combat with President Bamberger. When we walk into Miss Pistachio's room, she must have heard all the stories and more, because she drops her chalkboard eraser and comes right over to the four of us. She hugs each of us, holds our faces, looks with a sort of desperation into our eyes. "Are you okay?" she asks, two or three times. "Are you sure?"

Eventually, she gets the class to settle down, and settles down herself. She has to. Today's an important day. It's our first research report day. When it's our turn, Tinley and I turn to each other. "Do you have a way to get them there?" I ask. We have an excellent plan. We just never got around to planning it.

"Trust me," she says.

The class lines up and we lead them across the MHP campus, through a gate, and into a lush wood. "My backyard," she whispers to me. "My dad showed me the shortcut."

As the trees grow thicker, the class gets quieter. Soon, they follow us in a sort of respectful silence, aware today that we're capable of anything, us revolutionaries.

We arrive. The butterfly grove.

"What is this?" someone whispers.

"Look around," I answer. "Look up at the trees." It takes them a few seconds. When we look at trees, our brains expect to see leaves, and so we do see leaves. But then our eyes kick in, and we see what's really there.

It's like fifteen pairs of eyes kick in all at once as a collective gasp rises through the trees. *Look! It's butterflies! It's all butterflies!* The branches drip with gold-and-orange-and-black monarch wings.

"How do they *do* that?" Box Tuttle asks. "How do they hang on to the branches without breaking them?"

"Each butterfly weighs less than a paper clip," Tinley answers. "Imagine a hundred paper clips on that big fat branch." A few startle and leap from their branches. Their wings catch the sunlight and they flit around our heads like loose wishes. I can see why a group of butterflies is called a kaleidoscope: a single butterfly is beautiful, but a group of them actually forms a whole picture.

We begin. I talk about the blue morpho first, with its double-sided camouflage wings, the way it's brilliant blue on top and woodsy brown on the bottom. Tinley talks about swallowtails, how their young caterpillars are black and white and disguise themselves as bird poop. "And the older caterpillars," she goes on, her eyes widening, "they're more colorful. They have this orange band around their neck, and when they see a predator, the orange thing blows up into a big bubble. And it smells like *pineapples*."

When I get to our last butterfly, I wait for silence. "Miss Pistachio said we had to commit to a lens. So Tinley and I figured we couldn't just come out here and talk about butterflies for fifteen minutes." I look up at the monarchs. "So here's our lens . . ." Just now, I don't know why, but waves of sadness and happiness surge through me, gripping my throat, shaking my voice. I try to keep going. "Our lens . . ." I have to stop again. The words are all gummed up inside me. I think I might cry. I look over at Miss P., who smiles and nods and puts a hand on my shoulder. One breath in, one breath out. "We always say that butterflies are from Mariposa. But really, they're not."

She squeezes my shoulder. I go on. "Some butterflies are migrants. Monarch butterflies migrate two to four thousand miles to get from one climate to another. And they migrate over generations, because they don't live very long. Well, some of them do. I'll get to life spans later." I look over at Tinley, and suddenly I'm very aware that I've been talking, that every set of eyes rests firmly on me. Suddenly, I want to be invisible. I want to camouflage like a morpho and melt back into the trees.

Tinley's watching me, too. "Monarch butterflies travel from South America to Canada every year," she says, picking up where I faded off, "and on the way, they stop in Mariposa. That's why we see so many in the spring. They lay eggs as they move from place to place." From the corner of my vision, I feel the weight of everyone's eyes, but I gather up my courage, because I have something to say.

"So really," I cut in, "Bamberger's monarchs? The butterflies on the flags? They're not native to Mariposa. They come from different parts of the world. But they're as Mariposan as . . . rain. They're as Mariposan as the beach. They're as Mariposan as—as—me!" The class laughs. "Monarchs are Mariposan because they love this island, and this island loves them." I look at Miss P., who smiles back down at me. My face has gone hot, but looking at her calms me. For a second, I step out of myself, and I see this: I've grown up. I'm breaking out of my chrysalis. I'm becoming something new.

It felt strange, just then, saying Bamberger's name. His voice, his face, his version of Mariposa—they all feel far away from this grove. Bamberger was no butterfly. Butterflies are colorful, like Paati in her saris. They travel across continents to make new homes for their children, like my parents, Raju's, and Fabi's. They form a hard chrysalis to protect against predators, like Amma. Sometimes, they pretend to be other creatures, like Dad, the chemist, the samosa maker, the man all the customers look for. Like Tinley, butterflies navigate a world without their mothers, but they're tougher than they look. Like me, they're shape-shifters, masters of camouflage. I think of Paati again, who is all those things—traveler, secret agent, chrysalis builder.

Fabi whoops, and a whole branch of butterflies sprinkle from above—not just monarchs, but swallowtails and purple hairstreaks and emperors and blue morphos. They swoop down to flutter around our faces, tickling our ears and noses, and we have to laugh. I think of all of us who've migrated, who've put on new faces, new Mariposan wings, who wear those new wings like scratchy school sweaters, until they become part of us and we take flight. Me and

Paati and Amma and Dad, Fabi and Flip and Raju and everyone in Oceanview. Our wings have crossed continents. Our hearts have traveled oceans. We are all butterflies. Every one of us.

Acknowledgments

This book couldn't have reached your hands without the tireless efforts of my wonderful agent, Lindsay Edgecombe and my editor at Katherine Tegen books, Benjamin Rosenthal, who loved and understood this story from the get-go. My immense gratitude also goes to Shehzil Malik for her incredible art.

I am grateful to my Wednesday morning writing buddies, Nayomi Munaweera and Natasha Singh, and for my writing group—Laleh Khadivi, Mūthoni Kiarie, Keenan Norris, and Joel Tomfohr—who coaxed this manuscript along, month by month, read its first full draft, and helped me make it better.

Spencer Dutton, my husband and purveyor of morning coffee, gave me the support, time, and space I needed to write. My parents gave me my earliest understanding of home and family, past and present, ideas which form the foundation of this story.

And finally: *The Samosa Rebellion* began as a nightly bedtime story for my two sons, Avinash and Ashwin. As they asked for more, the story grew and grew. I couldn't have written this without them.